DIAMONDS FROM COAL

www.diamondsfromcoal.com

by CLARE WHITE

Published by:
Chipmunkapublishing
PO Box 6872
Brentwood
Essex
CM13 1ZT
United Kingdom

www.chipmunkapublishing.com

Proof-read by Ruta Skinkyte

Cover Photos by Di
ISBN : 978 1 84747 012 6

The development of this book was made possible by a grant from The Arts Council, London.

THANKS

It is always important to recognise and express gratitude. I always found gratitude one of the most difficult of emotions to express and understand, sometime it made me feel like I was in love with someone or indebted. Once I'd broken down I realised it was OK to simply recognise that some people are brought into our lives to bring out what is already within. There have been many examples of gratitude in my life and it is important for me to have sorted through and acknowledge them. Abuse leaves ones emotions in a mashed up mess, we don't always know what we are feeling or why we are feeling it. We are not used to people being 'nice' to us we are used to being abused or taken advantage of or we always think there is a price to pay. When we stumble across those precious few who simply input without demanding back they deserve recognition and acknowledgement. These are a few of those very people.

To Trish, Roz and Margi who started me on my healing journey you taught me so much about life but most of all you taught me about me.

For my family, through so much and against so many odds we have fiercely fought to hold our little families together, not always getting things right but always having an incredible love for each other and a closeness that only we can understand. Invisible bonds and ties that have almost separated us from the 'normal' around us forcing us almost to stick together and never let each other down. Only we as a family understand what we have been through, my love for you all is indescribable.

Stevie, your belief in me as a writer and encouragement meant this book actually got written! I know without your influence and place in my life it may never have happened. You echo every feeling and thought I have ever had about gratitude and how fucked up it can get.

To my children, I don't know if I could ever cope with you reading this book, but if you do there is a huge part of me that hopes you understand a little of why I have protected you so closely. I am incredibly proud of you all and I thank you for your support when I was healing, writing, growing and learning as a person. Even when you never knew or understood what was going on you loved me, hugged me to distraction and were my ever flowing source of unconditional love and kisses.

Laurence and Trish for superb editing, I remember so clearly the flying back and forth of manuscripts horns locked over certain parts and the closeness that developed that was hard to understand, I think this comes under gratitude..

My darling Frankie, I hope I honour you in my memories and every day I pray you are proud of our children but more I hope you are proud of me. I limped through life for so long without you but look I can walk again.

To my precious Fi, you believe in me and pointed me in directions I never knew existed. Your unfailing love support and trust in ME as a person overwhelms me at times. I love you with all my heart and soul.

This book in all its gut wrenching and sickening honesty is dedicated to the one who I felt could never fight for herself, who struggles daily with life, love and sanity. Who has held her own, never given up and silently pushed on through so much. Cath I love you and admire you more than you will ever know.

PROLOGUE

"Jesus fucking Christ I don't believe it – I don't fucking believe it. What the hell is going on? What is it about short men that breaks my fucking heart every time, every fucking time?"

Annie was on a roll, her anger connecting with anyone in her path. The children, knowing this side of her so well, scampered up the stairs and made themselves scarce. Mike, her husband, moved towards her. He towered over her by a good six inches.

"Don't fucking touch me." she yelled. "Keep your distance."

His blue eyes pricked with tears, he felt so useless when Annie was like this. Shit he hated the pain she dealt with on a regular basis. Being a gentle giant, violence had never entered his being but today, seeing Annie so out of control again, made his fists clench and his usually laughing lips clench in a thin angry line. He knew what to do, he knew how to support Annie. He had done it many times before. His anger and frustration was aimed at so many others, never her. He had done so much for her and would always do so; this was almost a life pattern. The times between the breakdowns were love and laughter and fun, during them it was a fucking nightmare.

Annie would move between different times of her life, yelling, screaming and flinging things out of her path, nothing seeming to register. Mike knew his part well and worked with it. He knew to let her ride it out and exhaust herself then he could step in. He moved back from her, giving her the space she demanded. Her green eyes were afire - flashing and darting trying to see, but not seeing.

"I can't fucking believe it," she ranted, "how the fuck did it happen? I have worked so hard I thought they had gone, I thought they had gone. Will they ever fucking go, will the demons ever fucking leave or are they going to be with me until the day I fucking die? What.... what more do they want? For fuck's sake is it never

5

enough, do I never do enough? Why always more, always more, it's just not fair, I never asked for this, what did I do to deserve this – what?" she yelled at Mike.

Mike moved into his role and started the process of bringing her down. "I know babe, I know." He soothed. "Fuck off and stop patronising me," she yelled at him, "I know what you are doing I just fucking know. You think you are so fucking smart, you think you are some kind of fucking genius, you feel so in control when I'm freaking out don't you? You fucking pervert you get such a perverse sense of delight from it, don't you? You love it when I can't cope, don't you? Fucking pervert." She spat at him. "You get some kind of sexual zing from this, don't you – don't you? I'll bet your cock is hard – come on show me, I know it is – all you ever want is to fuck me isn't it – that's all they have ever wanted from me – never me, never to love me, just to fuck me – why should you be any different?" Mike flinched, but only barely. "Its okay babe, just get it all out."

He had seen it building for weeks now and had been powerless to stop it – she had to do it alone. He had to allow her the space to work through this stage if she didn't it would just keep coming and coming and coming. She started moving for the stairs. "Jesus the kids," he thought. Knowing her so well he knew what would happen if she ventured up the stairs – the children would be in for a verbal abuse on the state of their bedrooms. Annie would find fault where no fault lay. He took his chance and moved to her. "Touch me and you're fucking dead!" She screamed at him.

He continued, he had to get her past this. Annie was no small lady. She was a good five foot ten inches tall and very well proportioned. She had large breasts, which rose and fell with each breath she took, her feet were large and she had pinned them flatly to the floor as if to try and steady herself. Long shapely legs met with a well-proportioned arse. The only area where Annie held on to her anger and pain was in her stomach – it was the one thing she hated most about herself but it was her protection – that was what kept the men away. She had worked so hard to put it in place – she had worked her negative features to counteract her positive ones, almost as if to hide her attractiveness.

Mike was winning, he moved closer and a whimper escaped her mouth, the pain waves were starting to roll. "It's okay babe," he soothed. "No – no, its not." She pleaded. Her eyes weakened, now softened and child-like in their appearance and Mike knew he had broken through the barrier. The tears started, huge globules of salty tears almost shot from her eyes so intense was the pain she felt. He took the last step to her and she met him there. Leaning on him she allowed his frame to take her full stature. Her knees went weak and the deep pain of the child within her rose, she felt so small, so very small; she sank to the floor, no sounds just immense tears breaking through her armour. She hugged her knees and felt so vulnerable, so exposed - almost naked. She looked down and saw she was dressed. Yes, she was dressed, but then why did she feel so naked and exposed? Her eyes darted around the room, looking for protection. In an instant she was up and making her way to the dining area, she crawled under the table hugging her knees. She always felt safe hiding somewhere. Mike moved some of the chairs out of the way and climbed under after her. He sat next to her and merely held her, no words were spoken. He held her as the deep wrenching sobs escaped her body. He took off his shirt and gave it to her to blow her nose in. He always marvelled at how one person could shed so many tears.

She buried her face in his shirt and took a deep breath, inhaling his smell, it always seemed to calm her. He stroked her hair, held her tight and she clung to him like a baby monkey. They sat there for a good hour and he let her cry it out, knowing she would talk when she was ready. Mike readied himself for what was to come, he had a pretty good idea and he could handle it, they had always had such an open and honest marriage and he knew she could never keep anything from him for long. He could accept all parts of her complex character for he knew forces outside of her control had formed it. He loved her wholly, unconditionally and passionately. He would do anything for her. His reward was her complete love for him and her commitment to their marriage. He felt as if it was his place in life to just be there for her, that's why he was here.

As she came down he brought her out from under the table and he put her to bed. He knew she would not sleep but she felt safe in her bed and even though the temperature outside was hot and humid she was shivering with an internal cold he could not relate to. He tucked her up and went off to make her a cup of tea and check on the children.

Annie lay there shivering and shaking and not thinking. She couldn't think, to do so would bring it on all over again. Yet she needed to talk, she needed to get it out and try to sort it out once and for all. Again. Mike returned with the tea and she sat up, he had only half filled the cup knowing how she would be shaking. Her words, when she began to talk, would come in jumpy, shaky, monotone sentences. They had been here many times before. She sipped her tea and reached for a cigarette. Finally, after watching her struggle to hold the flame still, Mike lit it for her. She drew deeply on the cigarette and felt the calmness begin its entry. Her head pounded and as if by magic Mike got up to get her an aspirin. No words were needed here, they both knew this routine so well. She took the aspirin and then the shame surfaced.

"Oh God babe, I'm so sorry." She choked out.

"It's okay," he reassured, "don't worry it's okay."

"Oh fuck my kids," she sobbed, "my kids, where are the kids, oh shit my poor babies are they alright?"

It's okay,' he reassured her again, "they are fine Annie, just fine. This is not the first time hey – they know the beat they are safe we'll talk to them later. They are watching television and are calm."
God, Mike was so capable. What would she do without him? For sure she'd just curl up and fucking die.

Understanding how hard this was for Annie, Mike started

the ball rolling. "So come on now, let's get this out, tell me how it started and how the hell did he get past your well-placed barriers? We can work through this Annie, you can get through this, you have survived so very much, this is just a hiccup, we'll get through it, you just have to trust me and talk to me, don't shut it in, don't shut me out, let me in and let me help." Mike pleaded. Annie double took, fuck, how well he knew her, nothing escaped him. In silence she struggled to find the words, fuck where to begin.

Seeing her struggle for words Mike left it – the time was not right now to push her, she was too vulnerable, he would let her sleep. Tomorrow they would talk. It could wait until tomorrow.

The nightmare came again that night – she awoke sometime between late night and early morning. She wasn't sure which. The silence was deafening. She became aware of the thumping of her heart and she allowed the rhythm of it to soothe her. Once the panic left, the tears came. They slid slowly down her cheeks as if they too were just so tired of this long and lonely journey. The journey to peace and release. The panic began to rise and with it came the years of self-taught, calming self-advice.

"It's okay, we've been here before, this is not new, we can work through this, just keep calm, breathe, remember to breathe, take in your surroundings." Panic hit her.

"Oh shit, where am I? Calm down, calm down, let your eyes adjust to the dark and work out your surroundings."

The years fled, she was unsure of her age at that exact time. "Okay, think, think of something, anything to bring you back. Oh God no, the nightmare, the nightmare!" That was what awoke her, she searched her memories looking for the answers, hoping to find something familiar to bring her back to the present. A picture filled her mind and as it painted over the pain and confusion of that present time, with it came the fitting together and the peace that she had searched so long and so hard for.

It was Tuesday, Tuesday early morning, she was safe in her bed. Mike was snoring quietly beside her. Why had she not noticed that before? How come there was someone right next to her and she still felt so alone? Fuck why do these shitty nightmares still come? Sleep had left now. She crept out of the bed, picked up her cigarettes and made her way to the lounge. She placed a CD on the stereo and made herself a cup of coffee with just a hint of brandy. She watched the sun rise through the curtains, watched the start of the new day and for the first time ever, felt control and peace.

She felt her completeness. It was like coming home, it was the season. The explosion with Mike the night before and the nights sleep had helped to bring the clarity. As she sat quietly awaiting the start of the new day she made decisions and with each decision she made, a calmness appeared. And with each wave of calmness that entered, the sun seemed to rise a little higher, giving Annie the confirmation that this was what she had needed to do all along. She had needed to take the time to look within herself and see exactly what her strengths of character were. She had needed to set her own rules, based on who and what she was. All her life she had been made and moulded by others into something or someone that she was not. It was time to take control of her own life. She rose from the chair suddenly feeling much lighter and made her way to the bathroom to prepare for the day ahead.

CHAPTER 1

Her nightmares had begun thirty odd years earlier. The only difference being their reality. Some odd sixth sense always woke her before he actually entered the room. She would then begin the act of pretending to be asleep. She had mastered her breathing technique, always remembering to breathe slowly and quietly, adding just a little snort at the right time. Sometimes he would bypass her room and go to Beth's room. On other occasions though, she was not so lucky. Tonight was her night. He gently shook her and she rolled over, grunted and feigned sleep, but he was persistent. Even at her tender age she could almost feel his erection in his fingers, prodding, poking and willing her awake. Finally she gave in; she always did, for she knew no different.

Knowing the ropes well she obediently followed her naked father to the lounge, tip-toeing so as not to awake her mother or her sister, holding her breath. The lounge door quietly closed, no words exchanged she knew her part. Without being told, she removed her panties, lifted her night dress and lay spread legged on the floor.

Her heavy dinner was still making its presence felt in her gut and she silently prayed tonight he would not force his penis into her mouth. She almost gagged at the thought. Saliva filled her mouth and just as quickly disappeared as he began sucking his middle finger, she braced herself for the pain that would follow – no matter how many times he did this to her it still hurt. Tensed and waiting, she began the process in her mind of disappearing so she could not feel what was happening to her. As his finger entered her vagina she gasped and a tear escaped her eyes. Willing herself not to feel or cry, she felt the lift of self from self.

Now she was free, she could do anything and feel nothing. As she rose above her body she watched her father hard at work. Determination in his eyes, his erection larger than real to her small eyes, his dirty grease filled fingernails and the roughness of his skin chaffing the softest parts of her body. As he manipulated her vagina to try and stretch the opening she caught sight of her face. Eyes closed, she looked so peaceful, almost asleep, but every now and again as his finger entered and withdrew, a grimace would faintly appear on her face. Beads of sweat began to break out, but she was one-step ahead the whole time, she always knew what would come next, he was going to try again, she just knew.

He lifted himself up, spat onto his finger and rubbed the saliva onto the tip of his penis, opening her legs wider he attempted for the umpteenth time to penetrate the tight walls of his daughter's vagina. She inwardly yelped in pain, always remembering to be quiet, never knowing why. Childlike thoughts, thinking if she stayed quiet it would be over quicker, knowing that if she made a sound and woke up her Mum she would be in big trouble. If she did not move maybe he would give up or maybe it would all be over. He pushed and pushed, with each push a tear appeared, she felt the burning in her vagina, the stinging of skin tearing, she knew it well. Tomorrow when she sat she would still feel it, when she urinated it would sting like shit.

Professionally coached she returned to her body and at the tender age of seven proceeded to seduce her father so that she could return to her bed. Withdrawing from him she looked him seductively in the eye and said, "Daddy make the white stuff come."
"Touch me." he said.

She moved her hand and touched his penis – her little fingers could barely close around it her hand was so small. Expertly she moved her hand up and down in rhythmic jerks trying to hurry, feeling his impatience at her slowness, she tried to go faster. Her arm began to ache and she was unable to go as fast as he wanted. He grabbed his penis with one hand and her head with the other and roughly pushed his penis into her mouth, she felt herself gag but suppressed the urge to vomit, she knew it would be over soon. He withdrew from her mouth and shot thick spunks of sperm over her face. The smell so familiar, the smell of sleep-time and peace - for a while.

12

He reached for his handkerchief and wiped the sperm from her face. She put her panties on, and completely in the routine of things, kissed her father good night and tip toed back to her room. She climbed back into bed and gave herself ten out of ten, her bed was still warm. Tonight she was lucky, she had done well. Tomorrow she would not be falling asleep in class or staring vaguely out of the window at school. Tomorrow she would not be yelled at by the teachers for not concentrating. Tomorrow would be better. She snuggled down and wept, waiting for sleep to come. The familiar pain and stinging in her vagina peculiarly comforted her abused body and emotions.

Tom went to the bathroom, sniffed his fingers, washed his hands and threw the sperm soaked handkerchief into the laundry basket for his wife to wash in the morning. Then he made his way back to bed and drifted into sleep, satisfied, as his daughter cried herself to sleep once more in the next room.

CHAPTER 2

There was nothing special about the day Annie was born. No fan-fare played. Sarah, had just turned seventeen and this was her second child. The gin and hot bath had not worked, Annie was determined from conception. The drive home from the hospital was silent. Sarah's usually rollered jet-black hair hung limp on her young and slender shoulders. Sarah was lovely, a natural beauty that always made the men take a second look.

Tom drove with an air of irritation. Not being very tall, about five and a half feet, and small of stature Tom always looked as though he sat on top of the steering wheel. He was almost hunched over it, his wavy blonde hair blowing in the wind from the open window. His baby blue eyes intent on the road ahead. Normally they were soft and warm, today they were cold and hard. He refused to talk to Sarah. He was in one of his moods. Tom drove the car expertly, fast as always, being a confident driver he always felt in control at the wheel. Beth sat in the back and peered at her new sister. She was only eighteen months old and the baby meant little to her. Boredom got the better of Beth, and Annie's introduction to her big sister was Beth's now removed shoes thrown into the carrycot.

Tom and Sarah were both thinking the same thing - how were they going to cope with another child, both financially and emotionally? The reality had now set in, they were taking her home, there was no going back. They had to accept this new child into their lives. Arriving home from the hospital, Tom had stopped the car but had not switched the engine off. Leaving Sarah to battle with the two children and baggage, he stared vaguely ahead. He blamed her for this new intrusion. Let her do it alone. After Sarah had closed the door Tom drove off without a word. He was heading for the nearest pub, he needed a drink. Sarah simply had to learn to cope.

*   *   *   *   *   *

They were hard, the early years for Tom and Sarah. Tom was an apprentice, Sarah stayed at home and raised the girls. Sarah

14

learnt the fine art of making a meal from very little, yet she always managed to have beer in the refrigerator for Tom when he came home. She was terrified of his temper and would do anything to avoid incurring his wrath. It was a difficult time for Sarah, yet she juggled the finances and two young children with relative ease, considering her own young age. To say Annie was difficult would be an understatement. She hated sleep. Conformity was not in her makeup.

When Annie was two, things began to change. Tom was offered a position in a different town, but that would mean Sarah would be without her mother's help. After much debate, they made the move and settled down with relative ease. Annie did not notice the change.

It was at the age of three when Annie's little world became unsafe. Tom would, on most evenings, return home at five thirty on the dot. Annie adored her father and was always waiting for him to come home. She would patiently sit on the kerb outside the gate to their home, kicking her bare feet in the dust, enjoying the feeling of the soft powdery soil between her toes. Time never seemed to matter and she would happily sit for hours waiting for him, knowing her reward would come eventually. When Tom approached the high wrought iron gates that surrounded their property, Annie would bounce up and open them for him. Then she would climb into the car and onto his lap and help drive the car into the garage. Once they were inside the house, her first task was to remove his shoes and socks, then she would raid his lunch box for leftovers.

One night Sarah had survived a trying day and Beth and Annie were not yet bathed. Tom totally out of character, offered to bath the girls. He invented a game that night in the bath called 'find-the-soap'. He would drop the soap into the water and feel around trying to find it. As he was looking for the soap he would tickle the girls and make them squeal with laughter. He also lingered at Annie's vagina, as if it were the most natural thing, making it part of the game. The game took on a new phase. The tickling lessened and the lingering increased. He prised open the lips of Annie's vagina and

15

felt for her minute clitoris and opening. Suddenly everything changed.

Words cannot describe it, but from that moment Annie took on a woman's job at the age of three. She suddenly grew up and her childhood left. Now she was to learn about things most people did not experience until they were adults.

Sending Beth to Sarah for dressing, Tom called out that he would bath with Annie. He undressed and Annie's eyes widened at the size of his erection. He climbed into the bath, took her little hand and placed it upon his penis. Cupping his hand over hers he masturbated into the water. His orgasm came quickly, the thrill of a new conquest fuelling Tom's penchant. He loved little girls. Annie was his third. The first he had to leave behind when they moved and he was beginning to bore with Beth and her sullenness. Annie's laughter, love of life and total devotion to him was just what he needed to enhance his sexual pleasures. Annie did not question his actions – it just seemed so natural – and she knew no different. Tom sternly told her never to tell anyone. He spoke of his love for her and how special she was to him. Annie felt loved and adored. He had never paid her this much attention before. Tom then bathed Annie in the sperm contaminated water and from that moment on she never, ever felt clean again.

CHAPTER 3

Tom had worked long, hard hours and saved enough money to put down a deposit on a house. There was great excitement. They would have a home of their very own. Annie remembered going with Tom and Sarah to see the house when they were considering buying it. It had seemed so very large, but in reality it was a modest home. Three bedrooms, a lounge, dining room, kitchen and bathroom. It was on a smallish piece of land – one third of an acre. The garden housed a garage and a small outside room with it's own ablutions, standard in those parts, as most people had their own domestic servants who lived on the property. Sarah though, chose to do her own housework and the quarters would be used as a playroom for the girls.

Sarah busied herself with the move and Annie and Beth spent long hours playing together. Beth was Annie's hero and Annie adored her. She so wanted to be like Beth. Beth always sat with her legs crossed and never shouted. Beth was quiet and shy, Annie loud and outgoing. Not long after the move Beth started school and Annie was alone at home. She hated it. Beth and Annie were tied by something stronger than love. They both knew what their father did to each of them but it was never mentioned between them. They refused to break the silence imposed upon them.

Annie always played outside in the garden during the day, busying herself with whatever she could find. She learnt that bugs did not taste good, but donkey weeds did. She discovered a chameleon in her garden, and made it into a pet. She was devastated when it ran away. She would climb the trees in the garden and loved the feeling of being bigger than she actually was. She could observe much up in the trees and no one would know she was there. Uncle Jack used to come over sometimes to visit her mother, and Annie was never allowed near the house when he was there. If she needed to urinate, she would relieve herself in the garden so as to avoid the wrath of Sarah.

One day Annie's curiosity got the better of her and she peeped through the window. Being aware of sex at such an early age, she could smell it a mile away. She watched with curiosity, as Sarah and Jack petted in the lounge, then they moved to the bedroom and Annie could no longer watch. This became a fairly regular routine but Annie never said a word. Sarah and Tom argued a lot during this time, having screaming rows whilst Annie buried her head under her pillow trying to block the sound out. Doors would slam and things would get broken. She always felt so scared. She saw Tom's anger on many occasions and it reinforced her fear of him.

Sarah became pregnant again. Tom was furious. He could not understand how it had happened, they were always so careful. Tom accused Sarah of having an affair. She denied it. The tension between them seemed to last forever. Daina was born late in the year. Tom did not look at her. He refused to touch her or love her, as far as he was concerned she was not his child. Daina was a feisty child and everyone else loved her. Stunningly beautiful, she captured everyone's hearts, except for Tom's.

Sarah adored Daina from the moment she was born and Beth and Annie felt pushed aside by Sarah. Tom turned his attentions and love to Beth and Annie. They were his release and life now. Annie started school and hated it. She carried such huge secrets within her, that she always felt different from the other children. She had no friends and would always look for Beth at playtime. Beth, being that bit older, shunned her younger sister and preferred to be with her own friends. They were lonely years for Annie. Her only source of love came from Tom's advances. Tom, now well into the abuse of his daughters, took amazing chances. Sunday in their house was fishing day.

The family would drive a few miles to a large lake on the outskirts of town. Tom would waken early and prepare his bait for the day, pack up his beers and fishing tackle then make coffee for all and get everyone motivated. They were such fun days - sometimes. Tom's favourite trick was to wake Annie early on Sunday mornings and take her with him to the kitchen. He would make her lie down on the dog's blanket, with her panties removed. Tom always slept naked and never hid his nakedness. He would stand at the stove cooking his bait concoction and stare at Annie's nakedness, his desire growing. Annie would be terrified that someone would walk through. She always felt that if someone was to walk in she would be the one in trouble. She hated the smell of the dog's blanket, the musty dog smell and the dog hairs covering her. Even later in life she could not bear the thought of a blanket touching her skin – it just brought back too many memories.

She remembered one particular morning, Tom had finished his cooking and came near to where she was to switch on the kettle. She knew not to say anything, just lie there waiting for him to do what he wanted. It was almost as if she lay watching him deciding what he felt like that day – like watching and waiting for him to choose a breakfast cereal or a sandwich filling. This time she was relatively lucky. He knelt between her legs and rubbed his penis over her clitoris asking her if she liked it and did it feel nice. Annie just said yes because that seemed to make him happy and then it would be over quicker. He masturbated onto her vagina then rubbed his sperm over her and pushed his finger inside her. At least it was not so sore today, the sperm helped lubricate his rough finger.

Annie always felt so very clever when it was over quickly, like she had done a good job. Some Sundays it had been terrible. The worst part was never knowing what Tom would do, the fear of never knowing seemed worse than the actual abuse. Annie hated having Tom's penis in her mouth, especially first thing in the morning and whenever she got out of having to do this she would feel that she had achieved something. Worse than this would be when Tom would try and force his penis into her vagina, it would be so very painful and Annie was not allowed to cry. If she did Tom would get angry with her. She had to keep quiet and lie still. She was not allowed to move, she just had to take whatever he felt like dishing out. When it was all over she was allowed to tiptoe back to bed and pretend to be asleep.

Tom would then make loud banging noises yelling "Come

on kids, we're going fishing!" Coffee was made and an air of excitement would infuse the house. Annie felt like she was living in two totally different houses. What had happened five minutes earlier would be totally forgotten about, as if it had never happened. Sometimes she wondered if maybe she had just dreamt these things. Tom would always put a record on the hi-fi on Sunday mornings and 'Oh Oh Candida' rocked the house that morning. Everyone was so jovial and happy, but Annie was crying inside. Sarah finished packing the lunch whilst all three girls helped to pack the car. Breakfast was eaten and worms unearthed and packed. Tom kept worms under the tree at the back of the house and Annie would watch fascinated as Tom would peel back the coverings and expose thousands of earthworms. She hated them.

Usually friends would come with them for the day and today Auntie Mary and her six children were joining them. There were thirteen of them squashed into Tom's car and the mood was light and cheerful, the day still young and full of expectation. Tom loved to sing and would make up funny songs causing them all to be in absolute fits of laughter. Tom could be great fun, everybody loved him when he was like this. He would change the words to well known nursery rhymes and songs and have all the children in hysterics.

"Doh a dear, a glass of beer, ray a drop of golden sun, me a name I call myself, far a big fat motor car!" Shrieks from the back. They adored him when he was in this mood it somehow made the other side of him seem unreal and Annie could almost believe that the things that happened to her were just a dream. They were not reality, this was, the fun and the laughter. In contrast, Sarah seemed to have no sense of humour during those years. She rarely laughed unless Uncle Jack was around. Sarah would get so frustrated with the children and yell at Tom.

"For Gods sake Tom, please speak to those bloody kids!"

Tom would reply "Hi girls, how you doing?"

And the four of them would shriek again. Sarah was never amused. She always felt so excluded from their fun. The day at the lake fishing was always an adventure and great fun. The first Christmas present Annie could remember receiving was a fishing rod. She became very good at fishing. Beth, on the other hand, only tolerated fishing. Annie would put the worms onto the hook for her because Beth hated getting her hands dirty. Annie would be fascinated at how the worms would kind of explode and shit when you pushed the worm onto the hook. She would watch them wriggling on the end of the hook knowing that after a while the wriggling would stop. She knew that if you wanted to catch a good fish you needed a live wriggling worm, and once the worm stopped struggling, she would take the dead one off and replace it. Annie would always catch something but after a while would lose interest, especially if the fish went off the bite.

Tom would happily sit all day fishing and drinking beer. Sarah would prepare lunch and tend to the children. The children would run off and play, never fearing, they explored caves and made up nature walks and talked for hours. Tom's favourite thing to do when he had not had his morning fix before leaving home was to explain that he needed to move spots as the fish had gone off the bite. This always seemed to happen just before lunchtime when Sarah was busy. Of course Tom would need someone to come with him. Sometimes it was Beth who had to go with. Never Daina, he never touched Daina.

Annie could vividly remember her times of having to go with Tom to find a new spot. They would walk for ages through bush and thorns, carrying rods and bait and drinks. Tom always hurrying her, her little legs could only move so fast though, and she was scared of falling. Her nerves were on edge anyway, for she knew what was going to happen. She hated it. Why couldn't it be like other days when he wouldn't do this? She knew Beth would know what was happening and it made her feel funny. She didn't want Beth to know. But Beth would be breathing easy. Beth's knowledge came from the number of times she herself had endured Tom's passions.

Tom would find a quiet spot with no one around. He would set up his fishing rods, cast the line and then tell Annie to remove her panties and lie back. She hated this, she felt so exposed and always feared someone coming or walking past. Tom never seemed to worry, something stronger always seemed to drive him. There was no stopping him. He couldn't stop until the white stuff came, then it would be okay. It would all be over then. But until then Annie would endure the pain and humiliation.

This day he rinsed his hands in the dirty lake water to remove the worm and fish crap from his fingers, undid his shorts and exposed his erect penis. He came to her, knelt beside her and whispered, "Kiss it". Annie closed her eyes and lifted her head and gave his penis a quick peck. God, she hated that thing, it always looked so ugly and he was so proud of it. "No," he whispered hoarsely, "kiss it like I showed you, kiss it properly."

Annie lifted herself up and placed her young mouth around his penis.

"That's better," Tom cooed, "now suck, Annie, suck it."
It would never stay in her mouth, it would always come out and he would get so angry. She tried so hard to suck it like he wanted but she just couldn't get it right. She began to cry.

"For fuck's sake stop crying!" He commanded. Annie stopped crying but sobs heaved in her chest. She could not breath, he was suffocating her. The combination of his large penis in her small mouth and the sobs echoing in her chest made her panic. She couldn't breath, but Tom didn't care, he was past caring. He was too intent on his own pleasure. He held her head and pushed his penis down her throat, she gagged.

"Suck," he demanded. A tear escaped from her eyes, she closed her eyes tight in the hope that he would not notice. Annie never felt like she could float away at these times, she always had to have her senses aware in case anyone came and saw what they were doing. She would have died if anyone had seen her like this. She had to stay and try to push past her fear and urges to be sick. She had to try and hurry things, to get it over and done with quickly. He must have loved being outdoors, his orgasm came quickly. Hot, thick spurts of semen pulsed into Annie's throat. Swallow," he insisted.

Annie crying and choking swallowed the revolting tasting sperm. It always seemed to stick in her throat and afterwards she would cough and cough trying to get rid of the taste but it would not go away. She would drink large cups of juice but the taste persisted. Tom adjusted his shorts and Annie, without being told, got herself dressed. She was heartbroken, she was so sure he would leave her alone today. She had heard Tom and Sarah only last night doing 'it' and she thought she would be okay today, it seemed so unfair. He had ruined the whole day.

She sat quietly on the banks watching the water, tears rolling down her face. Tom whistled as he fished. Annie explained she was going back and Tom said that was fine. She walked and walked, picking grass and watching the ants scurrying to and fro. She did not want to go back, she did not want to go and pretend all was well, she wanted to cry and be sick. But she couldn't, she had to pretend everything was okay. She made her way back eventually. She and Beth could not look at each other. For some reason there was always an underlying jealousy between Beth and Annie, even though they both hated what was happening, they secretly hated the other getting Tom's attention. It was becoming almost a competition. A silent competition between the two sisters and their mother. They all played the game but never showed their hands.

*   *   *   *   *   *

Tom was fire and ice, laughter and pain, he was two different people. One minute on the floor with his girls tickling them and laughing, the next sullen and moody. Annie knew his moods well and could pick them up at a glance. She knew when she could climb on his lap for a cuddle and when she couldn't. She knew when she could joke around and when she couldn't.

Sarah was different. Not being a demonstrative mother she showed her girls little affection. Cursed by her own demons she battled emotionally to keep it all together. She did not know what Tom was doing to the girls but Annie always believed that somehow she did. Annie hated her mother for so very much. She hated her mother for allowing Tom to do the things he did to their children, she hated her for doing those things to Tom, and she hated the fact that Sarah slept around. Sarah had moved past Uncle Jack and there was a new man on the scene. Annie did not know his name, she just knew of his existence.

Sarah was violent and had the most terrifying temper. The girls knew when it was brewing and they would make themselves scarce. Her favourite was to pick up Beth and Annie by their hair and bash their heads together when they would not listen. She would then literally throw them down the passage to their bedrooms where they would sit in absolute silence to "wait for your father to get home".

This was nerve wracking stuff. Beth and Annie would never know how Tom would be when he got home. Sometimes he would bring out his belt, pull their panties down and beat their bare bottoms. Sometimes he would shout at Sarah and rescue the girls, and other times he would just shout at them. Once in a while he would take the opportunity to fiddle. They never knew what mood he would be in when he walked through the door. Tom and Sarah were both so unpredictable. The girls lived a roller coaster existence, never knowing from one moment to the next what would happen. It could happen any time without warning, either sexual or physical abuse. They learnt to suppress their personalities, knowing they could never show them.

Occasionally Uncle Errol would come to visit. He was an old family friend, and was such fun to be with. He loved the girls and would sit them on his knee and tell them stories about places he had visited and things he had done in his life. Annie did not know life existed outside her country. She would sit wide eyed taking it all in.

24

Uncle Errol would make them laugh and he always brought sweets – a rare treat. One night Uncle Errol came to say he was going to San Francisco, the place like the song where you wear flowers in your hair. Beth and Annie were fascinated. It became their favourite song and they would dance around the garden with flowers pinned in their hair.

Uncle Errol promised to take them. He told them to go and pack their suitcases. Annie needed no encouragement. She was up in a flash and off to her bedroom. She grabbed her small school case and packed what she saw as her essentials - her favourite shoes, some spare panties and her teddy. She was ready to go.
"At last I am saved," she thought.

Uncle Errol was only joking though and they all laughed at her when she came through with her case all packed. She was heart broken and never forgave him for his ill timed joke. Her life was a misery and he was supposed to be her way out. Something died within her that night. Perhaps it was her spirit, her fight for self and with it's loss came a resignation to the life she led.

Being a bit older now, she was able to see her life was not normal. Her friends' fathers never did those things to her and her friend's fathers were so nice. Her best friend Belinda had the best dad. Annie would go and visit there and he would make her laugh and laugh. She would knock at the door and he would sing to her, "I hear you knocking but you can't come in," Annie would shriek with laughter. She would beg to stay there every weekend. Sometimes it was not possible, or Tom would say no and Annie would be devastated. Belinda and Annie were inseparable.

Belinda had a huge double bed that they would share when Annie stayed over. Annie and Belinda used to delight in each other's bodies. Even though Annie was only eight her body was orgasming. And Belinda was Annie's release and outlet. She adored Belinda and they would take any opportunity they could to be alone together. Annie could make her body climax in a short space of time. She would masturbate regularly.

Belinda and her family moved away, and they took a part of Annie's heart with them. She never got over her loss of Belinda but most of all she missed the healthy relationship she had had with Belinda's father, he was such a nice man and in so may ways she hated Belinda for the fact that she had a nice dad. Annie wanted one just like him.

CHAPTER 4

A whole array of new emotions were beginning to enter Annie's life, and her body was changing and responding to Tom's advances. She hated the way her body reacted to Tom and hated the fact he could make her climax. She would always pretend it was not happening but Tom always knew. She began to wet her bed and Sarah would be furious with her. Her school work deteriorated and her reports were always the same, 'could do better', 'lacks concentration' and 'untidy'. Annie hated school and mathematics and having to conform. She always felt like she was living some kind of double life and was always in trouble but it never felt like it was her fault and she never knew why. She could tell nobody, and no-one seemed to understand.

Nightmares came almost every night and she could never work them out, they were so real. She was running, running away from someone and all around her were huge black holes and she had to watch her footing so that she did not fall into them. They never ended and she could never see the bottom of them, they were just so huge and deep and dark, the area between them narrow and rocky. She would run and run sometimes wishing she could just fall into a hole so as to escape whoever was chasing her. She would wake up exhausted and fearful. There was no-one to call, no-one would hear her. What she thought was sweat in the bed was urine - she would always wet the bed and then spend the rest of the night panicking that Sarah would find out.

She began the eating cycle. She loved to hide and her favourite hiding place was the pantry and in the dark she would feel around for things to eat. When she could she would mix herself weird concoctions and eat them hidden under her bed or at the top of her cupboard. Tom became even more blasé with the abuse and Annie's fear heightened. She was terrified someone was going to see.

The girls had been in town with Sarah one day and when they had finished they popped into Tom's workshop to visit him.

Annie loved it there. There were always a large number of big lorries to look at, and Tom's friends would make a fuss of them. She loved looking down the pit but was always afraid of falling into it. They reminded her of her dream.

The workers were packing up and it was time to go home. Annie went to get into the car with her mother and sisters but Tom stepped in and said he wanted Annie to go with him. She knew what would happen, but she had no choice but to go with him. Sarah left first and Annie longed to be in that car. They drove off without looking back.

Tom's Zephyr had one long seat in the front, and this was not the first car episode. She knew her part. She moved to another being and removed her panties. She lay on the front seat with her head pressing against the door handle, it took her mind off what was happening down below. Tom would drive with one hand on the wheel and one hand fingering Annie's vagina. The terror of being abused in the open was always scary. She was convinced the whole world could see what he was doing and no-one did anything to stop it. Tom always drove fast and Annie would be terrified they were going to crash. She would lay ever so still and disappear in her mind. Tom would alternate between masturbating himself, feeling Annie and changing gear. He would always stop abusing her for a while to reach into his pocket for his handkerchief, lay it on the seat ready to receive his sperm. He would then clean up, adjust his shorts, put his handkerchief away and call Annie back down by telling her to dress. He did all this while driving. He never missed a beat.

Some days he would stop the car somewhere quiet, and open the front and back doors. He would try to force his penis into her tight vagina. He would lay her on the front seat and pull her legs out the door and open them as wide as he could. Then he would kneel on the edge of the car, levering himself to her. He could never get his penis into her. She was too tight and he could not risk injuring her. It was always so painful for Annie, the pain would last for days afterwards as if forcing her to remember what had happened. She tried so hard to hide it. The days after the abuse when the pain was

28

bad she would make herself come out of her body and float around. She was so proud of how good she was at this. Her favourite was to lie on her bed and make herself touch the ceiling. Other times she could go into her cupboard or under her bed where it was cool and dark, she could count the springs on her bed or pull the horse hair out of her mattress. It was the most fun she had, she felt so in control.

Tom by this stage had also moved up the road, so to speak. A large family lived two doors away and the youngest child was a girl, Kerry, who was a little older than Annie. Tom would chase Kerry in the pool and Annie could see him pulling her costume aside and fingering her vagina. She hated Kerry. She hated Tom and what he was doing to Kerry. She hated the fact he had someone else and she had to share him. Her love for him was changing, she was starting to mature and huge amounts of jealousy and rage would course through her. She could never express them. She never understood them. Beth became another enemy and she and Annie fought constantly. They fought for Tom's attention and affection and fought each other for the power they had over Tom, the power to wangle money out of him, or treats, or just his undivided attention. Beth and Annie never, ever spoke about what went on even though they both knew what was happening to the other.

Once, when Beth had a friend to stay, Tom abused her, and she never came round again. No one asked any questions. "Strange girl, that one," was all they heard their parents say. Tom was on a roll, he was brave and open and no one ever questioned what was going on. Tom was popular at work and in social circles. He could tell jokes that made everyone laugh and flirt outrageously with the women. Everyone loved him, adored him almost. Tom began sleeping with other women, his huge sexual appetite bursting its walls. He thrived on the secrecy and the power he had over women and children. He could make them do anything, anything he wanted and they did. He was never questioned or refused. Apart from Daina. Once he tried it with her and Daina firmly told him that if he ever did that again she would tell her mother. Knowing how close Sarah and Daina were, Tom never tried it with her again. However Daina was very aware of what was happening in the house. The only one who never seemed to know was Sarah.

Annie had an infection. The doctor was called to the house and Annie suffered the humiliation of having a male doctor examine her vagina. She slipped off her panties as if in a routine and lay spread legged on the bed and disappeared out of the room in her mind. The doctor took swabs and told Sarah he would have the results in a few days. Annie had a pelvic inflammation infection. No one thought to ask how she had got the infection. She was medicated and life carried on. She got another infection a few months later and again, no one questioned it. Annie though it was her own fault for playing with herself as much as she did. She felt so dirty. She thought she 'smelt' down there and was convinced everyone around could smell it too. She felt even more ostracised from the girls at school. She became a loner, lost in a world no one knew existed.

*　　*　　*　　*　　*　　*

Tom fell in love with Debbie, Sarah's best friend. Debbie had come to Africa with her husband and two children, a girl and a boy. She also fell in love with Tom. They decided they wanted to ride off into the sunset together. At this stage Sarah was involved in a fully fledged affair with George, a man ten years her junior. Tom left home, but more to the point Tom left Annie and she was heartbroken. The months that followed were some of Annie's worst ever. She completely lost her voice, and could not talk. It became a joke to everyone around her, but to Annie it was her only way of expressing the silence she had been forced into for all those years. She could not tell how much she missed Tom and in what ways she missed him. She pined for him daily and wept for him constantly. She was supposed to be his favourite how could he leave her? Why didn't he take her with him? She would sit for hours at the gate listening for his car, willing him to fetch her.

Living with Sarah was a nightmare, she was drinking, her temper was worse than ever, and she could not bring her relationship with George out into the open because her divorce was going through. She was angry, hurt and fierce. The girls became her pawns. She would use them in whatever way she could to get at Tom and Debbie. She demanded money, she phoned them constantly and went through all the pains, frustrations and insecurities of being left for another woman. The house was full of land mines waiting to be stepped on. Annie just withdrew more and more into herself.

Tom would take them out for weekends. Annie was at her happiest during these times. She would wait for him for hours at the gate, totally frustrating Sarah. Annie could hear his car coming miles away and would always run down the road to meet him. She would fling open the driver's door and throw herself into his arms.

They had such fun during the times away from Sarah. Debbie seemed to fulfil his sexual desires and he more or less left Beth and Annie alone. It seemed the most normal months of their childhood. Tom was happy, really happy and so in love. Debbie brought out the best in him and he put on weight, grew a moustache and his boyish good looks just seemed to get better. When they were with Tom and Debbie, they were like a big happy family, always laughing and joking. Tom hardly fished and instead they would picnic, go for drives or visit friends. The atmosphere was relaxed and happy. Beth, Annie and Daina got on so well with Debbie's children and they believed they were just one big happy family.

The worst part of these weekends was when Tom took the girls home. Annie always clung to him sobbing begging him to take her with him, but he never did. Sarah tried to stop his visits claiming they upset Annie too much. She was impossible when Tom returned her home and Sarah could not deal with her. Tom refused Sarah's request. He felt Anne would eventually settle down into the new routine of things and that they would get better. This did eventually happen, Annie got used to letting Tom leave as long as he promised to come and see her again.

The school holidays came and Tom asked Sarah if he could have the girls for the month. Sarah agreed, albeit for selfish reasons, she and George were getting on so well and needed the time alone to cement their relationship. Tom fetched the girls from their house and they began the three hour journey to the town where Tom and Debbie lived. They sang all the way. Tom always drank and drove, he would nestle a bottle of beer in the steering wheel and when it was finished he would open his car window and try and smash the bottle on passing signs. The girls thought this was hilarious and always cheered him on. They sang and acted totally manic. The car stereo was always blaring – Elvis and how life was sweet.

Having his daughters under his roof again disturbed Tom a lot. He could not control himself. The urges had always been there so why did he think he could ever stop them? The nightmare began again. After months of release it was back. The cycle continued and Annie began to lose herself again. Changing from a happy child to a quiet and lonely girl. No-one seemed to notice the change, it was just put down to Annie, going through a weird patch again. No-one bothered to try and understand why. Tom always had plenty of excuses to be alone with Beth or Annie, saying he needed time alone with his daughters, he missed them, he needed to see how they were doing. Debbie totally loving and trusting, did not give it a second thought. The girls returned to Sarah after the holidays and Tom turned his advances to Debbie's daughter. She never told anyone what he did to her.

*   *   *   *   *   *

Tom had to visit his parents, they lived in a town a good five hours away from where Sarah and the girls lived. He arranged to pick the girls up on his way through. Tom's mother hated Debbie and Debbie was never invited to her home. So it was Tom and the three girls that weekend. Tom's parents had a small cottage on their property where Tom and the girls would sleep. Annie never understood her grandmother, she gave Annie the absolute shits. A domineering and fierce woman, all the girls kept their distance from her.

Saturday afternoon was rest time. They made their way to

the cottage and Tom gave Annie and Daina some money to go to the shops and buy sweets. Annie did not even know where the shops were. Tom pointed them in a general direction and told them to walk, following the railway track. It seemed to take forever and they were scared. But they knew better than to question. They took their time and bought the sweets, but could not eat them. Something was stuck in their throats. They both knew what was happening but neither said a word. The ambled back and walked into the cottage. Tom was naked and so was Beth. Tom was forcing himself into Beth and Beth was silently crying. Beth looked around and saw them standing there and Annie would never ever forget the look on Beth's face. Annie knew it so well, the shame, the pain, the humiliation. Beth had not wanted Annie to see her like this, just as Annie would have died if anyone had ever seen what Tom did to her. Tom screamed at Annie and Daina to get the fuck out. They hurried out and sat on the step in total silence. Tom was persistent. He was not giving up, Beth's virginity was his and today he would take it, no matter what. They heard Beth quietly sobbing. Annie and Daina held each others hands and never said a word. They just sat there in total silence, staring straight ahead only shuddering when Beth's cries could be heard. Their sweets lay scattered on the ground, untouched.

That weekend took on a huge surreality. Tom acted like nothing had happened and Beth was her usual quiet self. Annie and Daina were now bound to each other in a mutual knowledge and pain that seemed to exclude all around them, as if they were in some kind of bubble. Their love and commitment to each other was born that day. They were connected by a bond that excluded all those around them. Annie knew from that moment on that without a shadow of a doubt she was next. Tom had finally succeeded with Beth, there would be no stopping him now. Annie simply had to accept the inevitable. No words were spoken and a fear seemed to envelop them both. Daina now fully understood what Annie would go through – it was the first time Daina had been confronted with what Tom did to her sisters, she too could no longer live in the innocence of her childhood. That had been taken from her that day. They had both seen the reality. It had happened and would happen again.

That day was never, ever mentioned by anyone.

CHAPTER 5

Sarah's romance with George heightened, the divorce had come through and Sarah was now free to pursue her new relationship. Annie began to get to know George, and being that much younger than Sarah he was great fun. He would take the girls to play pin ball and buy them ice cream. The girls loved him, he was a breath of fresh air to the house and Sarah took on a new lease of life. She was fun and witty and happy. She and George announced they were to be engaged and they were moving house. They were still in the house Tom and Sarah had bought all those years before. The divorce agreement was that if Sarah remarried or cohabited with a man, she had to move out of the house.

They moved to a new area. Annie was due to start high school and her body had started developing early almost as if it knew she was a woman before her time. Her periods began when she was twelve and for the first few months she did not tell anyone. Preferring to keep this secret to herself.

Beth was turning in to a real stunner and the boys were starting to sniff around. Beth was not interested. George got pissed one night and made a move on Beth. Beth told Sarah but Sarah simply refused to believe her. No-one was going to burst Sarah's perfect bubble. It was like reliving a nightmare for Beth, she never recovered from it. After months of an ideal home life it had been totally shattered again by a man's lust. Beth just became quieter, whilst Annie became noisier.

Annie began to make friends with the rebels and had started smoking, she loved the way it made her feel grown up, and it somehow fitted her grown up psyche. Sarah was so involved with George, she so totally adored him that she never really noticed what the girls were getting up to. Annie had freedom and would go out whenever she could. She never bothered with the boys, she just liked the freedom of being out and she loved to smoke. High school was great, Annie loved it, she made friends with a girl named Megan who had recently moved from Australia. She was a total rebel and non conformist, Annie loved her total 'fuck you' attitude. They became firm friends, totally inseparable and hated by their teachers.

*　　　*　　　*　　　*　　　*　　　*

Annie's thirteenth birthday was approaching and Tom had asked her on the phone what she wanted as a present. She begged him for a watch. It was all she had ever wanted. He said he would see what he could do. Tom made an arrangement with Sarah for the girls to spend a weekend with himself and Debbie. Financially Tom was struggling, after starting his own business. He, Debbie and her two children lived in a two bed-roomed flat. It would be a squeeze with three extra, but who cared.

The girls took a bus to where Tom lived. Tom and Debbie's previously happy relationship was showing signs of the financial strain and there was an atmosphere in the house the girls had not felt before. Debbie did all she could to make the weekend special for the girls but it was hard going. Tom suggested they go out for lunch on the Saturday to his favourite hotel. The owner was a good friend of Tom's and they were always treated like royalty in his establishment. Tom was so well liked.

They arrived at the hotel just before lunch and the atmosphere was light and jovial. A hot sunny day, it made everyone feel lazy and totally un-energetic after lunch. They sat around chatting and catching up. It was a blissful day. Annie felt so relaxed and safe. There was no way Tom could try it on with her this weekend, there was no time or space. She basked in the security of her thoughts. The time to leave came and they all went to bundle into Debbie's beaten up old Volkswagen Beetle. Tom had joined them at the hotel once he had finished work. He still drove the Zephyr and it was still immaculate. Annie hated the fucking thing. It always seemed to send shivers down her spine.

As they were loading up Tom called over to them to wait up. He explained to Debbie he wanted to take Annie, as Sarah had mentioned she was not doing well at school and he wanted to talk to her about it. Annie's heart sank. She knew, she just fucking knew. Debbie and the other four children followed Tom's car out of the hotel, Tom then put his foot down and left them way behind. The plan was for them to meet up with Tom and Annie at the workshop. It was a long windy mountain road home and Annie sat almost on the door handle she was so nervous. Tom drove fast and expertly. He asked Annie about school and she began to relax. She fed him some bullshit and he seemed happy enough.

Halfway home he told her to come and sit next to him. She moved over, slipping easily in to her well known role. He told her to remove her panties and she did. She kept trying to separate but she was too nervous. The sharp corners and winding road coupled with Tom's fast driving made her very nervous. She was scared but her fear was deeper than the road. She knew that somehow Tom had it all worked out. Today he would not stop, today was the day, today he would do to her what he had done to Beth months earlier.

She was terrified and stifled a sob. Tom drove well and confidently, all the while fiddling with Annie's lightly hair covered vagina. He drove home. No words were exchanged. Annie wondered what Debbie and the rest must have been thinking. They arrived and went upstairs. Tom ordered her to remove the rest of her clothing. Annie refused. Her voice sounded foreign to her, she had never thought of refusing him before. Tom was totally unmoved and again demanded she take off her clothes. She did not have it in her to refuse again.

She removed what remained of her clothing, her panties were still stuffed in her bag. She had just finished her period and her bag went everywhere with her - 'just in case'. He told her to lie on the bed and she obeyed, it was no use fighting. He always won. He had that look in his eyes, the one she knew so well, the one the world never saw. It was as if something drove him, he lost all connection with reality, so intent was he with the task ahead. There was no taking of time. He just took her. Roughly he forced his penis into her vagina, the resistance he met with only seemed to excite him more. Annie was sobbing with pain and fear, she was begging him to get off her.

"Please Daddy, please get off, your hurting me," she cried.

He ignored her, it was as if he did not hear her. She sobbed louder.

"If you don't get off me I'm going to scream, I'm going to scream Dad," she sobbed.

It didn't matter if she screamed now, Tom was finished. He was very pleased with himself, he had finally achieved what he had tried to attain for all these years, to own his daughters' virginity's.

Tom lifted himself off the bed and told Annie to get dressed. As she got up off the bed Tom looked down at the cream bed cover and swore. Annie looked down and there on the bed cover lay the evidence of her virginity. Like a blob of jam plopped on the bed, it was hard to comprehend. That small stain on the bed should have been her choice. He had taken what should have been the most precious thing she owned. For years afterwards she pondered who she would have freely given her virginity to if it had not been taken from her so forcefully.

Annie ignored Tom's outburst and made her way to the bathroom to clean up. She was so pissed off because Tom's roughness had re-started her period – or it may have been the blood of her virginity, she didn't know, she really didn't care. She was somewhere else. She was going through the motions. He took more than her virginity and choice that day he seemed to have taken her very soul and spirit. She separated herself into two lives, the 'when she was' and the 'when she was not'. Nothing seemed to matter any more, she felt like the fight was finally over. She knew he would never come near her again, she had lost her appeal, she was a woman.

Tom cleaned the bed and they went to join Debbie and the others. Tom totally ignored Annie, confusing her further. In so many ways she felt so grown up and special, and in so many others she felt like a vulnerable child. She wanted to cry but could not understand why. Everyone acted like everything was fine and Annie just played her role.

On Sunday it was time to go home, and Tom presented Annie with her birthday present, her thirteenth birthday was just weeks away. It was a watch, that which she had so desperately wanted. She was thrilled, she put it on straight away and Tom drove them to the bus station to get the bus home. Annie sat quietly staring out the window on the way home, occasionally glancing lovingly at her new watch. The watch packed up before they reached home. She felt so cheated and finally the tears came. That was the last time Annie was to see Tom for many years.

CHAPTER 6

It was early morning in the middle of the week, and the house was filled with the usual morning arguments and panics. Sarah emerged from the bedroom looking like death. No-one seemed to notice George's absence until they sat down for breakfast. Daina asked where he was, and Sarah simply explained that she did not know. The fact that he had not come home the night before was all they could get out of her. As if on cue, George drove up the driveway.

The girls sat at the table desperately trying to force down their breakfast while a huge row erupted. Naturally, Sarah wanted to know where he had been. He refused to answer. But he would not get off that lightly. Eventually he spat out that he had been with another woman and that he wanted Sarah and all her bloody children out of his house. It was just the sort of challenge Sarah thrived on. She went through to the dining room and told the girls there was a problem, she did not know where they would be staying that night. She told them to meet her at the petrol station at the end of the road after school and she would take them to where they would be staying. They all set off for school in silence. They were devastated, they thought George loved them. They loved him, he was such great fun and they loved living with him and living with the happy person Sarah had become. The fist part of the ride to school was silent, none of them said a word.

Annie, though not the eldest, always seemed to take the lead in situations like this. She eventually spoke to Beth and Daina and tried to make light of it. "Its okay," she said, "by the time we have finished school they would have sorted it out, they have fought before and always worked it out. You will see, it will be fine."

After school they met up at the designated place. Sarah had been busy, very busy. In a few short hours she had found a flat for them, and had organised to have the electricity, water and phone connected. She had borrowed a truck from work and she had moved every single item belonging to herself and the girls from the house

40

they had shared with George. She had left the lounge and dining room suite that was on hire purchase and had taken literally everything else. She closed the remaining curtains, locked the door and walked out. When George returned home that night there was no evidence to prove that Ninety-two Victoria Drive had once housed Sarah and the girls.

Sarah took them to their new home. Naturally it was a shambles, but Sarah had done a remarkable job in a few short hours. The girls were stunned. Sarah and Daina were to share the main bedroom and Beth and Annie the second bedroom. The flat was tiny with a small garden at the front. After living in a huge four bed-roomed mansion it was a bit of a shock for the girls, but Sarah's determination won them over. Annie's respect for Sarah grew that day.

Everything had changed so quickly from there, Sarah was broken and began seeing men. Any men, many men. The girls were confronted with their mother's promiscuity during their teenage years. Daina had it the worst, she shared a bed with Sarah and whoever else was around. Annie had been moved into the dining room because Beth had demanded privacy. She had a boyfriend now, a boy two years younger than she was.

Annie was beginning to notice boys but did not let anyone near her. She kept her distance and preferred to keep her sexual urges or desires to herself, preferring her fantasies to the reality she lived in. Beth was stunningly beautiful and Daina still young and almost boyish looking. Annie's body was showing the signs of over indulgence in the food line. She survived the mockings of school friends, usually telling them to fuck off or she would beat them up. She and Megan were still firm friends.

It was New Years Eve and Annie and Megan were going out, Sarah thought Annie was staying at Megan's house and Megan's parents were never to bothered about what their children got up to. Megan had a boyfriend years older than she was and they all headed for the local hotel. It was Annie's first taste of alcohol and she loved the feeling it gave her. They made their way into town, Annie wild and free. Kissing everyone on her path, laughing, shouting and having a great time.

Megan's boyfriend had a friend with him, he was keeping an eye on Annie to make sure she did not get lost in the crowds. He took her to an alley and raped her. Annie was too drunk to notice, it was so familiar anyway. What was the difference? He finished and took Annie to a taxi rank to get her home. They arrived and Annie slid down the wall turned her head and puked her guts out. She was coming down from her drunken buzz and this animal had just ripped open all her nightmares. Her 'date' then swore at her, bundled her into the back of the taxi and sat in the front, away from her. They drove her to Megan's house where they deposited her in the garden and left. Megan found her there a few hours later and managed to get her inside and into bed where she slept it off. It was a good few years before Annie touched alcohol again.

Things were getting out of control, Sarah could not seem to handle her life and the pressure of the girls. Annie frustrated Sarah terribly and the one was as stubborn as the other. Annie was terrified of Sarah, the childhood memories of Sarah's temper were always lurking just below the surface. Sarah would lose her temper for the slightest thing and the girls were terrified of her. If the flat was not spotless when Sarah came home from work there would be hell to pay. Sarah would just lose it completely. The girls tip-toed around her. One night Sarah called Annie to the kitchen.

"I want to ask you something, Annie," she said. "And I don't want any of your bullshit or lies, I just wanted the truth." Annie sat on the counter kicking her legs and said, "Okay."

"Are you still a virgin?" Annie had just turned fourteen. She saw no point in lying so she gave Sarah what she had asked for, she told Sarah the truth.

"No." She answered

"Okay," said Sarah, "I want to know who it was Annie, I want to know who you have been sleeping with. No bullshit."

"Okay, if you want to know I will tell you but I just know you won't believe me. It was my father." Annie spat out.

Sarah was furious, "Of all the lowest of the lows Annie, how can you sit there and say that – you are a lying little bitch."

"Well if you don't believe me, ask Beth," Annie spat. "Because the same thing happened to her."

Sarah called Beth through, but Beth denied everything. Sarah sent Annie out and asked Beth again, Beth confessed.

All hell broke loose.

*   *   *   *   *   *

The next few weeks passed in a blur for Annie, there were policewomen, social workers, priests, psychiatrists and doctors. Annie was terrified. She had been sworn to secrecy, and now she had to tell all these strangers what had happened. She did not now how to tell them or what to tell them or how much to tell them. How does one, in the space of a few hours, describe a life of sexual abuse? Statements were taken, examinations done, reports made. The girls were not allowed to talk to Tom under any circumstances. They had not seen him for over a year now – he seemed to have lost interest in them. Maybe that's why Annie blew the whistle on him, because he had so totally cut her off after raping her and she was so mad and hurt.

The weeks that followed were carefully planned. A holiday was organised for the girls. They were to go to friends in a neighbouring country. Sarah was to follow a week later. Sarah felt she had to get the girls out of the country. The girls did not know what was going on, no-one told them, they were just interviewed and then left feeling confused and full of unanswered questions. Sarah did not explain to them what she was doing or what was happening. They just thought they were going on holiday and were excited by the prospect.

The plane for Malawi took off at fifteen minutes before two o'clock on a sunny Tuesday afternoon. At two o'clock on the dot the police were knocking on Tom's door. Debbie answered the door, and could not believe what was happening. She thought it was some kind of joke. Tom was arrested and put in jail. The court case went by quickly. Tom had read the evidence, the girls had not said much. He pleaded guilty, he could not afford to let the girls give evidence in court. Tom was given three years imprisonment. For the continual years of sexual abuse on his two daughters he served a mere twenty months in jail, time was taken off for good behaviour. It was a complete farce, the girls were sentenced to life.

Sarah joined them in Malawi, they had a great holiday, everything seemed so perfect. Sarah did not tell the girls what was happening at home. They returned home three weeks later, none the wiser. Annie thought it had all just gone away. Sarah dropped a bombshell. Annie was to go and live with her grandparents in a town five hours drive away, she would go to school there and live with them indefinitely. She was not told why. She thought is was her punishment for telling on Tom. She was convinced Sarah hated her and just wanted to get rid of her for causing so much trouble. Annie had no choice, she was shipped off, away from her sisters, mother and friends. She never understood why.

She was placed in a school a good ten miles away from where they lived and she had to cycle to school. Her grandmother put her on a diet, so she ate in secret. One day after school her grandmother sat her down and told her Tom was in jail. Annie was devastated. She felt so guilty. She had put her own father in jail. "How he must hate me," she thought, "he will never forgive me." It was all her fault she should never have told. He had warned her, he had warned her and now look. She was so angry with Sarah, Sarah had lied. Sarah had said he would not go to jail. Sarah lied! Annie felt as if she was existing rather than living, choices were made in her life for her and she never seemed to be able to have any say in it. She was terribly unhappy. She missed Beth and Daina passionately. They had always been together through thick and thin and now Annie was alone. So very alone. And to top it all she felt so very responsible for Tom's fate.

CHAPTER 7

Annie's grandmother, Agnes had organised for Annie to join the St John's Ambulance Brigade. She felt it would be good for Annie. Annie lost herself in it and did very well. Every Saturday she was there, always the last to leave, striving to achieve, yearning for love and attention. She was top of the class. Life saving was her passion and she was an excellent swimmer. There was to be a display the next weekend of the services St John's offered, and Annie was asked to demonstrate life saving skills. She was thrilled. Agnes and Ted, her grandfather, promised to come and watch. Annie spent the morning looking out for them, they were still not there in the early afternoon when Annie's turn came. She did extremely well, swam as though her life depended on it and successfully showed how to save the lives of two people at once. Her picture made the local paper. No-one she loved or cared for was there to watch her.

There was a disco in the evening and Annie was determined to enjoy herself. It had been a shitty day. She was so depressed and pissed off. She knew something was up but did not know what. There was a boy, the best looking one there, and he asked Annie to dance. They had one dance and headed for the rugby field. Annie at this stage did not care – she was no longer a virgin so what did it matter. She reasoned that if two men had taken her against her will then she may as well just do it – it was all they wanted. The fight had left her. They screwed, Annie just lay there watching the stars waiting for him to finish. She did not even know his name.

From a distance she heard her name being called. Agnes was there to fetch her. "Oh fuck, she is coming over," Annie thought. She quickly adjusted her clothing and ran to meet her, full of false bravado. Agnes asked where she had been, she said she had been talking to friends. She was lucky there were quite a few people around. Agnes had been crying, she was dealing with her own demons that day. She accepted Annie's explanation about why she had not been at the disco and why she was out on the rugby field. Agnes drove them home and told Annie her grandfather was drunk, very drunk. Annie would not be able to come into the house, she would have to sleep in the car. There were pillows and a blanket ready for her in the back seat. They arrived home, her grandmother said good night and left Annie in the car.

Ted was on a roll, screaming and hurling abuse and ornaments, he was very far gone. She heard her grandmother yelp in pain, she also heard the blow that had struck her. She was furious. Her grandmother did not deserve the sort of treatment that was being dished out. Annie lay perfectly still in the car, terrified. This was not the first time Ted had become so drunk. Memories came screaming back.

Annie was about six years old, they were spending the weekend visiting both Tom and Sarah's parents, all of whom lived in the same town. They had travelled by train the night before. Annie loved the train and its rhythmic movements and the smells, and best of all the coffee in the morning. They were staying with Ted and Agnes. Ted had taken her out to buy sweets. They had gone to the club where Ted had given her money for sweets. It was a fortune to the small child. She had carefully selected her sweets, taking ages, they had put them in a little bag for her and she was so pleased. She refused to eat them because she wanted to share them with Beth and Daina.

Ted was taking his time drinking, Annie was getting scared. It was getting dark and she was alone on the veranda. Ted came out and told her they were leaving. Ted drove an old Morris Minor and on the way home stopped at his favourite haunt for one or two more drinks. He left Annie locked in the car. She was so scared. She needed the bathroom, and in the end she had no choice but to urinate in her pants. She curled herself up in a ball and cried. She fell asleep still clutching her sweets. She was awoken by an almighty row, Sarah had opened the car door and was pulling Annie out. When she got out of the car, Tom was beating Ted up. Ted lost a few teeth that night and was never allowed to take any of the girls out again.

Annie returned to the present, there was silence, she peeked her head up and looked around. Her grandmother was standing smoking a cigarette and crying at the gate. She flicked her cigarette end away, turned and walked into the house. A few hours later Agnes came and rescued Annie from the car and quietly slipped her inside to her bed. Agnes and Annie became friends after that, they built a special bond and love that excluded Ted. They just seemed to understand each other's pain. In the years ahead Annie was able to look back fondly on her time spent with Agnes, it had bonded her and her grandmother together for a life time and their strong bond and love for each other strengthened over the years.

Annie hated the school she had to attend whilst with Agnes and Ted. She had made no friends, she felt like a total outsider and was treated as such. She had slept with a few boys but had no boyfriend. She wanted to go home. She had had a pregnancy scare. She hated being away from Sarah and her sisters. She started stealing, not much, a few cigarettes from Agnes and Ted, some odd silver lying around to buy sweets or treats. Anything to defy the confines of the strict diet and her mundane life.

Sarah's reasoning for sending Annie to her mother was because she did not know if she would still receive maintenance from Tom once he was in jail, and she did not know if she could afford to survive financially. Annie was the easiest option as Beth was writing exams and Daina was too young. The money from the sale of the house Tom and Sarah had bought was in an account and Sarah was paid regular maintenance for the girls. Annie begged to come home. Sarah relented but with conditions. Annie was to attend an all day school. Annie would have agreed to anything, just to get back home. It was a joyous homecoming, Daina clung to her and even Beth cried. Sarah just looked tired and worn out. Annie was delighted to be home. She rang all her friends and her social life picked up again.

CHAPTER 8

Beth was in her final year of school and still going out with Shane, her boyfriend of many years now. Daina was in her final year of junior school and still showed no signs of breasts, or anything that would tell the world she was embarking on womanhood. She was tall and lanky with skinny legs and a wicked sense of humour. Annie looked older than her years and made the most of it. She preferred older men. Annie was not short of admirers, they would have preferred Beth but she was taken so Annie would do – literally.

Annie had lost all respect for her body, she did not care, her life pattern was made and moulded. And not by her. She flitted from one male to the next, never staying for long, never able to commit to one man at a time. She was fifteen and sleeping with men well into their twenties. She hated the immature boys in her own crowd. Except for Boyd. He was her first love. He was different, his family had come to Africa from England. He was soft and quiet and totally loving. Annie adored him, and he broke her heart. They started going out and were blissfully happy for a few months. Annie would rub herself against him and delight in embarrassing the poor guy. On more than one occasion he left the flat with his shirt pulled out to cover the embarrassment of what Annie did to him. She was an expert. Naturally it was not long before they were sleeping together. Boyd spoilt her, bought her gifts, phoned her and made her feel so very special. She began to feel like life was not so bad after all. But Boyd fell for one of Annie's friends, a pretty slim blonde and Annie never forgave either of them.

Annie's outlet was her swimming. She trained for her life saving medals at the local swimming pool. Every day she was there training and swimming, she was determined. She was also heart broken. She would phone Boyd at least twenty times a day just to annoy him. She was so pissed off with him. She would have done anything to break up his new romance. One day Annie decided she had hit on a winner. She phoned a taxi company and sent a taxi to Boyd's house. It seemed so funny at the time. Boyd knew it was her and directed the taxi back to her flat. Annie, Daina and their friends all hid in the flat laughing and quietly shitting themselves. Annie decided to answer the door, the taxi driver was very persistent. Annie offered him all the money she had on her, it was about a fifth of the fare. He took it and went to the police. He said Annie had tried to bribe him. Annie was training when her name was called over the loud speaker. It was Sarah, Sarah said two words and Annie crapped herself. "Get home".

She dressed and rode home, racing so as to try and beat Sarah home so that she could quickly tidy the flat. Sarah was angry, very angry, and Annie did not want her going ballistic over the flat as well. It was school holidays and they had had many friends over. There were coffee mugs everywhere and Annie had not cleaned the ash tray. She was in deep, deep shit. They arrived home together. Sarah sent Annie to the bedroom. Sarah related the taxi drivers story, Annie denied it. She was so scared, she lied through her teeth. Sarah knew. Sarah took the belt to Annie, lashing her a good twenty times. Sarah broke the skin and Annie had bleeding welts from her shoulder blades to the back of her knees. Sarah was not finished with her. Grabbing her shaking, sobbing and bleeding she pushed her into the car and drove her to Boyd's house. She made Annie go in and bring Boyd out and apologise to him in front of Sarah. Annie hated the humiliation more than the beating. Sarah then took her home and locked her, Beth and Daina in the flat. She grounded them all for two weeks.

For the first week Sarah locked them in the flat. They would hang out the windows talking to their friends. Annie would get the caretaker to go and buy cigarettes for her, and she and Daina would sit with their legs hanging out the windows smoking. The second week Sarah let them go out into the garden. Sarah was no fool. She would phone to check on them, asking to speak to each one in turn. She would phone at odd times, they never knew when the next call would come. She would ring and then ring again ten minutes later, or sometimes four hours later. They did not dream of disobeying her.

Annie's life saving days were over. She missed the exam

and lost the desire to train and do it all over again.

Sarah was battling financially, there was never enough money. The girls shared clothes and shoes, things did not come easy, and life was hard. Agnes sent the girls pocket money every month. She also paid Sarah's phone bill and helped in other areas whenever she could. Annie hated seeing Sarah so consumed with money worries, she also hated having to go without so much. She hated never getting new clothes or shoes, she was fed up with having to settle for Beth's hand-me-downs. Annie became an expert thief. She could smell money a mile away and was always careful never to take too much. They would go out visiting and Annie would slip a few dollars out of someone's handbag. When they got home she would slip the money into Sarah's bag. Sarah could never work out where the money came from but it always came when she needed it the most.

School was a complete gas. Annie never did homework and always just scraped by academically. She was more interested in her social life. She had a large circle of friends and there was always a party or a disco on. Megan had moved house and they barely saw each other. Annie never really noticed as she was so busy with her other friends. Annie was sleeping with Karl, a family friend who really fancied Beth but could not get past her walls. So he settled for Annie. She was so uninhibited and they would fuck anywhere. It was just different faces for Annie. Same shit just different men. It meant nothing to her, absolutely nothing. It was usually a means of getting something she wanted or a means of getting back at someone.

Karl was home on army leave and spending a night at the flat. There was a war going on in their country, all able bodied men were called up on a regular basis and sent out to fight. It was a bush war, and people the likes of Annie never really knew what was going on. The newspapers and television were always careful what they told the general public. The population at large were kept in the dark. Only the men who went to fight knew what was going on. The flat was usually a central meeting place, there was always coffee and of course the girls. All four of them. The army guys would usually bunk down in the lounge for a night or two, it was never a problem. The girls almost felt as if they were all doing their bit for their country. Annie was just doing a bit more than most.

Annie had decided to bunk off school the next day so that she and Karl could spend the day in bed. Given to terrible migraines she used these as an excuse to stay home. It was weird. Annie could not figure out what was happening. Sarah always left for work at the same time every morning. That morning she had fed Annie aspirin and tried every trick in the book to get Annie out of bed and off to school. Annie would not budge. Neither would Sarah. Eventually Annie won and Sarah stormed off to work. Annie and Karl spent a wild morning in Sarah's bed. Karl went out for a while to see his family and Annie cleared his trunk to get his washing done. She found some letters. She could not resist, they were all in Sarah's writing. Karl was doing Annie and Sarah, alternating between the two all the while declaring his undying love for Beth. Fucker. Annie confronted Sarah and a huge row erupted. Annie told Sarah she was also sleeping with Karl. Karl being the wimp he was packed up his things and left. Never to be seen again.

Beth started work, she was seventeen and had done well in her O' level's. She got a job at a bank and quietly got on with her work. Her boyfriend, Shane, was only fifteen and still at school. They all mocked Beth about how fat she was getting. Usually Annie was the brunt of the fat jokes but Beth was definitely putting on weight. Beth was four months pregnant before Sarah realised. She sent Beth to South Africa in the hope of getting an abortion, but Beth was too far gone. Sarah was in a state. She could barely manage financially as it was and Shane was still at school.

Sarah made all the decisions. She promised Beth to keep it all quiet from the family and in turn Beth would give the baby up for adoption. Beth had no choice but to agree. Annie and Daina took it upon themselves to watch out for Beth. They were in love with this baby growing in Beth's tummy. They would sit for hours feeling it kick. The three of them were desperately trying to find some means of keeping this baby. Shane had no say – he was too young. Even his family were excluded from the negotiations. Beth went into labour and gave birth to a healthy baby boy, a baby she never saw. She never recovered, nor did she ever forgive Sarah. The three girls would cry together for that baby, they felt as though they had all lost something. Sarah seemed to be the only winner. She got her own way and had got rid of Beth's so called shame. She also broke her promise, everyone knew and Beth never felt as if she could hold her head high again. Beth found a flat and moved out of home soon after that. She and Shane were still so in love and would plan their future together, it would be them against the world.

Daina started high school. She and Annie were now at the same school. They were inseparable. No one dared touch or bully Daina because Annie would have fucked them up. One of Daina's friends told her that Annie was a slut. Daina was so upset, she went to Annie and told her. Annie grabbed the friends older sister, dragged her into the girls' toilet and beat the crap out of her. No one messed with Daina again. One of the boys in Annie's class pissed her off, she grabbed him and pushed him up against the black board, lifting him off the floor. No one fucked with her. She was big for her age, taller than most of the boys as well as the girls. She was also larger than most of them. Being tall meant she carried her weight well, she just looked big, not fat, big.

Annie and Daina did everything they could together, they rode to school together, ate lunch together and rode home together. Daina loved Annie, idolised her almost. Their bond was so strong. Annie would slip into the toilets most lunch times to rummage through various school bags looking for money to buy cigarettes or food. She was usually lucky. Daina was her look out. Annie was sixteen and due to write her O' levels the next year.

Tom had been released from prison for good behaviour. The girls did not know. They were not told anything. The conditions of his release were that he would attend regular psychiatric sessions. Tom received intense psychiatric treatment at the government's expense. Sarah and the girls received nothing. No-one helped, they had just been dropped and left to try and live some semblance of a normal life. No social workers or psychiatric help was made available to them, almost as if the world thought they could cope. They did not have the problem, Tom did. What no-one seemed to realise was the huge impact and destruction Tom had caused in all their lives. If anyone needed help it was Sarah and the girls. It never came, they slogged through life, trying so hard to be normal but all the while feeling so different, ashamed and almost like outcasts. Each and every one of them was screaming for help in their own way, but their screams were just never heard. They were the innocents, Tom was guilty and he got all the help. It was just so unfair.

Annie was so out of touch with her feelings and herself, she would sleep with anyone. She was not too fussy, everything seemed fine, as long as there was someone to show her love in the only way she knew how to receive it. No one had ever told her she was innocent, that she had done nothing to deserve the treatment she had been dealt in her life. She always assumed it was her own fault and the nameless, faceless men were some form of punishment. She did not deserve to be loved, only used. She was only good for one thing. She was not a person but rather a convenience for men.

One lunchtime at school Annie and Daina were in the toilets, Annie was rummaging through someone's bag. It gave her such a thrill, she loved the excitement of it and the reward when she found money. Usually she and Daina would run off to the tuck shop and buy drinks and sweets when they were 'lucky'. On that particular day Annie did not know that two girls were in the next door toilet, standing on the cistern watching her. The school authorities were clever, very clever, they did not call Annie in, they called Daina in. They totally intimidated her and put the fear of God into her. They told her they were calling in the police and that the police would take finger prints and then she, Daina, would also be implicated. They broke her, she confessed to what had been going on. Annie was expelled that very day.

Her cry for help had gone unheard in a pile of bureaucratic

paper work. The system failed her totally. It should never have got to that, Sarah and the girls should have been looked after by the powers that be, but the system simply served to abuse them more. The only one who came through it okay was Tom. The injustice of it all never left Annie and she never forgave those in authority at the school. She lost her trust in those who were supposed to be looking out for her. It was her against the world now. There was no other school in the area for her to go to, Annie was sixteen and had to find a job. As unqualified as she was, she was totally unprepared for the world at large.

Her first job was in the post office. She sat in a large office, almost like a school room with about twenty other girls and they stamped savings books all day. The only difference from school was the fact that she was allowed to smoke and did not have to wear a uniform. She hated it. It was like a prison and she would rebel at any given opportunity. She would wear revealing clothes and be called in for it. She would talk on the phone constantly to her friends. She seduced the manager. She got fired. Sarah was so pissed off with her.

Annie put the whole nasty experience behind her and looked for another job. She found one doing Tele-sales. It was time to knuckle down and work. She did very well and worked her way up, absorbing all she could, always looking to learn. Always trying hard, wanting desperately to better herself. It was time to move out of home, a friend suggested Annie move into a commune with a few other people. It was perfect, Annie was having an affair with one of her married customers and needed the privacy. She tired of him a couple of weeks after moving, one man could never hold her for long, there would always be more than one man on the go. Annie was always looking, searching but never finding. Totally unfulfilled sexually, she never really thought sex was about mutual pleasure, it was only ever for them – the men. It was the game and the power it gave her that was the biggest thrill. The chase and the satisfaction of always getting whoever she went after. No one ever turned her down, she was popular and sought after. Annie dictated, took control, it was never about the ones who fancied her, it was only about who she wanted. Married or single, involved or not, old or young, it did not matter Annie got who she wanted. Annie had no conscience. She had never been taught that lesson.

The commune folded up and Annie moved into a flat near Beth and the two of them found they enjoyed each other's company and had great fun together, they got on better as adults, they felt more equal and respected each other. Beth and Shane had broken up. Their foundations were destroyed before they had even started building. It would never have worked with the odds they were dealt. Beth was involved with a divorced man who had two children. Beth tried, she really tried, but she could not cope with it.

For others, things seemed to be coming together. Sarah had met a man. A special man. Quiet, intelligent and totally devoted to Sarah. He was pleasant looking and although he did not make Sarah feel as though a thousand violins played when he touched her, she loved him. He was secure and established and very mature. He adored Daina, the only one left at home. Sarah and Daina moved in with Will. He had a lovely home in a good suburb with a swimming pool and lots of room. As far as Sarah and Daina were concerned, it was a palace. Will was divorced, his first wife had left him for another man and he still carried the scars. Sarah was happy, Daina was happy, she was at a new school and no-one knew what her sister had done. She was accepted for who she was and not discriminated against and constantly watched because of Annie's mistakes. Will raced stock cars.

Every Saturday afternoon they would all meet at the track to watch the racing. Annie loved everything about the racing. She loved the smell, the sound of the v8's, the feeling coming up from the ground when they drove past her, it kind of hit her right at the spot, it seemed to vibrate in her groin, God she loved it. The speed, the excitement and most of all, the men. She fell for Gary, he was shorter than her, a good fifteen years older and probably the ugliest man there. But he had something. He was ruthless in his racing, a rebel, a total speed freak. He didn't give a shit about anyone. He never looked well groomed. His dark hair was never combed, he had teeth missing and rough dirty hands. He was a mechanic. To Annie he was divine. She wanted him and she would get him. Men were so easy. But Gary was different, Gary really liked Annie, he loved her spirit and zest for life, he loved the way she, like him, did not give a shit about what people thought. He loved her individuality and her sexiness. He loved her youth, it made him feel younger. Gary had three children, two boys, both of whom were snotty, badly behaved brats, and a daughter. The daughter was a beauty, a miniature version of Gary's wife, but she was a complete little bitch. Spoilt and arrogant.

Gary was not short of money he just never really cared about it. His business was successful even though his workshop looked like a bomb had hit it. Gary's cars were always breaking down. He only drove Chevy's, and Annie loved them, they were so fast, so powerful, so big. Annie made it perfectly obvious to Gary that she fancied him, she would always be where he was. If she had to go and order drinks from the bar she would always stand next to him and lightly brush past him to place her order. Other times she would ask him to dance. There would always be a barbecue and disco after the races. Annie would watch him all night. When he went to the toilet so did she, just so she could bump into him as he came out. She waited and watched for her opportunity to make her move. It did not take long. Gary went down to the pits to get something from his car, and Annie followed. They met up in the dark, both knew exactly what was happening. Gary grabbed her and kissed her passionately, Annie was floating. She took the chance and invited him over to her flat the following week. Gary agreed and they decided on a day. Then they both returned to the club house, Annie went in first and acted like nothing was going on.

The war was a fantastic excuse for the married men in those days, with all the secrecy, the men could tell their wives they had been 'called up' and could disappear for days, and their wives never questioned their whereabouts. One did not question what was happening in the country. The general public was constantly reminded that 'walls have ears', 'careless talk costs lives' and 'big ears is a terrorist'. No-one ever spoke about the war. It was a taboo subject. It gave Gary all the freedom he needed.

He arrived on the chosen night, he had wet and combed his hair and he was clean. Annie had to stifle a giggle, he looked so unreal. He held a bottle of Southern Comfort under one arm, and a bottle of coke under the other. Southern Comfort was a delicacy during this time in Rhodesia, totally unobtainable. Gary had managed to get some imported on his own behalf. They sat and had a few drinks and chatted, feeling very at ease with each other. Beth had popped over to say hello and have a drink and then she had left them to it. It was bed time. Annie was a little nervous, which was strange.

Gary could not perform. Gary could not get it up. Annie was astounded, she had never had this problem before. She tried everything. Nothing worked. She was beside herself. She moved her mouth towards his penis, he stopped her, "No," he said, "not that." Fuck, he made her cry. He was so gentle and loving and considerate of her and her body. They lay together the whole night holding each other. Just talking and loving each other without inhibition. Gary's wife was a bitch on wheels. She did not love him, she only took and took and took. She had totally demeaned him.

They saw each other every spare moment they could. Annie moved to a bigger flat. Gary never humiliated her by paying her rent. He was, more than anything, her friend. He would always bring the booze, because she could not afford it. Her meagre wage never went far enough for her tastes. Her life became a routine of watching and listening for Gary, she could hear his car a mile away, and was always so pleased to see him. They spoke to each other twice a day on the phone. They adored each other. After three months or so Gary was finally able to make love to Annie. It was beautiful, gentle and loving. But Annie did not know how to take it, she only knew abuse. Gary never knew what she got up to when he left.

CHAPTER 9

Sid was a parasite. He had plenty of money and always found the girls who wanted to take it. Annie was no exception, but she worked hard for it. Sid loved to take pictures, pornographic pictures. At first Annie didn't care, he paid her well. He had a flat set up near to where she lived, and one or two evenings a week, after Gary left, she would go over to Sid's so he could photograph her. He was revolting. Dark greasy hair, a huge beer belly and one leg. Annie did not knew how he lost his leg, and she never asked. They never really talked, he would just instruct her on what to do, and she would slip into the old familiar pattern and do as he said. She could handle it, she would suck and wank him off, he would fuck her and ejaculate over her vagina and take pictures of it.

She marvelled at his ability to get in to the positions he did to take pictures. She could handle almost anything. The only thing that turned her stomach was when he would take his false leg off and she would have to blow him. His stump was just in view and she would keep her eyes tightly shut and just do her job. She never knew how much Sid would pay her, it was never discussed, it must have depended on her performance or his generosity. Some nights it was hardly worth it, but most nights he made it all worth her while. The money she got from Sid paid the bills and meant that every now and again she could buy clothes or other luxuries. Sid, on the other hand, had his shoe box full of Polaroid pictures of Annie.

The strain started to show. Annie began to hate the trips to Sid, she hated the fact that she was now dependent on him, just the way he wanted it. She hated the fact Gary always went home to his wife and children. She hated waiting for Gary. Gary was feeling the pressure, and his wife was getting suspicious. Annie had begun phoning him when she shouldn't. His wife would answer and Annie would hang up. The wife knew, she just fucking knew, but could never prove it.

Annie was in a whirlwind and did not know how to get out.

The call came one day at work. She was totally unprepared for it. She answered the phone in her usual bright and cheerful voice. "Hello."

There was just silence. "Hello," she said again.

"Annie?"

"Yes, hello who is this?"

"It's Tom." Not dad, not your father – just Tom.

Her mouth went dry, she was petrified. He was coming for her, she had told on him, he had warned her not to and now he was coming for her. She did not know what to do, she kept silent. She spoke all at once, feigning false bravado. He was quiet, so quiet, where was his spark, where was his sense of humour, where was Tom? The father she had loved and adored, who was this stranger on the phone? He apologised for not contacting her sooner. "I was not allowed to," he said. "But now that you are working I can phone you..... do you mind?"

"No," she said "not at all, anytime." She had mixed emotions. Her heart was beating so very fast, she was so pleased to hear him, she had missed him so much, she loved him so much. She hated him. She did not know which was stronger. She felt as if he were two different people, one part she loved so much and the other she hated passionately. The latter part was the one that had hurt her so badly.

They finished their shallow conversation and Annie went to the toilets, she sat on the floor shaking and crying. She vomited her heart out. Her entire existence became a huge mess of emotions. She could not settle them, she did not understand them or even know them, they were just there, all of them, flying around her being, pulling her up, throwing her down. She was being thrown to and fro in a whirlwind of conflicting emotions, she hated him, she loved him, she so desperately wanted to see him, she never wanted to see him again. His voice so familiar, so loving, so forgiving, but why did she need forgiveness? She told on him, she had told. She knew he was so angry with her. He sounded so sweet on the phone but she knew, she knew him, he was coming for her. He was going to make her pay.

"Oh God what have I done?" she yelled at herself. "I should never have told, he warned me, he warned me. It's my own fault, it is all my own fault. He is going to kill me, what am I going to do?" God she was so scared of him, but she loved him so much, she wanted to see him, she wanted him to hug her and hold her. In some warped way she wanted him. It was all so confusing, she did not try to work it out, she did not know how to. She was never given the tools. She had to go home. She could not work. She blamed it on woman's problems.

Gary became Tom – Gary was always Tom – she had just never seen it. The same build, the same height, the same trade, the same smell, grease and sweat, the same hands, rough with grease under the fingernails. All she had done was replace Tom with Gary. How would Tom feel now that she was sleeping with another man? Oh God he will be so angry, how was she going to cope. Did she still have to sleep with Tom?

"Will he still want to do that to me? I hate it, but I know it and it feels good and normal. Oh fuck, what a mess!" She thought

Tom phoned often, she did not see him, but they would chat. It was strained and stiff and difficult, she never knew what to say. He wanted to see her. Part of her wanted to see him, but another part of her did not want to. Finally, they arranged that they would meet at Tom's sister's house. Annie had confided in Beth and Daina that Tom had been in touch and organised for Beth and Daina to come with her, they were all so curious. They had all missed him in their own way. As Beth was now mobile transport wise, it was arranged that Beth and Annie would fetch Daina from home, telling Sarah that they were spending the afternoon together. From there they would then drive on to see Tom.

Annie saw him first - she always did, she got out of the car and went to him. She was stunned to discover that she now looked down on her father. She had grown since they had last been together, and was now over four inches taller than him. "He has shrunk," she thought.

She wanted to kiss him, but was confused about what to do. "How do I kiss him, do I kiss my father or my lover?" she thought. She did not know which one was standing before her. He held her tightly, and they cried. They both held each other and cried. She did not let him out of her sight that afternoon, she touched him all the time. Beth and Daina were more reserved, they seemed to be able to control their emotions. Annie had moved to another place in her mind, she was somewhere but she could not work out where. Her emotions and her body were a mess, too much screaming round, too many feelings awakened. Too many senses reeling. It was surreal, it was scary and Annie simply could not deal with it. Annie's whirlwind was gaining momentum.

Things in Annie's life were getting out of control. Annie hated the trips to be photographed by Sid. She tried to put them off, to make excuses, but he had control of her now. She was dependent on him, and simply could not refuse his requests. She did not know how to. Her reaction to this was to put more pressure on Gary. Annie had begun phoning him more and more when she shouldn't. When his wife would answer now, Annie would bravely ask to speak to him. His wife fucking knew what was going on but could never prove it. Annie felt like she needed to own Gary, like she was trying desperately to replace Tom in her life on a more permanent basis. She wanted his wife to know, she wanted him to leave his wife, she wanted him all. He, on the other hand, only wanted the fun, not the commitment.

Tom had fucked her mind as well as her body and no one seemed to notice. Annie had learnt to hide herself well. No-one around her knew the torment in her mind, how things would scream around and make no sense, how questions would rush in all at once, questions that there were no answers to. No-one saw what Annie classed as her weaknesses, the nights laying awake sobbing or the confusion in her head. The hammering of her heart and the fear that seemed to grip in the early morning hours. There was no-one to tell these things to, Annie could not have explained them to anyone for she never understood them herself. When the demons came, she would split from her body to escape them. She would fly away in her mind to safe places until she felt calm enough to come back again. Outwardly Annie appeared calm and together, deep inside of her was a little, lost girl trying very hard to play the game called being grown up. Her emotions seemed to swing from being in control one minute to feeling as if she was slowly falling into a deep black hole the next. Annie just kept going, desperately trying to move past this stage of her life, trying to ride out the whirlwind or simply trying to anchor within it. Gary was supposed to be the anchor. But Gary was not solid ground.

She sat one night sipping vodka on the balcony, she could see the road from there and was watching the passing cars, waiting for Gary. She had no telephone installed at home, because she could not afford one. Gary could not phone her when he was going to be late. Today he was late, very late. Annie did not know that an irate customer had kept him at the workshop.

Annie drank more and more. Beth was out, she had nowhere to go and no one to talk to. She was falling deeper and deeper into a well of misery and self pity and did not know how to stop. She could not cope, life had become too much. A calmness appeared, almost a resignation. "I can't go on another minute," she said to herself. She went to the bathroom and got her razor. It was a disposable one, and she sat for ages cutting the plastic to get the blade out. Eventually the blade was free. Annie stood in the bathroom, telling herself to be brave and strong. She closed her eyes and cut, holding her breath. She opened her eyes and looked down, there was a small nick on her wrist. "Fucking useless," she muttered. She drew in a big breath, poised the blade, squeezed her eyes closed and slashed at her wrist, she opened her eyes and watched in amazement as the white of her flesh turn to red as the blood came. It was like slow motion. Annie watched the blood start oozing out of her wrist and drip onto the floor. She grabbed some toilet paper and applied it to the cut holding it tight. "Oh fuck, I don't want to die," she thought. "I don't know what I am doing!"

Annie was inwardly screaming for help, but there was no one to hear her, no-one was listening. She ran downstairs, and approached two young men walking down the street. She was crying, drunk and her words came out in sobs. "Please help me," she begged, "I don't know what to do."

One of them calmed her down and asked to see her wrist, the other went to telephone for an ambulance. Beth came home while Annie was sitting on the pavement waiting for the ambulance. She was distraught, she asked Annie what had happened and Annie showed her. Beth was not good at the sight of blood and very impolitely threw her dinner up into the hedge. Annie felt like she was watching a movie, she felt removed from what was going on around her. Suddenly the police were there, blue lights flashing, then the ambulance with red lights and right behind the ambulance was Gary's car.

Annie freaked and ran. She hid behind a bush. The police came and talked her out. The ambulance was waiting. She allowed a policeman to lead her to the ambulance. She clung to him shivering. As she got to the ambulance she saw Gary talking to Beth trying to find out what the hell was going on. Annie saw him and turned on him. "You bastard," she ranted. "You fucking bastard, where have you been, where have you been, you said you were coming to see me, where were you?" She sobbed.

Gary came to hold her. "Fuck off!" she screeched. "Just fuck off, I don't ever want to see you again." Gary was distraught, he could not understand what the hell was going on. They sat Annie in the ambulance and placed a blanket around her shivering body. She looked out the doors and saw Gary standing there, just watching and she broke.

"Please Gary, please come with me, please don't leave me, I am so scared," she sobbed. Gary followed the ambulance to the hospital. He was at Annie's side constantly. Annie needed five stitches. The doctor was a friend of Gary's, and joked with Annie. "Now Annie," he said, "you won't die cutting yourself like that, you will only bleed a lot, it would take ages for you to die that way. If you want to do it again make sure you do it properly, don't slit across the wrist, cut up the whole arm along the vein then you will definitely die quickly." Gary took her home, tucked her into bed and went home to face his own music.

The police went to Gary's work the next day to find out what had happened. Attempted suicide is against the law, Annie could get into trouble. Gary did his bit and calmed the whole thing down. Annie never knew what Gary told them, only that she did not hear anything else ever again.

CHAPTER 10

Once again Sarah was totally pissed off with Annie. Annie always seemed to piss her off – and she always did such a good job of it. It had all come out, the affair with Gary and the visit to Tom. Sarah had pitched up at Annie's flat after Beth had tearfully confessed to Sarah that Annie had tried to kill herself. When Sarah came to confront Annie with what she had heard, her timing could not have been worse. It was the night after Annie had slit her wrist, Sarah had marched into Annie's flat to find Annie and Gary sitting together holding hands and talking. She was livid. Gary and his wife were friendly with Sarah and her new husband, Will. Sarah and Will had married a few months earlier. Sarah demanded answers and got them – it all came tumbling out, Annie's affair with Gary and someone – probably Annie, mentioned the visit to Tom. The suicide attempt was not mentioned, Annie's bright white bandage said it all.

Once Sarah got over the initial shock she took control of the situation and decisions were made. No more visits to Tom, and Annie was to move in with Will and Sarah. Annie agreed, she was in no fit state to look after herself. She gave up her flat and freedom and moved in with Sarah and Will the following week. Annie's affair with Gary was not mentioned, there was no way Sarah could stop it, but she could control it by having Annie staying at home. It was a nightmare. Daina and Annie fought constantly, the jealousy was rife. Daina was spoilt, she had received the freedom and love and support in her teenage years that Annie had always yearned for. It was not fair, it was as if Daina had a father now and Annie didn't. Annie was also trying to recover from a traumatic ordeal and there was no one to talk to about it. It all had to be forgotten and life had to move on, Annie would often sit and stare at the scar on her wrist and wonder why the hell she had done it.

Annie did eventually settle down relatively well with Sarah and Will. She still saw Gary, he would come to the house to visit her and they would sit for hours talking outside. The physical side to their relationship had been put on hold, neither of them could face the intensities of their feelings for each other. But they couldn't let go of each other either. They clung to each other, lost and bewildered, unsure what to do. Gary's visits began to dwindle, and they saw each other less and less.

Annie did not see Sid again, she simply disappeared from his life and he had no way of finding her now that she had moved. By this stage Annie had also changed jobs, she had needed a fresh start and she had to leave things behind and let them go. This also meant Tom had no way of finding her either – well, for a while at least. She never knew what Sid had done with her pictures. "Maybe he wanks over them," she would joke to herself. She did not miss him at all, and was pleased to be rid of him. Annie started to see men again. She was very discreet, if Sarah guessed what was happening she never said anything. Annie always had a string of men, she could phone any of them at any time and they were available. She was always out. She had a few liaisons with married men but it was not the same.

She had one steamy afternoon with one of Gary's friends. He had tried for ages to get Annie into bed and finally she had given in. Colin was an amazing lover. He knew all the buttons to press. When they had finished Annie was embarrassed to see a huge wet patch on the bed. Many years after her abuse, she had experienced her first orgasm at a man's hand. No-one since Tom had been able to do that to her, it was as if she had shut down her body after he had raped her. Colin had played her body so beautifully, she was amazed at the feelings he uncovered inside her, and at her own body's reaction. She was scared shitless. She refused to see him again. He had managed to get too close. He had found something no-one else ever had.

*　　*　　*　　*　　*　　*

The war was climaxing, drawing to an end. Daina had met a guy called Lance, and she was desperate for him and Annie to meet. He was in the Rhodesian Light Infantry, a feared regiment in the country's army. Despite that, he was gentle and kind and very sweet. His girlfriend had broken up with him and he was nursing a broke heart. Daina decided he needed Annie. She arranged for a crowd of them to go out to the lake so that Lance could meet Annie.

Six of them had squeezed into Lance's Alpha, with Daina sitting on some guy's knee. Lance was sweet but not her type, she fancied the guy Daina was sitting on. He started to speak, and to Annie's surprise, she could not understand him. He had a broad Scots accent that made him difficult to understand. He was not tall, about five foot eight inches, dark haired with laughing brown eyes. Naughty eyes. He had a stocky build, and his body was decorated with tattoos. He had a large scar down the one side of his arm, which was about eight inches long from the wrist up. It was the weirdest thing Annie had ever seen. He had been shot right through one of his tattoos and the tattoo looked as though it was split up the middle. Annie could not take her eyes off him.

He introduced himself as Mitch. They arrived at the lake and poured out of the car, they had all been drinking on the way. Mitch explained that he was knackered. He had been on duty all night and was going to sleep for a while. They left him in the car and went off to enjoy themselves. A fire was lit, food brought out, and a tape deck played the latest songs from Goombay Dance Band. This was the band of the moment, they played the tape over and over and over again. They swam and joked around getting more pissed as the day went on. The sun was setting and Mitch was beginning to wake up

Annie decided to sit in the car and chat to him. After a while she managed to understand his accent. She liked him, he was different. Well travelled and mature. She discovered that he was ten years older than her. So mature, so good looking, so sexy. They went for a swim, Annie knew the game. She wrapped her long legs around his waist and leant back in the water. She felt his cock harden. She teased, and he took the bait. They came out the water and sat on the banks, it was dark now and Annie explained that she needed the bathroom, and asked Mitch to accompany her because it was dark. They went off together hand in hand. They detoured on the way back and made love on an anthill under a tree, with the moon shining through the branches. It was delicious. Annie was smitten.

He was gentle, loving and almost appreciative. Afterwards they sat and chatted until they heard the others calling them to come back, because they were leaving. They arrived home at midnight. Sarah was fuming. Daina had school the next day. She asked them why they had not phoned, explaining that she had been worried. Lance had walked them up the driveway, because Mitch was urinating at the gate. He was embarrassed at the way Sarah was doing her nut. Eventually he asked where he should put the barbecue they had borrowed. "Over your fucking head!" Sarah screamed at him. He dropped it and ran. Meeting Mitch at the gate, they climbed into Lance's car and made a hasty exit.

The days passed. Mitch did not phone. Annie was confused and angry all at the same time. He had not seemed the sort.

Annie was enjoying her new job, it paid better and there was more for her to learn. She was ambitious and eager to learn anything she could. She was determined to succeed and better herself in her career. She was now finding life at home with Sarah and Will stifling. She had recovered well from the ordeal with Gary, and was beginning to feel claustrophobic. She missed her freedom and privacy. Annie and Daina were having their days, sometimes they would get on well and other days were a nightmare. Annie found it very difficult to control her jealousy of Daina. Daina played on it. Annie decided the time had come for her to move out again. She needed her freedom and space.

She found herself a garden flat not far from Sarah and Will's house. Will had helped her buy her first car, an Anglia – so Annie was mobile. She loved her car, and named it 'Betsy'. Annie just loved driving. She was a confident and fast driver. It must have been something she inherited from Tom. Annie felt as though she was finally in control of something, she could drive and not be driven. She was setting herself up for the move, gathering bits and pieces together. Sarah lent her a refrigerator and curtains. She was all set and could not wait for the day of the move.

Mitch had slipped through her mind as just another arsehole. A user. She was getting wiser now. Out of the blue a call came, not to her but to Daina. Mitch was turning twenty-eight and asked Daina and Annie if they would like to join himself and Lance for dinner. Daina phoned Annie at work to tell her, but there was just one problem, Daina was still grounded, after their late night at the lake. "Leave it to me," Annie said, "I'll get around Sarah and call you back."

As she had promised, Annie got around Sarah. The date was set, they were being fetched on Wednesday night at seven thirty. Annie was fairly nervous and could not really understand why. Maybe she liked him too much, or maybe he was not the same as all the others, maybe he was not just a user. There was something about him Annie reasoned, something she could not put into words.

Wednesday arrived, Annie found she was still feeling fairly nervous. She had dressed carefully and done her hair and makeup, taking more care than usual. She wanted to look good. The men arrived on time, broke the ice with Sarah after the previous week's drama. They all left. They went to a local Scottish restaurant, and what Annie could remember of it was superb. After the restaurant they went on to a night-club for a while. Annie loved to dance, loved the way the music vibrated through her body and the way her body seemed to take on a life of its own. It made her feel sexy. Mitch and Annie danced for ages, the spark was there, so there, she could feel his desire for her through his trousers. "God what a man," she thought.

They had to get Daina home, as she had school the next day, so they left fairly early. The men saw them to the door. Daina went in, Lance went to the car and Mitch chatted with Annie. Annie was not available. She had given in far too easily the first time and was not about to be used again. They were both so hot for each other but Annie was stronger, her own strength astounded her. She had resolve, she had fight, she could say no if she wanted to. This was a relatively new experience for her. She told Mitch she was moving at the end of

70

the week. She told him he was welcome to spend the weekend with her at the flat if he wanted to. She told him to ring her before Friday lunch time as she was moving on Friday afternoon. He did not ring. She was confused and angry.

She got home from work that Friday lunch time, having taken the afternoon off to move and began to pack, swearing and cursing. Daina returned from school and Annie let out all her frustrations. "Fucking men," she spat, "all the bloody same. Just take, take, take. Do they have no feelings?"

The phone rang. It was Mitch. He would love to spend the weekend with her, could she fetch him from barracks on Saturday morning? Annie did not hesitate. Oh God life was suddenly on the up – things were looking up – a new flat, a new man, a new life. She felt such an excitement, something here was just so different. She worked like a demon getting the new flat ready for Saturday, she worked late and Daina helped. She was a bit nervous that first night, all the new sounds and smells, but sheer exhaustion won her over and she slept well. She was up early on Saturday morning, she bathed and dressed, and decided not to bother with make up. "If he does not like me just the way I am it is tough shit," she told herself looking into the mirror. "No airs and graces with this one, just the real me and he can like it or lump it."

She arrived at the barracks to pick him up. He was standing waiting for her his foot leaning on a crate of beer. Her stomach lurched, God he was so divine. She realised that this man did something for her. His stocky build, divine brown eyes, moustache and his olive complexion. "What a divine make up of a man she thought, God I am shaking."

He did things for her and she liked it. She got out to meet him and open the boot. All Mitch had brought for the weekend was a crate of beer, a bottle of brandy and a bottle of vodka. No clean clothes, no toothbrush, no razor - nothing. Just the booze. Annie could not remember the drive home. They chatted but she could not remember a word they said. The spark between them was so strong. He was divine, absolutely divine, and Annie had it bad, she had just not allowed herself to realise it, or fully absorb it.

They arrived at the flat and made their way in, Mitch carrying his stash, Annie moving ahead to clear a space. His arm brushed past her breasts as he placed the booze on the kitchen counter, the air seemed to be charged with sexual energies. Mitch turned to her and pulling her close to him allowed his mouth to find hers. The seal was broken, they pulled at each other's clothing while making their way to the bedroom. Annie and Mitch spent the weekend making love. Anywhere and everywhere. They laughed and drank and fucked. The weekend disappeared, they did not know the time or the day, they were just so lost in each other. Annie was completely uninhibited with him, so open, nothing mattered. It was like coming home for both of them. They were inseparable, so comfortable with each other. The rest, as they say, is history. Annie was in love, very much in love, she had found the man she wanted to spend the rest of her life with. She was ecstatic, bubbling and peaceful.

She took Mitch back to barracks on Monday morning and fetched him after work on Monday night, the same happened on Tuesday and Wednesday. On Wednesday night Lance and Daina had joined them at the flat for dinner. Although they enjoyed the company they hated the intrusion. They were in the kitchen and Annie said to Mitch, "Shit, you are here every night I don't know why you don't just fucking move in."

"What would your mum say?" Mitch asked. "What can she say? I pay the rent, stuff her." Annie replied bravely.

Sarah was furious. To say she did her nut is putting it politely. She ranted and raved and threatened. Annie did not care, she was in love, this time it was different.

"What are the financial arrangements? After all, I helped you set up home and I'm not happy about some lay about moving in

72

and sponging off you Annie," Sarah demanded.

"I don't know, we never discussed it, we just want to be together," Annie replied.

Sarah could not win, Annie was too determined. On Friday night Annie went to fetch Mitch after his Sergeant's meeting. She collected him at seven, he loaded his one bag of belongings into her car, and he held Annie and kissed her ever so gently. They drove away into their future, all looked so bright and promising. They were so in love, so full of hope and expectation. Their time had begun.

CHAPTER 11

Their first weekend of 'living together' was wonderful. They had unpacked Mitch's few belongings. Annie sat and looked through the photos of his family in Scotland, Mitch seemed to have a lot of sisters, every second picture was a sister and he whizzed through them so fast. It was only months later that Annie realised that they were pictures of old girlfriends and there had been quite a few. He was well travelled, he had been in the British army for nine years and the Rhodesian army for four years. He had been all over the world. Annie, on the other hand, had never been out of Africa and she would sit wide eyed listening to his stories of places in the world she had only ever heard about.

On the Sunday morning Annie told Mitch she needed to go to the shops for milk, he asked her to buy him a paper, and tossed some money at her. It was more than her whole months salary. "How many fucking papers do you want?" she laughed.

"Take the money for household expenses," he replied.

Annie left and her first stop was to see Sarah. "You see," she laughed, "you see, look what he gave me, just look. You worried for nothing, he will pay his way. I told you it would be fine – see he does care!"

They never had to discuss finances, it just seemed so unimportant, they always managed. There was always food and booze and they could go out now and again, it worked well, it suited them both.

As Mitch was ten years older than Annie, mature and wise she found she loved learning from him. The wars he had fought had not been easy but he never talked about it. He just loved her. He adored her. He was slightly shorter than her – not much – just slightly, yet he always made her wear the highest heels. He said he loved it when she was taller than him, he loved her long shapely legs. She loved the feeling. It gave her some sense of power to be bigger than him. It felt kind of normal and she felt in control – she could not explain it. It just suited her. She loved the fact that Mitch never complained about her being taller. She had always fancied shorter men, she had never found one that could deal with her height. Mitch did not seem to notice, it was so unimportant to him.

Annie had not seen Tom for months. She had been unable to face him after her 'freak out', as she called it. She had not spoken to him either, he did not know how to get hold of her now that she had moved jobs, in truth he must have known something was wrong and he could have found her if he had really wanted to. Annie was pleased he had left her alone for a while but she needed to see him again. It was not something she could really understand or explain – every now and again she would just yearn for him and become almost desperate to see him. She wanted Tom to meet this new man in her life, she was unsure as to how Tom would take to Mitch. How would he react to Annie living with another man? Annie was very concerned, her thoughts confused. Would Tom be jealous, would he be rude to Mitch or would it all be okay?

She had told Mitch what had happened, she relayed a story to him about her life, it did not feel like it was about her. It was as if all those things had happened to someone else, somebody that Annie knew. She was able to tell Mitch all the details, yet with no emotion, it just like telling a story. Her past did not feel real to Annie, it was more like a big nightmare – it was like telling someone about a dream they had once had. Mitch was fine about it, to him too, it read like a story. He had not met Tom and it seemed so unreal, Mitch was unable to grasp the full implication of what Annie had told him.

Tom still lived in the same town three hours away, he and Debbie had broken up. She had waited for him to come out of jail and they had been engaged for a while, but they could no longer hide behind walls of denial. They had to face the truth of what Tom had done, and their relationship could not handle it. In the end they had split up, and Debbie had left the country for greener pastures. She needed a new start. Annie never saw her again.

Since then, Tom had found new love, a single woman named Melanie. She had never been married. They had bought a house together and Tom was working, things seemed to be okay for Tom. The time had come for Mitch and Tom to meet. Annie got very brave and phoned Tom, she told him she had met someone special and that she wanted Tom to meet him. It was fine, Tom was fine, and arrangements were made. They would travel to the town where Tom lived and spend the weekend with him and Melanie. The weekend seemed to arrive very quickly and Mitch and Annie began the journey after Annie finished work on the Friday evening. Annie was nervous, quiet and withdrawn, with weird patches of giggles and stupid conversation. Fuck she was nervous, she was scared but she did not know why. Mitch was with her, and as long as she had Mitch she would be okay.

Tom and Mitch got on well. Annie was relieved, she was worried as to how Mitch would handle things but it was fine. Even Mitch had separated this Tom from the Tom who had abused Annie. They did not feel like the same person. They would sit at Tom's bar drinking and joking, having a great time. Tom had not lost his sense of humour and he could always make Annie laugh. God, it was so confusing, she loved Tom so much and loved being with him but there was always something, something lurking and waiting. At times Tom and Annie seemed to tip-toe around each other. Sometimes to Annie it felt as if she was watching a movie, she would separate self from self just like the old days, when she could not cope she could disappear and not feel it and everything was okay again. The main thing was that she had Mitch there with her, she was protected and it was fine. All in all, it felt okay.

One day they all went for a rest, Annie woke first and left Mitch sleeping. She went through to Tom and Melanie's room and sat on the bed chatting. Melanie was a weird sort, she explained to Annie that quite honestly she could not understand what all the fuss was about. She had no problem with what Tom had done. She claimed that it had all been blown out of proportion. Annie just agreed and wondered if Melanie was right – maybe she had blown it out of proportion, maybe it was not so bad after all. Melanie got up to go to the bathroom and on leaving the room she closed the door behind her. Annie nearly shat herself, she and Tom were alone. She shot off the bed and yanked the door open, her heart was suddenly beating fast and she was scared but she could not understand why. She made an excuse and left the room and went and lay with Mitch. He was always so calming. He had such a good effect on her. She loved him so much. Shit, she hated the ups and downs. How could she be fine one minute and then freaked out the next? Almost as if she were slipping between stages with Tom and she did not know where they were at. They never mentioned the whole abuse thing, it was as if it had never happened. Sometimes Annie wondered if she did just dream it. It was so surreal at times, it made her doubt her memories and her very self.

Mitch proposed. It was Annie's twentieth birthday when Mitch popped the question. Annie did not need to be asked, she had made it perfectly clear months before she was keen to get married. Mitch would not marry her until she was twenty one. They had a year to plan the wedding and get engaged. Annie was floating.

*   *   *   *   *   *

The war had finished in Rhodesia and the changes came, they now lived in Zimbabwe. Rhodesia, as the country had been called when Annie was growing up, had held a majority white leadership. Races had been segregated and Annie had only ever known racism. She had schooled only with white children and only ever worked alongside white people. The blacks, she had been told were the enemy. They were the ones who committed all the terrible atrocities in the country and who had killed the innocent women and children during the war. The blacks had been fighting for leadership of their country. They had won. Black majority rule was now the order of the day. The schools were to be opened to everyone as would be the previously white only suburbs and areas. Huge adjustments for all were now needed.

It all looked the same but the undercurrents were there. So many of their friends and family members left the country and it was a confusing time. Adjustments had to be made and slowly things began to change. Mitch found it hard. He had spent four years fighting the enemy and the enemy were now supposed to be your brother. After spending so many years of his life fighting wars he now had to find a job. This was something that was not easy for him. He managed to find a job doing sales. Annie had moved jobs again and now worked in the telex department of a large firm. She earned more than Mitch but it never worried them. Life was fun they were in love and the future bright. They got engaged a few months after Annie's twentieth birthday, and the wedding plans were made. They moved from the flat to a house and bought a dog. He was their baby.

The wedding was drawing closer. Some of Mitch's family were coming out from Scotland, his mother, father and sister. Annie was both excited and nervous. It would be the first time she had met any of Mitch's family and she badly wanted to make a good impression. She was dieting so that she could look good for her wedding, and she began dabbling with bulimia. She felt it was nothing serious, every now and again she would expunge a meal from her body. She liked the feeling of being in control of what her body could and could not have. She hated the deprivation of a diet but loved the freedom bulimia gave her. She did not have to say no, there was another way. She could eat anything she wanted to – the difference was the forbidden foods were not allowed to stay in her system – they had to be purged.

The wedding date drawing nearer was taking its toll, Annie was nervous and jumpy and she had a dilemma. Sarah and Tom were naturally enemies, and they had not seen each other for many years. Annie did not want Tom to give her away – she did not understand why, maybe it was just the hassle of it all, or maybe it was simply that he had never felt like a father It was almost like having an ex-boyfriend giving you away – it did not sit right – it felt abnormal. Sarah made her feelings about the wedding very well known, which only confused Annie further. Annie asked her grandfather, Ted, to give her away. After all, he had been a father to Annie for a while and this seemed like a healthy option, everyone would be happy. Except for Tom, but that could not be helped. It was all settled, no-one told Tom, they all just hoped it would kind of go away. Bridesmaids chosen, every one bickering and arguing, normal pre-wedding crap and nerves.

Mitch was nervous, Annie was nervous. Mitch would go out drinking and leave Annie at home. She became confused. Mitch missed the comradeship of his army days, he was battling with his own demons. Annie could not really reach him. It was happening again, she felt as if she was being pulled into the whirlwind again and did not know how to stop herself from being sucked into it. When things were going okay she could cope but as soon as things started changing she seemed to crumble inside and become fearful.

The company she worked for organised a golf tournament, all staff were to take part, irrespective of whether they could actually play golf or not. It was a social event, basically just an excuse for a major piss up. They would start drinking in the morning at work, everything was laid on - food, drink, clubs, the whole bang shoot. It was a wild and great time. Annie and the team she was in packed bottles of wine into their golf bags, and they had such fun. None of them could play, it took four hours to play nine holes. They giggled, lost golf balls, urinated in the bushes and generally acted like school girls having their first taste of alcohol.

They returned to the club house for tea. Annie was well pissed and told the other team members that she could not play the other nine holes. She told them she was going to have a rest and would see them later. Everyone went off to play the next nine holes. Annie sat and wept, but she could not understand why. It all seemed so good, she was getting married and should be happy so why now, why this same old shit? Why so down, depression just seemed to find its way into her and she could not shake it off. She could hide it now and again but when she was alone it would almost choke her and she found it hard to cope with.

She would get the urge to run, just run and run and run, going nowhere in particular, just to get out, move, get away, run from the pressures and crap and planning. It was all too much for her. She needed to escape. Annie found a phone and rang Gary. She asked him if he could come and fetch her. He was there in ten minutes. Words were not needed they both knew what Annie wanted. They drove out to a lake, peaceful and quiet. As soon as the car stopped Annie was all over him, pulling at his clothes, kissing him, feeling him, smelling him. Smelling the familiar grease smell sent her back, moving back in her mind to a familiar place and time. It did not feel wrong just predictable.

How could she ever think she could stay with just one man? She needed the flight from normality and routine, she needed the escape from pressures and problems. Sex was it. Oh God it was such a good way to lose oneself. She could easily move back into the role, she could play it so well. Annie could click her fingers and Gary would come running, she loved the power she had over him. She was a good fuck, so they always came back for more. Gary was no exception. God she was like an animal, sucking, biting, and writhing in stored up, unreleased passion. She was shaking she was so hungry. The tensions with Mitch had meant their sex life had deteriorated. Gary had not had sex for quite a while, his wife never slept with him. It was over before it began. Annie was left shaking and frustrated and he was spent.

Gary drove her back to the golf club, they kissed goodbye and he left. Annie went inside and had a shower. She sorted herself out manually, as she liked to put it, and generally freshened up. The players started coming in, the sun was going down and it was time to start partying seriously. Mitch arrived from work. Annie acted like all was fine. No-one ever knew. Annie put her liaison with Gary that afternoon down to pre-marriage nerves and a touch of cold feet. It seemed to do the trick and she settled down a bit. She did not feel she had been unfaithful because she had slept with Gary before. "Okay the dates don't work out exactly, but what's the difference?" she reasoned. No need to tell Mitch, I'll just add it to all the other fucks Gary and I had she decided. She pushed it out of her mind and got on with the wedding plans. She did not see Gary after that for another eight years.

The wedding was a great success, they had put up a marquee in their garden. They married at a church up the road, the only music coming from a single bag pipe player. Mitch and Ray, his best man, wearing kilts and as tradition dictated, no underpants. Ray was horrified but Mitch was insistent. Annie looked lovely, very plain, no frills and veils and crap. A plain long cream gown and fresh flowers in her hair. If she could have gone bare foot she would have, but Sarah would have had a heart attack and who needed the added stress. The whole wedding passed in a blur, they went home for the reception and had a great party.

Tom was there, keeping out of things. Tom's parents had flatly refused to come to Annie's wedding because they did not want to see Sarah. For some weird reason they blamed Sarah for their son going to jail. They had reasoned that the whole affair was not his fault, it was Sarah's. Annie wondered what bullshit Tom had fed them. They cut the cake and went through all the wedding motions. It was a gentle loving day and Annie totally enjoyed it. She and Mitch saw everyone off and went to bed. Mitch's parents and sister were staying with them. They climbed into bed and Annie said "Well I suppose we had better do it legally for once, hey?"
They went through the motions of making love and they slept after a long day.

The next day family came over and they 'finished off' all the alcohol from the wedding, it was more of a party than the actual wedding. Annie and Mitch then went away for a night on their own to Victoria Falls. Bugger the Falls, they spent the time in bed. Mitch's family joined them after a day and Annie and Mitch did the showing around bit. From there they all went away to the mountains for a week. A huge cottage was booked through Annie's work and there was ten of them going up. Mitch and Annie lacked privacy but they were not too bothered.

One day Mitch and Annie went to climb the mountain outside the cottage. It was wonderful, they reached the top and literally felt that they were on top of the world. Nothing could touch them, they were going to be fine, happy and content, children and the whole works. The clouds came down and they could not get back. They passed the time making love, the feeling of being out in the open but completely out of view was beautiful. They took their time, the feeling of the clouds on their skin was so dreamy. There was no rush. When they had finished Annie sat on a rock and stared out over World's View, it was so amazing. She was dreamy and fulfilled and content. Mitch took her photograph, it was an amazing picture, it so captured that moment.

CHAPTER 12

Mitch's family all went back to Scotland and Annie and Mitch continued with their own lives. There was no real change, just Annie's name. Mitch, on the other hand, was restless. Seeing his family again seemed to have unsettled him. War had broken out in the Falklands and Mitch was itching to get involved. Every day he would check the post box hoping and praying he had been called up by the British army. Nothing came. Mitch was taking strain, drinking more and communicating less. Annie threw herself into her work. She loved it. It was her release and outlet from the strains in her now tense relationship with Mitch. They just seemed unable to reach each other. They knew they loved one another deeply but they seemed unable to reach out to each other. Annie wanted her marriage to work, her thoughts were "If Mitch is happy then I am happy."

They finally sat down and had a good heart to heart, decisions were made, they would make a move to Scotland. So many of their friends had left, maybe they knew something Annie and Mitch did not. Secretly Mitch was hoping to somehow get to the Falklands. Plans were made, household goods were sold or packed up, boxes stored with Sarah, air tickets bought and suitcases packed. They were off. Annie was like a kid, so excited, she had never been out of Africa. She was going on a plane, going to a new country and a new life, it all sounded so very exciting. They would stop first to visit her grandparents, Agnes and Ted, in Liverpool. Her grandparents had moved there a few years earlier, their only visit back since then had been for Annie's wedding.

They had a few days with Agnes and Ted. Agnes delighting in taking Annie shopping and showing her things she had never seen before. They spent time chatting and enjoying being together again. Annie loved the fact she was close to her grandmother again. She had missed her terribly when her grandparents had left. They spent Christmas with Agnes and Ted, Annie was so childlike in her excitement. There were so many new experiences, her first sight of snow, the cold and the wetness of England, which was so totally different to the heat and dryness of Africa. Annie loved the contrast.

After Christmas they made their way up to Scotland. They lived for a month with Mitch's parents. It was a nightmare. Annie had lost all her weight before the wedding and was looking good, but unhappiness always led to eating and weight gain and Annie was very unhappy. Mitch's parents were so different in their own country. Annie felt suppressed and stifled, she hated the life, she hated the way Mitch's father treated his wife. His mother was a slave, she would work all day and come home and have to cook the dinner. Annie would help but she never felt at home. She would just hang around and help as and where she could, she never felt she had access to things and always had to wait for permission.

The final straw for Annie was when she asked Mitch one morning to put the water on for her for a bath. When she came downstairs an hour later the water was not on. "Shit," she said to Mitch's mother, "I asked him to put the water on for a bath for me." Mitch's mother looked her straight in the eye and said, "Please could you limit your baths to one per week, if you need to bath more than that you can use the public baths down the road."

Annie was horrified. She was used to bathing every day, sometimes twice a day. She hated feeling dirty, dirt held too many nightmares. She felt the panic beginning to rise, she had to get out. She could not stay there a moment longer. They found a place of their own, but Mitch was unable to find work. He was down and things were not working out as planned. Annie was terribly homesick. They had fallen out with Mitch's family – Annie never quite knew what had happened. Annie's weight escalated. She let herself go and moped around. Money was very tight and she hated it. She hated the fact that neither of them could find work, she had tried so hard, but there was nothing available. She felt like a freak. People would make her talk to hear her accent and almost make fun of it. Mitch saw his father now and again, and they would go out drinking, Annie was never included. One evening at the pub Mitch's father told him "I feel very sorry for you son married to that woman."

Mitch's family wanted nothing to do with her, if his mother saw her on the street she would cross the road to avoid her. Annie never understood what she had done wrong, she felt like a failure. Mitch and Annie fought, they had terrible rows. Annie would rage and scream, she would be totally unreasonable. Annie wanted to go home. So did Mitch, they had had enough. They flew back to Zimbabwe five months after leaving. They stayed with Sarah and Will for a while until they got back on their feet.

Annie was ecstatic to discover that the girl who had taken over her job in the telex department was leaving, her job was available again, and they asked her to return. She leapt at the chance. They settled back into the Zimbabwean way of life with ease, picked up their social life and built up a home once more. They had found a quaint little cottage fifteen miles out of town, it was set in rural surroundings and bush and was perfect for them. The house had two bedrooms which had a thatched roof, and the rest of the house was under corrugated iron. They both loved it. A huge two acre garden fed Mitch's bush hunger. A swimming pool and out buildings completed the picture and they were once again happy in their surroundings.

Mitch had managed to find work in the sales department of a large motor vehicle business selling cars, he was working with an ex-army friend. Despite all the happiness, there were still problems. The main one was Mitch's drinking. Every Friday night after work Annie would wait for what seemed like forever for him to come home. She hated being so excluded. She hated taking second place to his army friends and alcohol.

They decided to have a baby. It was the norm – you get married, you have children. Mitch desperately wanted children. And deep inside of her Annie knew she too wanted children, she knew she would be a loving mother – she had lots of love to give.

Annie fell pregnant the very first month. They were both over the moon. Annie continued to work throughout her pregnancy, it was a fairly easy pregnancy, the only drawback being that she piled on weight. She finished up with her telex job but stayed on at the firm doing part time work. She was sitting one day in the office and things started happening. She went and did some shopping, excited and nervous, it was two weeks early. She got home cooked a nice meal for herself and Mitch. They knew it was now a waiting game. They went and saw a movie and timed Annie's contractions, when they were about seven minutes apart they went home, Annie bathed and they left for the hospital.

Annie was examined and told she had a few hours to go. They gave her an enema and put her to bed to wait. It was midnight. By nine o'clock the next morning Annie was totally fed up. She had only dilated a few centimetres and wanted to go home, the gynaecologist broke her waters and told her she had to stay in. She was hungry and thirsty and very tired. By three in the afternoon her contractions had disappeared all together. Mitch had been with her all night and had popped home to bath and change. They put her on a drip and induced her. From that point on Annie thought she was dying, the pain was so intense. They gave her pethadine, which had little effect, so they gave her more. She was as high as a kite, and had no idea where she was or what she was doing, her entire existence became the pain, she screamed the place down.

No-one could calm her or get through to her. By the time Mitch got back to her she was in another world. He left a fed up and tired wife and came back to a screaming mad woman. She was so tired and sore. She had never known pain like it – all her childbirth classes were totally forgotten in the waves of pain. She would fall asleep between contractions and wake up in the peak of her next contraction, unprepared for it and out of control. She was wild and scared and nothing could calm her. She felt as if she was awake through some horrible nightmare, and could not understand what was happening to her.

Ben eventually made his appearance at seven thirty that night. The umbilical cord had been wrapped around his neck and he was blue. Annie hardly even looked at him she was so tired. She had held him briefly and they then took her to the ward and placed Ben in the nursery with oxygen. Annie slept, a heavy drug and exhaustion induced sleep. She awoke during the night, blood pouring from her. She tried to find the toilet and was wondering around the hospital blood running down her legs, fuck she was so confused. A nurse found her and helped her clean up and put her back to bed.

They brought Ben to her in the morning. Annie was now well rested and full of excitement to see this baby she had waited nine long months for. The events of the previous night were all coming back. A boy, they had their son, just what they had wanted. His name had been decided months earlier, they both knew the baby would be a boy. She wished Mitch was there with her at that time to share this special moment. The nurse placed Ben in her arms and she studied this amazing bundle. The sheer awesomeness of reproduction hit her and she was stunned, totally stunned. A love she never knew existed welled up in her and she wept with the intensity of it. He was so beautiful, so perfect, so small, she would kill for this little person in her arms. That was the best way she could describe it, if anyone came anywhere near him she would kill. It was a peaceful, protective kind of feeling. Deep and true and healthy.

The nurse showed Annie how to feed Ben, he almost attacked her nipple and Annie laughed, his little mouth seeking and knowing. It was wondrous. Annie found it hard to absorb. Ben suckled away, and Annie watched, totally content. The nurse left them to it and Annie took time to discover her son. He was so perfect, perfect little limbs and fingers. He was just perfect. He had finished suckling and Annie lay him on the bed to examine this little person further. He seemed blue around the mouth, yes he was still blue she could see it. She panicked, oh fuck she panicked. She picked him up and ran to find the nurse. They told her off for carrying her baby in the hospital, she was supposed to have wheeled him. She was confused and scared. They took Ben from her and called the paediatrician. Ben was placed in an incubator with oxygen.

Flowers arrived, so many huge bouquets. Mitch had sent the

most enormous bouquet Annie had ever seen, it had to sit on the floor in the corner it was so big – she was totally overwhelmed. Mitch arrived to visit her. He was drunk, and Annie was heartbroken. She needed him, she was scared for their baby and she was awash on a sea of emotions. She needed his calming effect and logic, and he was drunk, out celebrating the birth of his son. She needed him and in her mind he had failed her. They went up to see Ben, they were the only ones allowed to see him. Mitch held his son and just stared at him. He could not absorb it. It was just too overwhelming. A tear slid down Mitch's cheek.

Annie would go and feed Ben every few hours she would have to scrub and wear a gown before she was able to touch her son. She hated it. She hated leaving him there. She wanted to be with him and couldn't. Gradually his condition improved, his colour returned to normal and Annie was able to take him down to the ward with her again. She was sore, stitches making her movements small, but she and Ben were together again. This was how it should be and the pain seemed a small price to pay for this new love in her life. Then Ben went yellow, it seemed he now had jaundice. He was taken from her again and placed under ultra violet lights. He would lie in his little crib under the lights, his eyes bandaged for protection,

The blues set in, and Annie became a sobbing wreck. Things were not as she had thought they would be. No-one told her anything and she sat for hours staring into space wondering what was happening. Ben soon recovered from his jaundice and Annie was allowed to take him home. There was great excitement when Mitch came and fetched them to take them home. Annie felt more comfortable in her own home but she was nervous and depressed. Breastfeeding was hard and sore, the sleepless nights began to take their toll.

There was another problem too, Beth. Beth had not come near the hospital. Annie had not heard from her. Beth was reliving her own nightmares. She was grieving for the son she had given up all those years ago. The pain had never left Beth, and she had never recovered from her loss. Beth could not cope with the fact that Annie had a son and that everyone was so happy. No-one had wanted her son. But they loved and accepted Annie's. Beth was totally illogical and in very deep emotional pain. It only made Annie feel worse. She and Beth had become so close over the past few years. Beth had been involved with a married man for a few years. He had made her pregnant, and she had given birth eight months earlier to a beautiful baby girl, now Beth was a single mother. She battled with so very much and she adored her daughter, yet it did not fill the gap in her heart left by the son she had given up. It was a hard and confusing time for both Beth and Annie.

When Beth had fallen pregnant for a second time, Mitch and Annie had discussed with Beth the possibility of them adopting Beth's baby. This way she would not have to give up another baby if she had felt she could not cope with single motherhood. Throughout Beth's pregnancy Annie and Mitch had been there for her. Annie had been at the hospital when Carrie, Beth's daughter, had been born. They had been so involved in each others lives. Annie could not understand Beth's rejection of her and her son. It seemed so unfair and she did not know how it would get better. It took Beth a good six months before she could even look at Ben, let alone hold him. It was just too painful for her. Annie tried so hard to understand and kept her own pain and confusion to herself.

*　　*　　*　　*　　*　　*

Annie was not working, she was at home with Ben. He had recovered from his earlier problems and was a happy, well behaved baby. Annie adored him. Mitch almost idolised him. He would rush home from work so he could bath Ben. He would feed him his dinner and put him down. Mitch was born to be a father. He was amazing, nothing was ever too much hassle. He would never grumble about helping with night feeds and nappy changes. He would let Annie rest at the weekends and enjoy his time alone with his son. There had been no word from Mitch's family in Scotland, which was hard for Mitch. He had so wanted his family to know about his son and had secretly hoped it would cancel out all the history. It did not.

The excitement and newness of everything had gone. Despite the joy he received from his new son, Mitch was battling with his own demons. The birth of his son had stirred up so much for him. He was deeply hurt by his family's rejection of his wife, and their refusal to acknowledge his son. He withdrew and Annie could not reach him. But there was more. One night they sat and had a few drinks together and Annie tried to reach him.

He told Annie that when they were fighting the war they had gone into a known guerrilla camp. The army had surrounded the camp and moved in slowly. Mitch's task was to clear one of the huts. He had kicked in the door, his rifle was loaded and ready, he had slowly moved into the room, his rifle aimed and ready for anything at a moments notice. There was a mattress against the wall and something under it moved. Mitch had instructed whoever was under the mattress to come out or he would shoot. Nothing happened. He gave the command again in the local language. Still nothing. His survival instincts and army training took over and he opened fire spraying the mattress with bullets. "It's him or me," were his thoughts. He stopped firing and waited, no movement. He slowly made his way to the mattress and pulled it away from the wall. He never got over what he saw. There were three little children, they had been hiding in fear and Mitch had killed them all. He never got over it and having a son of his own made the whole nightmare of it harder to cope with.

Their mutual friend, Lance, committed suicide. His demons could not be exorcised. Mitch and Annie were devastated. He was their start, he had always been there, almost a part of them and now he was gone. Mitch took it very badly. Another very close friend of theirs committed suicide. He had taken an overdose and hung himself. He was determined to die. It was a hard time for Annie and Mitch. Mitch found his solace in a beer bottle. He and Annie grew further apart. Mitch started staying out late after work, drinking. Mitch would drink at lunch time. It was turning into a vicious circle and the more Annie complained the worse it got. It all just seemed so out of control. The war had left a very strong mark on everyone and only now things were surfacing and in true style they were not being dealt with. The men were finding their escape in a bottle and for those like Lance who simply could not cope, the only way out was suicide.

CHAPTER 13

Daina had moved out of town to live with Jamie, the new love in her life. She had finished school a few years earlier and had been working for a while. She was a bright woman and a hard worker. She had grown into an attractive woman. Still ever so slender, but well proportioned. She attracted looks wherever she went and was not short of male admirers. She had met Jamie one weekend when she was out with friends. Jamie lived in a small town two hours away from Daina. It was hard for them to conduct a relationship with the distance between them, so they decided to live together even though they had only know each other a short while. "It will be make or break," Daina would joke. She packed up and moved to be with Jamie.

Mitch and Annie would often go and spend the weekend with them. They enjoyed getting away and it was always a huge party from the beginning of the weekend to the end. One weekend they went up to see Jamie and Daina after Mitch had finished work on a Friday. They arrived late and Ben had been quite fractious, he was coming down with something and Annie was tired. She was trying hard to lose weight, and in the process was not eating enough. On top of that she was bulimic and had no energy, what little energy she got from the food she ate was vomited up a short while later. On this night she could not settle Ben and Mitch was drinking heavily at the bar. Annie was furious, she had had enough and also wanted to party. She called Mitch through to ask him to help with Ben. Mitch was very drunk at this stage and Annie should have known better. They had a huge row, Annie was holding Ben and screaming and crying at Mitch. She was cracking up and could not cope. Neither could Mitch. He lay into her, punching her in the stomach and on the arms, whilst she was still holding Ben.

She never forgave him for that. He killed something that night. He had never hit her before, nor abused her, but that night he broke her heart. He hit her again that same weekend. They were travelling back home and she was in the back seat feeding Ben. Mitch had not stopped drinking all weekend. Annie was tired and weakened by the recent events. She said the wrong thing. He turned round and slapped her across the face and told her to shut up. She did. She shut up very well. She closed a part of herself to Mitch that day. It was never the same again. He had totally destroyed her illusions. He had killed something in their marriage and there was no getting it back. The remorse did come a few days later, but it was too late – the damage was done.

The restlessness began again when Ben was about two years old and Annie went back to work on a part time basis. She was lucky enough to get her telex job back with the same firm. She loved her job, the people and the parties. She loved the escape from motherhood and the independence it brought. She felt alive and worthwhile at work. Her sense of humour always made her popular with all around her. She had spent the last year losing the weight she had put on after having Ben and was feeling good about herself. She had made slimmer of the year at her local slimming club and she felt like a mini celebrity. Her pictures in the national paper showing her before and after pictures made people turn and look at her in the street.

At the correct weight for her height Annie was lovely. Her long legs seemed to go on forever meeting her firm well proportioned buttocks. She was never happy with her stomach, no matter how hard she dieted or exercised it would never be flat, she would never have a bikini figure. Her breasts had just been reduced and lifted surgically and they were firm and still ample. Her dark hair was cropped short and her green eyes were laughing and shining, always with a hint of sexuality lurking just below the surface. She could have her pick of men, they seemed to sense and smell her wild sexuality. On the outside Annie was riding high.

What no-one knew was her battle with bulimia had overtaken the healthy desire to lose weight. People praised her efforts, she felt so in control and, in her own mind, she was. She would eat what she was allowed but if she went over by one mouthful, up it would come. She became an expert bulimic. She knew exactly how much to bring up before her eyes ran and her make up smudged. She could quietly and effortlessly vomit anywhere, and did. Any meals eaten out were never allowed to stay in her body. She would feel so ill after a big meal she could not sit still. No-one suspected. They all praised her sheer hard work and determination. Her greatest fan at this stage was Sarah, proudly she would boast to her friends how well Annie had done and freely show the paper cutting to all who would lend an ear. Annie loved the feeling of the control over her body, she loved depriving it and she adored the continual abuse on it. If felt safe and familiar and she knew no different.

Her weight loss, and the fact that she could wear Daina's clothes, gave her such a sense of power, she felt invincible. She could own the whole fucking world, she could have anyone she wanted. "So why," she thought "am I stuck with a man who falls asleep at seven o'clock every night in front of the television and only makes love to me once a week?"

The age gap between Mitch and Annie was starting to show and Mitch was beginning to wind down, just as she was starting to come alive. As always happens, it started subtly, she couldn't remember how or when it started or what the attraction was. Curt was younger than she was, single, not good looking and at least six inches shorter than her. None of the other girls found him attractive and he did not even have a girlfriend. He was not one of the party animals, he did not get drunk with the boys and told no rude jokes. He did not pinch her butt or make fun of her breasts like the others. Somehow, he was different. She fell for him, the poor sod. The married men buzzed around her like flies around dog crap and she gave them the brush off. Curt, well, he got her going. Confident of her effect on men and confident of her ability to seduce she began the mating game with Curt, but he wouldn't play.

She became obsessed and thought of no-one else. Her bulimia peaked and she became almost anorexic refusing to eat sometimes for weeks on end. She was caught in the whirlwind again and didn't know how to get out. The more Curt pushed her away the more she wanted him. She dreamt about him constantly and fantasised about him for hours. She planned and schemed her relationship with him totally in her imagination, and found the reality of it too much of a contrast. She would stay for drinks at work knowing he would be there, she would leave when he did and would follow him. She would ask his friends questions about him to find out his movements and she would always make sure she was where he was.

If he was playing cricket at the weekends she was there watching him, not the cricket, him. He became her saviour and she just knew that if only she could make him love her, life would be fine, everything would be fine. She would phone him at work and at home and ask him the most ridiculous questions. He was attending a sports dinner at a local hotel one night and Annie got so drunk she drove there and called him out of the dinner. As long as she could just see him or touch him she was fine, she just needed anything to fuel her fantasy. She lived in her mind and her only companion was Madonna on the radio – Madonna just seemed to understand where Annie was at – she felt such an affinity with her. She wanted Curt so badly. 'Crazy for you' was their song, the only difference was that poor Curt never even knew about it.

One night after a few too many drinks at work they all moved on to a sports club. Annie managed to arrive just after Curt and parked next to him. She asked him to wait before going inside as she needed to 'talk' to him. It was now or never, the perfect place, parked in amongst the trees out of sight she made her move. He never stood a chance. She pushed the buttons so well, just as she knew she could, he had just never given her the opportunity before. Oh God, it was like coming home, he kissed just as she imagined he would, God he was so passionate his hands were everywhere, on her breasts in her panties, his fingers expertly exploring her vagina. She moaned and melted to the moment. They were both so engrossed, she was living her every fantasy and it was just as divine as she had always imagined. A voice pierced the moment, Curt's friend was calling for him. He regained his composure quickly and the moment was gone.

Annie begged him to take her home with him and he quietly but firmly refused. He reminded her of her husband and child and said that he could never take her away from them. She had a commitment there and she needed to go home. She said she didn't care, all she cared about was him and being with him. He refused her. He had regained his composure so quickly, she was totally freaked. How could he be so hot for her one moment and so cold the next? He put her in her car and sent her home. She was heart broken, absolutely heart broken.

He refused her calls after that, would never stay for drinks and avoided her at all costs. She was crushed; all the schemes and plans had come to nothing, all she had received was a taste, a mere taste, and it seemed so unfair. She would write him lines and lines of outpourings of her love and lust for him. He did not reply, and she did not even know if he ever read her letters. The bulimia heightened, the eating worsened and the drinking took over. She was so calm and cool on the outside that no-one knew and no-one suspected. Inside she was in absolute torment. She shook constantly and the lack of fuel in her body made her speech feel as though it was coming from somewhere else. She could talk and laugh and joke but it was not from her, it was from somewhere else. She went through the motions, she cooked, she looked after Ben and inwardly she fell apart.

*   *   *   *   *   *

It was Friday night drinks at work. She had it all worked out so well. Her office could be seen from the pub and she would always have huge amounts of work on a Friday. She loved it – a total escape from her mind. Someone would always send over a drink for her. She worked and had a few drinks and then Graham, one of her married admirers, came to chat. She had finished working so Graham escorted her to the pub. She remembered to phone Mitch and tell him what time she expected to be home. Mitch was looking after Ben, Annie felt this was right, as she had spent too many nights waiting for Mitch to return home after drinking so it was pay back time. "If he can do it, so the fuck can I," she thought.

The pub always had a festive atmosphere, there was always joking and laughter. Annie was in her element – she loved it. Graham was so attentive all night and Curt so cold. She had been surprised to see him there but he had had no choice, he was entertaining customers. Fuck, her heart broke just watching him, remembering, seeing his hands and remembering the feel of them on her breasts and in her most private of places. She wanted him, she still wanted him. She had stolen a photo of him from the notice board and would stare at it constantly. As the evening progressed, she got drunk, and Graham became friendlier.

She needed a lift home and Graham obliged. He fed her ego and she felt so low it hit the spot. Taking the long route home they stopped at a quiet place and the petting began. She slipped off her panties as if stuck in some old habit and Graham fucked her in his car four houses away from where her husband and child were. Her reasoning left and they spent a very steamy hour in that car. Graham could not believe his luck. She fucked like a professional and gave head as if she had been doing it all her life, she was an animal, insatiable and wild.

They dressed and he took her home. She was so heady from the sex it was easy to feign drunkenness. She went straight to the toilet to clean up, Mitch hot on her heels, his senses screaming. She calmed him down by totally patronising him and his jealousy, then she expertly cleaned up without Mitch suspecting. Mitch forced himself on her that night. She didn't want to do it, the high was going and the guilt was replacing it. But he was so persistent she could not refuse. Mitch could not understand her tears that night, he just thought she was pissed. It was the first time she had slept with another man while married to Mitch and she felt such a failure.

The next morning the demons returned and the nightmares began again. She could not work out why. Mitch lost his patience with her and that made it worse. On the Monday while Mitch was at work she found a bottle of wine and began her day getting drunk.

Ben was being looked after by the maid and Annie was on a mission. The bottle finished she searched the cupboards and found a bottle of vodka, she snapped the seal and it was downward from there on. She rang Curt, he was out. "True fucking story," she thought, "he knows its me and won't speak to me."

She phoned Graham, he was full of fucking alcoholic remorse or some such shit. She asked to meet with him – how could he refuse? Annie waited for Mitch to come home, handed Ben over and told him she needed to go and see her aunt who was out from England. She did not give Mitch the chance to see how pissed she was, she verbally threw her plans to him over her shoulder as she left the house. She met Graham in town under a tree next to a top hotel. The vodka bottle was neatly nestled in the back of the car and she was flying.

When she met with Graham, he explained that he was not interested in anything further with her and that it had just been a night of fun, and wanted to leave it at that. "Fucking bastard," she thought, seething inside, but outwardly smiled and agreed. She left the car and went to the ladies at the hotel where she puked her guts out. She returned to her car to discover that Graham had left. "Yellow fucking chicken livered bastard," she thought. "Now where?" she schemed.

"Coffee, coffee would be good."

She drove to a coffee house, parking her car outside an all night pharmacy. It was now eight o'clock at night and she had been drunk for ten hours. As if totally removed from reality she went into the pharmacy and spoke to the pharmacist. She told him she had had some terrible news and was in a real state. One look at her confirmed this – she looked like shit. He gave her some tranquillisers and told her to go home and take one and sleep. He had given her twenty. She went to the coffee shop and ordered a cappuccino. She asked the waiter if he could possibly do her a favour. She wrote the name of the tablets down on a piece of paper and gave him some money and asked him to please pop into the chemist and get her some more. She

98

was shitting herself that they would not give them to him. The waiter returned with another twenty. She ordered a glass of water, she swallowed the first twenty tablets in one go and then the next twenty. It was over she had no more fight left in her, she couldn't go on another day, not one more day.

She removed a photo from her purse, the one of her on top of the mountain she and Mitch had climbed on their honeymoon. She recalled how they had made love, how they thought they were on the top of the world. God she had been so happy then, so full of life and the future looked so bright and hopeful. What happened to change it all? She wrote to Mitch on the back of that photo, placed it back in her purse and then panicked.

"Oh fuck I have taken the tablets now, but where do I go and die?" I can't just stay here because I will pass out soon," she reminded herself.

She paid her bill, leaving an extremely generous tip for the waiter, and made her way to her car. She got in and began to drive, she did not know where to go or what to do, she decided to travel the road leading home as it was quiet and there were no houses and not much traffic on that road. It was a long drive and when she felt too tired she could just pull over and die. She remembered looking at the speedometer on the dashboard because she was convinced she was driving too fast and was amazed to see she was only doing twenty miles an hour. She drove and drove feeling drowsier with each passing mile. Why she drove all the way home she never quite knew. But she found herself out side her home. "Now what?" she thought. Her brain was still going round and round. "I'll just go in Mitch will see how pissed I am and I will just fall into bed."

Mitch took one look at her and knew. He had learnt a lot during his fifteen odd years in the army. He grabbed her and shook her asking a million questions she could not answer, her tongue had seized up. Her head lolled and her eyes rolled back. He pulled her up and walked her with him to the phone where he rang their doctor.

The doctor asked what she had taken and Mitch did not know, he told the doctor to hold on and he rummaged through Annie's bag finding the empty pill bottles. The doctor freaked and demanded to know where she had got the tablets as he had never prescribed them for her. Mitch gave him the information from the bottles, as that was all he had. The doctor told Mitch to try and keep her awake and to take her to casualty. "And make sure you take her to the government hospital," he added, "it is so awful there, she will never do this again."

Mitch called the maid inside to watch Ben, bundled Annie into the car, opened all the windows and drove her to hospital, talking to her all the while, refusing to let her sleep. By the time they had reached the hospital Annie could not walk and her hands had curled into tight fists, which she could not open. They brought a trolley and wheeled her straight through to the emergency room. It was a fucking nightmare. All Annie could remember was them keeping her awake and making her drink the most foul liquid followed by glasses of water. After that was forced down her, there would be peace for a few minutes and then the vomiting. She felt as though she was bringing up everything from the bottom of her feet upwards.

This routine continued for several hours and Annie was abusive and violent. They had six staff in to restrain her and force the medicine down her. Mitch was by her side constantly. For him, the army medical training took over, and he remained in control. Finally at about two o'clock in the morning they felt they had managed to get everything out of her system. Then they had to placed her on a drip to replace the fluids she had lost. They could not find a vein. She swore at them all and ripped her arms away. They threatened to turn her over and insert it in to her anus, and finally something got through. The doctors were unable to get the drip in and Mitch took over and effortlessly inserted the drip into her wrist.

He said afterwards he was ready to just let her die at that point he was so tired of it all. They wheeled her to a ward to sleep. Every hour a doctor or nurse would wake her and start interrogating her as to why she had tried to take her life, but she couldn't answer.

They were so persistent. She couldn't answer in one sentence and she was too tired to talk. She awoke at eight o'clock the next morning devoid of all emotion. She wanted to go home, but had to wait for Mitch to collect her. The doctors did not want to release her but she insisted. They said they would phone Mitch. She had no money and worst of all no cigarettes. She had huge ten inch bruises on the inside of her wrists where they had tried to insert the drip and that was the only outward evidence of her ordeal.

Mitch left her there until four that afternoon. He had been busy. After leaving the hospital he had driven home and drank himself in to an absolute drunken stupor, he had then taken out his Suzuki Eleven Hundred and hit the open road with no helmet in the hopes of blowing the nightmare from his mind. He returned home and slept for two hours and then got up bathed, sorted Ben out and phoned into his work, explaining he was feeling sick. Then he visited all of Annie's friends to try and piece together what had happened. Her best friend Katie broke Annie's confidentiality and told Mitch it was about a man, but she did not know who. Mitch was so fierce looking that morning, the good Lord himself would have told him anything he wanted to know. He went to see Sarah and took her out for a drink and asked her advice. No one ventured near the hospital that whole day, until Mitch arrived to take her home. The hospital released her on the understanding that she would agree to psychiatric treatment every week. She would have agreed to anything to get out of there. They drove home in silence. When they got home Annie held Ben for as long as she could, then Mitch gave Ben to the maid and sat Annie down. He handed her a hand written note.

Dear Annie,

I know you have been with someone else. I don't want you to lie to me I want to know all the details and then as far as I am concerned this whole thing is over. I will never mention it again.

Mitch.

He looked so intimidating, not hurt, just very, very angry. Annie tried in very simple terms to tell him about the episode with Graham, she could not even mention Curt. For her the worst part was that her infidelity had actually been with Curt, Graham had just done the deed for him. Mitch bundled her into the car and made her drive him to the exact place where the deed had taken place. She could not do it. She lied and took him a few miles further up the road and said it was there. He asked for every detail, exactly what had happened. She told him what she could. They drove home in silence.

They got inside and Mitch said "Now phone him I want to talk to him." She was shitting herself. She rang the number and asked for Graham, Graham knew something was up when she had not been at work. Briefly she told him she had done something stupid and ended up in hospital for the night and that Mitch wanted to talk to him. All Mitch said was "What time do you finish work, and where can we meet?"

They agreed to meet in an hour at a golf club. Mitch got himself ready, took out a bayonet he had kept from his army days, put on his crash helmet, said goodbye and left. Annie was extremely nervous. Knowing Mitch as she did, she knew only too well he was trained to kill – it was all he knew – he had fought God knows how many wars and killed God knows how many people – this felt bad. She was powerless to do anything. It was all her own fault. She bathed and put Ben to bed and sat and waited. At nine that evening she could take no more and rang the golf club. She caught Mitch just as he was leaving. "All is well," he said, "Graham is coming home with me for a beer."

"Oh fuck," she thought, "how much more can I take?" They arrived home full of good spirits and proceeded to get totally rat arsed pissed at Annie and Mitch's bar. Annie sat quietly and sipped endless cups of tea waiting for this surreal nightmare to end and for Graham to go home. Graham left and Mitch never mentioned the evening or her infidelity to her ever again.

She spoke to Graham the next day and apologised for her part and asked what had happened. He explained that Mitch had given him the bayonet and told him to keep it in remembrance. He had also explained that if Graham ever touched Annie again Mitch would kill him. Graham believed him and so did Annie. Annie stayed clear of Curt after that – the pain of the repercussions was just too much but she never really got over him.

CHAPTER 14

In compliance with the agreement she had made with the hospital, Annie began her psychiatric treatment. It was a fucking joke. She arrived the first Friday for her appointment. She sat on a wooden bench with about fifty other people, all of whom were also waiting. She was the only white person there. She felt very uncomfortable and out of place. Her name was called and she was ushered into the psychiatrists office. She was still not eating and her hands shook constantly. She felt so very weak emotionally and physically, and had lost more weight. All her new clothes were now hanging on her. She looked drawn and had large black rings around her eyes. She still felt very fat.

The psychiatrist was Male, he asked her what her problems were. She was just so tired - "How do you try and fill in a life time of problems into half an hour?" she wondered to herself. She said something, some crap about marriage problems and how much she disliked herself. The doctor told her how beautiful she was. "Fucking hell," she thought, "don't tell me he is coming onto me now, I can't cope with this."

He prescribed medication for her and told her to return the next week. The next visit was a repeat of the first, sitting on hard benches, waiting. She was called through to discover there was a different psychiatrist waiting for her. "Here we go again," she thought, "same old shit."

Why did she try and kill herself and what are her problems. "Fucking hell – what good is this?" she thought. She was prescribed more medication and told to come back the next week. The next week was the same as the past ones. Same process different doctor. When she got into the office she was fuming.

"I have been here three times now," she said, "and you are the third doctor I have seen. This is bullshit. How do you think you can help me when I don't even get to speak to the same person every week and have to keep repeating the same things over and over again?"

This doctor was very nice, he calmed her down and promised her he would deal with her from now on. She would not have to see anyone else. He prescribed more medication and told her to come the next week to his private offices at the hospital. He prescribed two weeks medication. They would only prescribe it weekly in the past because of her suicidal tendencies. The next week Annie made her way to the doctors offices. She was alone there. He never showed up. She placed her bottle of pills on his desk and left. She never went back. Mitch fetched her and as they drove home she said to him, "Well Mitch this is it, you are stuck with a fucked up wife, there is no-one who can help me, you are just going to have to learn to live with me as I am and if you don't like it, well tough shit!"

It never got any better. Annie partied more. Curt's best friend made a move on her. She fucked him in his car and hoped he would tell Curt. She never knew if he did or not. There was another married guy who fancied her, she fucked him on his desk while everyone was partying downstairs. She did not care. Things were getting out of hand. Annie had to move on. She resigned and found a mornings only job. She thought she was safe. It was only her with a very ugly boss. Just what she needed, there was no way she would fuck him. She hid away there, worked hard and thought that she was starting to coming right. She began eating, but only small amounts, as she was paranoid about her weight. Life took on a form of normality again. She and Mitch were distant – like strangers living together. They would fight and never really make up. Their sex life almost disappeared and their only saviour was Ben. They both adored him. Mitch wanted another child, Annie told him in no uncertain terms to go and fuck himself - she wanted no more children. She had just spent over two years losing weight, and there was no way she was fucking up her body again. "No way," she thought.

A customer named John kept calling in, there was no reason for him to do so, he could have conducted his business via the phone. The truth was he fancied Annie, but she was not interested in him.

Been there, done that, no thanks. She had become a bit of a hermit. A routine of going to work, fetching Ben and then going home. Life took on an almost nothingness.

"This is the price I have to pay," she would think. "I can't trust myself, so I have to hide away. I don't know how to say no. I just keep fucking everything up." She began a small business buying and reselling things. She was making good money. She loved it, loved the thrill of a bargain and then selling it for a profit. She was good at it, and had an eye for bargains. She saved enough for herself and Mitch to go to England on holiday.

In the meantime, John kept calling.

He would phone Annie every day. She would laugh and joke and tell him to dream on. He was extremely persistent. Eventually Annie gave in to the pressure. After work one lunch time she removed her panties in the toilet, stuffed them in her bag and drove to John's office. She parked her car, walked through reception, ignoring the receptionist. She marched into John's office, closed and locked his door. He was busy eating his lunch. Annie walked round to where he was sitting at his desk, pushed his chair away from the desk, took his sandwich from his hands, placed it on the desk and pulled up her skirt. She hitched it around her waist, opened her legs wide, placing one foot on either side of his chair, up to this point no words had been spoken.

Now Annie instructed him to undo his pants. His desire was hard, Annie moved and removed his pants, then she climbed onto the chair with him and slowly lowered herself on to him, she took the full length of him deep into herself. She then sat perfectly still, staring him straight in the eye, her face devoid of emotion. Slowly she began moving only her internal muscles. He was history, he came gently and silently Annie felt him pulsating through her body. She raised herself up and got off the chair, pulled her skirt down, handed him back his sandwich and left. She got into her car, cleaned herself up with her panties and drove home. By the time she arrived home she had almost forgotten what she had just done. He phoned her even more after that, but she told him to fuck off. She hated herself more than she hated him. Eventually he got the message. It had started again, the men. It was just never enough. She wondered if she could ever be happy.

She was falling again, falling into the deep black holes of her nightmares, there seemed to be no way out. "I am destined to be like this for the rest of my life," she thought. "No hope, there is no hope for me."

* * * * * *

Hope came in the shape of a childhood friend, Rebecca. Rebecca loved Jesus and Jesus could solve all ones problems. Annie had never been religious, but she listened. Rebecca took Annie to church, it was a huge American type church with a full band and young beautiful people who looked so happy. Annie was shocked, church was not supposed to be like this. She got caught up in the emotion of it all. When the pastor did an alter call for anyone who needed Jesus, Annie found herself standing at the front of the church. She was shaking and crying. Yes, she wanted this love she wanted Jesus to make it all better, she wanted it all. She said the sinners prayer. She felt so unworthy of the perfect love that was on offer. But they explained that Jesus loved her, she was a sinner no more – she has been washed by the blood of Jesus. She was free of her past, and was a new creation. The past has gone and only the future is there to look forward to.

Annie did not know how to tell Mitch. He would laugh, she just knew he would laugh and tell her she was mad. The truth of it was that Mitch saw such a huge change in Annie that he believed what Annie had been told, that Jesus saves. He can save anyone, he loves you just as you are. Mitch came to church with Annie, and he too gave his life to Jesus. Sundays became a routine of going to church. Mitch and Annie would always sit near the front, like sponges they absorbed all they were taught. They did all the courses, and learnt all they could. The pastor was so amazing, his wife so

107

beautiful, their children were model children. Annie felt so unworthy in light of the perfect people around her. But she was determined. She and Mitch found a common ground and their marriage took on a new lease of life. They fell in love all over again.

Annie was always up for prayer, they explained that they were casting demons out of her. It was the demons that had made her do all the bad things. She believed them. Mitch and Annie were being professionally coached into Christianity. They would be good for the church, they would bring in large numbers of other people. Who could deny the changes in them. Annie was now serene and together. She smiled, she laughed and Jesus loved her, what more could she ask for? She and Mitch were so happy that they had found each other again. It was all working out so well. Annie's bulimia quietened down, she was more in control of it. Her weight steadied, she put on a bit but she was controlling it well. Jesus was helping her.

Mitch and Annie decided to have another child. Annie was ready to take responsibility for another life. She fell pregnant easily. Annie knew that this would be their daughter. Mitch would joke and say no way, it is another boy – if it is a girl, she is going back. They would talk for hours, they sorted out past differences and forgave each other for so much. Annie never told him about the other men. What for, she reasoned. She sailed through her pregnancy. She blossomed, she looked beautiful and radiant. She and Mitch went to natural childbirth classes, this time Annie wanted to be in control. She did not want it to be like when she had Ben. It would be perfect this time. Everyone would be praying for them and Jesus would be there too. It would be wonderful and perfect. It was.

Janna made her entrance to the world in a perfect, controlled environment. No drugs, no screaming, just peace and love. Mitch was there the whole time. They both held their daughter and each other and cried. She was perfect, a mass of dark hair and eyes already brown just like Mitch's. They felt the completeness. Annie went off to shower after Janna's birth and Mitch just sat and held his daughter, tears streaming down his face at the sheer beauty of her. She was just so beautiful. Such a completion of their family. Just what Annie needed. Annie was a good mother and now she would be complete.

It was just like they said. Jesus could make it all better. A new life in Him and be saved from all past sins. He came to bring hope and love. Mitch and Annie prayed together later thanking the Lord for all His blessings in their lives. Thanking Him for the completion of their family unit and the love they had for each other, for the rubbing out of all pasts and the promise of their futures now so bright.

It was a wonderful time, loving and special. Mitch too, had changed much, he had let go of many of his nightmares, he had his demons cast out in Jesus' name and he was also a new creation, pure and clean washed by the blood of Jesus. He had fallen once or twice and had a few too many beers but that was the beauty of Jesus, He always forgave. Smoking was something that caused a few problems. Annie had managed to stop, being pregnant had helped, and she was sworn off them, but would always be on at Mitch to stop. He found that he could not.

They took Janna home, she was so special and so loved and Ben, who was now four, adored her. They were complete and happy. There were only a few pains for Annie. Mitch was not allowed to change her nappy or bath her.

Annie would change her and see her minute vagina and clitoris and feel as though something had punched her in the stomach. Her daughter was so small and perfect and untouched. She would remain that way until Janna herself made her choice. And it would be when she was married. No premarital sex for Janna. She was God's child and would be raised as a strong Christian and be taught the strict Christian rules.

Annie was on the phone to Rebecca one Sunday afternoon, she looked across at Mitch, who was sleeping on the couch with Janna resting on his chest. They looked so peaceful, Annie felt as if they were in some kind of bubble, they were so happy. She had not had the blues and no stitches had meant that she and Mitch had begun making love again very soon after Janna's birth. It was just so perfect.

Sarah was so taken with Janna, she adored this child, the flowers and gifts that had arrived after she was born were overwhelming. Mitch was holding Janna one afternoon when Sarah was visiting and Sarah went to Mitch and said "So tell me when is she going back?" Mitch just smiled and melted, he held her tighter and said, "Never!"

Annie fed Janna, even with her breast reduction she was able to feed. This of course was an answer to prayer. They had prayed so hard for this to be the case. It was as it should be, natural and good and right. God was good.

A couple of months earlier their house had came up for sale, Annie and Mitch saved up all they could and managed to buy it. They had lived there for nearly six years and loved that house. Even though it only had two bedrooms it was big enough. They loved the space and quietness of it. They never wanted to leave it. It was just a part of their lives and were so pleased that they managed buy it. It had everything they needed, a pool, space and quietness, and now it was theirs. Mitch was good with his hands and could handle all minor repairs and maintenance.

Mitch and Annie now lived on faith. They believed the Lord would provide. Annie had applied for maternity leave from her job and had planned to go back after three months. Her boss had decided that he did not want to pay her maternity leave and fired her. She was heartbroken as she had worked there for over two years and had worked hard. She was devastated by her boss' actions. She fought him and he ended up having to pay her out a large lump sum of money which meant she and Mitch could buy a car for Annie. They had used Annie's' company car for years and had no car of their own, the lump sum meant they could buy a car for Annie to get around in.

Annie repaid the good Lord by being a faithful and

committed Christian. He had done so much for her, He was her saviour in so many ways, and had saved her from so much. Every morning she would sit and read her bible. She had a daily routine, she would bath Janna, then take Ben to school and do any shopping, then return home. She became the perfect housewife. Everything was done and in order.

It was the eleventh of November, an important day, Janna was a month old and it was the day Rhodesia had declared UDI (Unilateral Declaration of Independence). It was a day everyone silently celebrated, especially the ex-army guys. Celebrations of this nature had to be kept silent, the word Rhodesia was not to be mentioned, all Rhodesiana memorabilia had had to be taken down from peoples homes and hidden away, the new Government was paranoid about spies. If anyone was caught celebrating this day they risked being jailed. Mitch always had a beer on this day. It was the done thing in his book. It was a day of remembrance and little trips down memory lane, a time to remember friends and family who had been killed during the war. Silent toasts were made to them. It was a day that never failed to bring back memories and feelings of nostalgia.

They had been invited to a friends farm for the weekend. Faye and Annie had been friends since school and still kept in touch. Faye had recently married for the third time and she and her husband were farming out of town. Annie was looking forward to getting away with Mitch and the children. They loved going to farms, all the fresh air, God seemed closer too. Faye's husband Martin was getting a lift back to his farm with Mitch and Annie. Annie had spent the day baking shortbread to take with them. She had done her bible reading, packed up, organised the children and was ready to go. Mitch came home from work on time and quickly changed. They had a cup of tea and shortbread – it was Mitch's favourite and Annie baked it well. They packed up the truck. Mitch had a company double cab pick-up. It was perfect, room in the back and two rows of seats. The luggage was loaded in the back, Martin and Mitch sat in the front and Annie sat in the back with Ben and Janna. Annie had put off Janna's feed in the hope that she would be able to feed her in the car and then Janna could drop off to sleep. It was perfectly organised.

Mitch was just starting the car when the gardener came running over. "Boss, boss," he called, "the swimming pool is not working."

"Shit!" Mitch muttered. It could not be left, if the pool went green it would cost a fortune in chemicals to try and get it back to the right colour. Mitch went into the pool shed and fiddled around with the motor. It sprang back in to life. He came back to the car and started reversing. The gardener came running again. "Boss, boss it has broken again."

"Shit!" Mitch swung out of the car leaving it running, his cigarette burning in the ash tray his keys were swinging in the ignition, his door open.

Annie and Martin were chatting. They heard a scream from the gardener. "Switch it off, switch it off," he was yelling. Then there was silence. Annie knew, she just knew.

"Please go and see," she begged Martin. Annie's maid had run out of the house to see what was happening, she had run to the pool shed and run back holding her mouth, her eyes wide. Martin ran, Annie got out of the car with the children, and grabbed Mitch's cigarettes, she stood, clutching Janna and Ben. As the maid came over, she handed the children to the maid, and went to the shed, but could not look. She could not look. Martin yelled at her to phone for an ambulance, Mitch had been electrocuted. Annie's phone was not working, she called to the maid to bring the children and ran next door to a neighbour. She made three phone calls. The first to her doctor, he tried to tell her what to do, but she could not hear. She could hear nothing, she gave the phone to the neighbour, and the doctor told her to go and tell Martin what to do.

She left and Annie phoned Sarah. "Mum," she choked, "there has been an accident, it is Mitch, I think he is dead." Sarah screamed and threw the phone to Will. "We are on our way," he said. Then she phoned Rebecca and asked for prayer. She left Ben and Janna with the neighbour. A bottle was arranged for Janna. Annie went and sat on the road. She could not go back inside. She sat on the road and smoked. She smoked Mitch's cigarettes. She gazed into the half empty packet and at his lighter and could not comprehend what was happening. The world seemed to have stopped, all went quiet and time was meaningless. Annie had no idea what was going on at the house. She just sat and smoked.

Then things all happened at once, the doctor arrived, Sarah and Will arrived, Beth arrived, the pastor arrived, Rebecca and her husband arrived, Beth's lover arrived with an electrician friend. It was all going on around her, she did not know what to do. It was just so weird. "Why are all these people here?" she kept thinking, "What must I do with them?"

The pastor had gone to see what was happening. He came and got Annie and took her inside the house. They came through the back, Mitch had been moved into the back of his truck, someone had switched it off, there were papers and needles all over the garden – so many of them. The doctor was working on Mitch, Annie could not look into the back of the truck, all she saw were his feet sticking out, still with his shoes on. Someone had made tea and the shortbread was on the table. Annie could not look at it. The pastor sat Annie down and gave her a cup of tea. "Mitch," he said, "has taken too much electricity into his body." Annie sat and fiddled with the cigarettes she wanted another one but the pastor was in her house. "Thank goodness it is tidy," she thought.

The pastor continued, "We have three things here that can happen. One is Mitch can recover from this and be fine, the second is that he could recover but never be the same man again, the third is that he will die. You have to prepare yourself for either one of those options Annie."

Something got through, Annie looked at him and said "If

God can hear me now I will ask that if I have any say in this I would ask for Mitch's sake that the second option be taken away. Mitch would hate to be incapacitated." The pastor gently told Annie it was not her choice to make. The doctors radio was going mad, the doctor was trying to find a heart specialist, they were moving Mitch and taking him to the hospital. The specialist would meet them there. It was just after five in the afternoon, and the traffic was a nightmare. Rebecca's husband led the way, lights flashing hooter blaring, as if by magic cars moved and let them through.

Annie was just sitting around, she did not know why or what to do and everyone was looking at her. She got up and went to the bedroom, she picked up her bible and came through and said "I want to go to the hospital. Now." It was the exact time they gave up working on Mitch and he passed from this lifetime to the next.

They arrived at the hospital, Annie, Rebecca and the pastor. The pastor went through the back to casualty and Rebecca led Annie to the front reception. As they were walking Annie turned to Rebecca and said "You know, he was such a good man." Mitch had moved to the past tense. She just knew.

Annie came into the reception, Sarah and Will were there and so was Beth. Annie felt as if she were some kind of robot going through the motions of walking and talking. The pastor came from the back, he walked to Annie, looked her in the eye and said "I am so sorry Annie, he has gone."

Annie buckled and the pastor caught her, she just sobbed. She leant on him and sobbed – huge wailing's of pain tearing from inside her, like Mitch was being wrenched from her very being. Oh God, the pain. She saw no-one, Sarah was sobbing Will trying to comfort her, everyone was sobbing in the middle of reception and people walked past them. The pastor took Annie to casualty, she was shaking, shaking so much. The staff asked her if she wanted to see Mitch.

"No! No!" She screamed, "I don't want to see him." They

gave her his wedding ring, watch and wallet. Mitch's time had finished, he no longer needed these items, the realisation was immense. Staring at Mitch's wedding ring Annie realised she was no longer married. She was a widow at twenty-seven. The doctor came and spoke to her. It was his heart they said, his heart could not handle it. He did not die at home they said but Annie did not believe them. To her Mitch died the second he climbed out the car for the second time, because she never saw him again. The doctor said to Annie "Don't ask me for any pills because I am not giving you any. You go home and you cry and cry and cry. That is all you can do."

She did not need to be told that. That she knew by instinct. Someone took her home, she could not remember who – there were just people, faceless people around her. She gazed out the car window on the way home, she looked to the sky and saw a bright shining star. No one else saw it only Annie, it was Mitch shining, he was gone, he was with Jesus and she was lost.

Sarah and Will went to their workshop to make the phone calls. Mitch's family had to be told. So many people had to be told. There was no way Annie could do it.

The doctor returned to his surgery at seven thirty that evening. All his patients had sat and waited for him. They had been unable to leave. As if they all instinctively knew. So many needed to be comforted that night. It was as if a ripple effect had occurred and suddenly strangers were turning to strangers and comforting each other. It did not matter that they did not know Mitch or Annie. But they knew that night a woman had lost her husband and a child his father and a baby would never know her father. A deep sadness and grief settled over almost the whole town.

Rebecca was with Annie, they packed up clothes for her and the children. Someone collected the children from the neighbour. Everyone was in shock, going through the motions. Rebecca took Annie and the children home with her. She had a large house and Annie would have privacy to grieve. Annie could not handle being with her family and their grief at that time, her own was just too strong.

The pastor and his wife were at Rebecca's house. The children's pastor was called out to talk to Ben. No-one had told him anything yet. Annie did not know what to tell him. Ben and Mitch were so very close, how do you tell a four year old his Daddy is dead? It just seemed so very unfair. The children's pastor came and he and Annie went and spoke to Ben. They told him the facts as best as they could. They had no idea how much had got through. They just hoped the Lord would do his job and comfort Ben.

That night Ben woke up screaming – his first scream was for his Daddy – then almost as if he knew that was not longer right, it changed and he screamed for his Mummy. He had always called Mitch at night, never Annie, always Mitch. It had sunk into his subconscious mind already. He knew his dad was gone and not coming back.

Annie and Janna slept together in a bedroom far away from Rebecca and her husband. Annie cried the whole night, huge gut wrenching sobs, she sounded like a wounded animal, the sobs foreign to her ears. She had no idea where they were coming from, just from deep within, these huge waves of pain screaming through her body. It felt as if someone had stabbed her in the chest. The physical pain of losing Mitch stayed for months after. The emotional pain never left. Something was stuck in Annie's throat from the moment Mitch had died, she could not eat. If she put food near her mouth she heaved.

Annie got up, somehow she and Janna had survived the night. She was trying to feed Janna, but she kept crying as if she too knew something was not right. Annie nearly choked her by pouring gripe water into her mouth, she panicked and picked up Janna and held her and sobbed. It was so unfair.

The phone started ringing early the first Saturday morning after Mitch died, and after that it seemed as though it would never stop. "And the people, all these people, where did they come from?"

116

Annie wondered. Everyone wanted to see Annie. Annie wanted to see no-one.

The Funeral Director arrived at Rebecca's. Rebecca's husband had been a star, he had organised everything. The Funeral Director needed to talk to Annie about the arrangements. Annie had no idea what to do, burial or cremation? She simply did not know. She and Mitch had never discussed it, ever. Somehow, she made the decisions. They decided to wait for the funeral as Annie was hoping Mitch's parents would come over for their son's funeral. No date for the funeral was decided on. They took notices from Annie for the paper. Annie just seemed to go through the motions.

She was taken back to her house to receive people. She thought how odd that sounded – like she was an old woman, an old widow. There were people, a never ending flow of people coming to see her. Sarah and Will were there, Beth and her lover, Daina had come through with Jamie, everyone seemed to be there. People came in hordes and Annie did not know what to do. Every time someone else came she would start crying again. She was amazed at how many tears she had, she wondered where they all came from. She knew they would never stop.

Sarah wanted Annie and the children to go and stay with her. Annie could think of nothing worse at that time. She wanted to be alone but not on her own. With Rebecca she had privacy and a friend to talk to whenever she wanted. Rebecca was a star. She held her own grief in check when Annie was around and would cry quietly when Annie was not around. She was Annie's rock at that time. Annie would surely have sunk without her. Sarah deeply resented Rebecca taking over things – they were all fighting their grief in different ways.

Annie hated being back at her own house, she felt so unsafe there, she wanted to go back to Rebecca's that Saturday, she did not want to be at home. It did not feel like home anymore. She wanted to be alone, and she did not want to talk to anyone. Ben was wondering around as if lost, he could not work it all out. Annie went looking for him and found him in the kitchen. He was sitting in a cardboard box sobbing his little heart out rocking back and forth saying "I want my Daddy, I want my Daddy." Annie sat on the floor next to him and just held him and they sobbed together. Rebecca took them back to her home. Annie was shattered. She slept, only waking to feed Janna.

On Sunday morning Annie was awake very early, and got up, leaving Janna sleeping. She made herself a cup of coffee and found the Sunday paper. Rebecca's paper was delivered every day. Annie tried to collect herself and willed herself to open the paper. She wondered around coffee in one hand, paper in the other. She wanted a cigarette but Rebecca would do her nut. She could not smoke here. She had to be strong. They all said how strong she was and how well she was doing, she could not give in, she had to push on. She sat in the lounge and opened the paper.

It was so very surreal seeing all the death notices for Mitch. The ones she had written and all the others from family and friends. She had not really comprehended he had gone. It just did not feel like he had gone forever. Seeing it in print made it so very, very real. The funeral notice there saying date to be advised. Where is he she wondered? Lying in a morgue, but which one? At the hospital or funeral parlour? She simply had no idea. No-one had told her anything, as if they were trying to protect her from something that there was no protection from. She sat and cried. Not huge sobs now just gentle tears flowing down her cheeks, non-stop ones. Just flowing and flowing. "Leaking," she thought, "it feels like I am leaking. And I can't stop the flow."

Janna woke up, Annie felt so tired. "I can't do this," she thought, "I just can't do it."

Rebecca woke up and got Annie back together again. She told her to get ready they were going to church. Annie did not want to face anyone, she wanted to hide. Rebecca made her bath and dress and put some make-up on. Annie got Ben and Janna ready and they left. They dropped Annie at the side door so she would not have to walk past the thousand odd people that attended their church. She slipped in with Rebecca holding her hand. Rebecca's husband took the children to the nursery and joined them. The pastor came over and hugged Annie. She just wept. The pastor started the service. He told the church about the loss of one of the church members. As he told them what had happened the gasps and sobs from the congregation could be heard by Annie. It was just too much. She wanted to get out but couldn't, if she stood up they would all see her. She felt as though they were all looking at her anyway, like she was some kind of freak to be pitied.

The pastor preached the most moving sermon on courage. He praised Annie for her courage. They all prayed for her. She just wanted to get out of there. She could not cope with it all. It was too soon. The service ended, and they all came towards her in a wave. She backed off, turned and ran out of the church hall and waited in the car. It was just too much. Their friends, she could not cope with their friends. The ones they had got so close to during the ante-natal classes, the ones they had spent time with, the ones who had prayed for them and seen them through so much. It was all too sore, Annie could not handle their grief, she had enough of her own. They went home, Annie retreated to her room.

The following week was just like one long day, nothing made sense or had meaning, it just moved along. Annie had to phone people, she had to cancel Mitch's dentist appointment or they would charge her. She rang and said that Mitch had passed away and she needed to cancel his appointment. The dental nurse was rude to her. "Oh," she said, "so he won't be making his appointment then?"

"No!" Annie screamed at her, "he won't, he is dead, do you hear me - dead. He won't make his appointment!"

She slammed the phone down and sobbed. She could not do this.

Mitch's family had phoned, they said they could not get flights out to Zimbabwe. None of his family would be at his funeral.

They did not even send any flowers. Annie was deeply hurt and disappointed. She had so badly wanted Mitch's family with her, surely they loved him as much as she did, surely they would just have an understanding of each others deep loss and pain? Why could they not come? Annie never understood that they simply never really cared. She received no support from them whatsoever.

The funeral was arranged for Thursday. Annie was dreading it.

Tom arrived out of the blue. He cared about nothing but Annie. He walked into Rebecca's house, found Annie and just held her for the longest time. "He came," she thought, "he came when I needed him." He was a hated man, disliked by all who knew what he had done to Annie and he did not care, his only priority was Annie. It just meant so very much to her.

Annie needed a dress for the funeral. She refused to wear black. "Mitch is with Jesus," she said, "it should be a celebration of his life. I will be brave and I will be thankful for the time I had with him and I will be happy that he is in a better place."

She dressed herself in lilac that day. She went and had her hair done, her hairdresser was one of her best friends, they had not seen each other since Mitch had died, Vanessa simply could not control her emotions around Annie. She loved Annie and Mitch completely. She did Annie's hair, the two of them in silence, unable to comfort each other, tears freely flowing. Annie sat there shaking. Annie wanted to smoke. She had been sneaking off while at Rebecca's and smoking all Mitch's cigarettes. She had found them in his drawers. She had taken them and was working her way through them. She could not smoke now, she had to hang in there. She dropped Janna with Beth's maid, Ben went to school that day. Annie saw no point in taking him to the funeral. What could a four year old understand? Annie had asked for the service to be taped and that when Ben was old enough she would play the tape for him and explain things. She wanted to protect him.

Rebecca and her husband drove Annie to the church. It was a much smaller church than theirs but perfect for Mitch's send off. Rebecca walked her in. She saw no-one, she just walked. She had forgotten there would be a coffin. Mitch was in the coffin. The coffin was at the front of the church, she could not take her eyes off it. She wanted to open it and see what he looked like. She wanted to see if he really was in there. If he really was dead or if this was just one huge nightmare. She sat on her hands staring at the casket. She saw it was scratched and was so pissed off. It should have been perfect and it was scratched. The flowers she had ordered were there on top, peach carnations her favourite and baby's breath, a lot of baby's breath. There were a few other arrangements from Annie's family and Sarah had thoughtfully placed flowers from Mitch's parents. No-one asked – she just did it.

Daina sat next to Annie, Rebecca behind her and Sarah and Will next to Daina, Beth was next to Will. They all sat there, waiting. The church was full, there were not enough seats for all those who came. Annie did not look back, she just sat there hearing it all. A ripple passed through the church when Tom arrived. He held his head high and marched down the aisle, he came to Annie, moved everyone over and sat next to her holding her hand. He did not let it go. It was the most comfort Annie had received. His only concern was her and she loved him for it.

The service passed in a blur. Annie did not want singing. The pastor's wife played the piano, and it was beautiful, gentle and loving. Annie made it through the service, it ended and they all got up, Tom led Annie out. Mitch's coffin was removed by a side door and taken away for a private cremation. Annie stood on the steps outside the church greeting everyone. Gently weeping and not bothering to wipe her tears. Tom stood to the side of her and just watched over her. She coped, she coped through the masses of people at the tea laid on at her house. She wanted to be alone, and to smoke. She wanted to be with her children. She did not want to be here, living this part of her life.

She stayed with Rebecca for two weeks. The house was checked out by electricians. The pool pump fixed by experts. Everything was done for Annie. Half the time she did not know by whom, but she was so grateful. She needed to go home. She needed to try and start managing on her own. She had no choice now, it was just her and her babies. She had to look after them now, there was no-one else. She went to Mitch's work and cleared out his desk. She took all his personal belongings and all the cigarettes. It was as though he had some kind of paranoia about smoking, she had found cigarettes hidden everywhere. "He had no intention of stopping," she thought.

At home Annie went through his drawers. Everything was in place. His will and all the paperwork Annie would need was neatly filed. Everything was in perfect order and Annie wondered if he knew. It seemed as if he knew he was going to die. Pity he never told her.

CHAPTER 15

Annie was on some kind of automatic pilot, she paid the bills, saw lawyers, fed the children. The first night home was the hardest. She simply did not know what to do with herself. She bathed Janna and put her down, fed and bathed Ben and put him to bed. She could not eat. She tried to watch television, but saw nothing, just a blank screen. She put some music on, there was a bottle of whiskey in the cupboard, one of Mitch's Scottish friends had given it to her at his wake. She had refused to serve alcohol at Mitch's wake, she felt that it should not be a piss up, she could not have coped with the drink. She had simply left the scotch on their bar counter and told the true Scots that if they wanted a wee dram it was there for them. No-one touched it. It was still there in the cupboard.

"It would be so easy," she thought, "so very easy." She got up and found the bottle, she snapped the lid, she held the bottle to her nose and drank in the smell of it, it was lovely. She took the bottle to the kitchen and poured it down the sink. "I refuse to sit and get pissed on my own every night," she reasoned. "I will never drink alone here, it would just be too disastrous. There must simply never be alcohol in this house. With the Lord's help I will get through this."

She threw the bottle out, went back to the lounge, and sat there for five minutes. Then she got up, wondered around, and went to check her babies. She sat and touched Ben, tears slipping down her face. It all seemed so unfair. She went back to the lounge and made sure everything was locked up. She had never felt fearful in this house before, but now that she was alone there it was very different. In reality her neighbours were far away, no-one would ever hear her scream. The phone hardly ever worked, if someone tried to get in she would be powerless to stop them. What would she be able to do? How could she protect her children and herself? There was no way to do it. Fear grasped her. Suddenly she was scared, scared for their safety, scared for her future. It was so unfair, their babies so planned, so loved, only now they would have to grow up without their father's love.

"No-one will ever love these babies as much as Mitch did," she thought. "No man would ever love another man's children as his own. They are destined to a life without a fathers love, it is not fair, just not fair." She had a good cry. After a while she calmed herself down. She got up and made herself a cup of coffee, listened to some comforting Christian music, read her bible and then decided to try and sleep. She re-checked that the house was locked. Then panicked again, a subconscious thought, that if Mitch were to come home he would not get in. "He is not coming home," she told herself. "But I can't believe he is gone, maybe he has just gone away and when he comes home he won't get in."

"He is not coming home!" She told herself. She had this conversation with herself for over an hour. She switched off all the lights, Mitch had usually done that, it felt so foreign. She got into bed alone, it felt so weird. She simply lay there. Every time she closed her eyes she saw a picture of Mitch. The pool shed was just behind her head where she lay, when Martin had pulled him out of the pool shed he had lain Mitch on the ground, Mitch's head must have been touching the wall of their bedroom. He would have been laying almost head to head with her as she was now, it was freaky. She remembered she had seen his legs, when she had gone over to see what was going on, all she had seen were his legs. There were large burns on them, the exit for the electricity they had told her. No other marks on him, just large burns on his legs. But his insides, they explained, would have been frizzled, cooked.

"God, what a horrible way to die," she thought. She moved over to Mitch's side of the bed, his smell was still on his pillow, still there. She threw the pillow off the bed. "How dare his smell be here!" she screamed inside. "How dare it, he is gone, gone, gone, gone, get it through your thick skull, he is not coming back," she sobbed. Eventually she fell asleep, exhausted.

She awoke a few hours later, all was quiet, so very quiet. What had awoken her? Someone was trying to get into the house, she was sure of it, someone was breaking in. What should she do? She heard her breathing, fear breath. She told herself to calm down. A peace seemed to enter the room, her eyes adjusted. There was someone here, someone was in the room, she looked and she saw the most amazing sight. Standing at the end of the bed was an angel, she knew it was an angel, he was huge, so big – his shoulders were so wide, and he was tall, so very tall. He was standing with his arms folded, he had the most gentle, loving eyes, they looked like golden lights. And a smile, a warm and gentle smile, almost patronising, she felt as if he was saying "Why are you worried? I am here, I am watching over you all – look."

Annie looked to her left, Ben was in bed with her, she looked to her right, Janna was on the other side, they were all together, the threesome, safe. They were being watched over. Annie closed her eyes and slept, waking only to feed Janna. She never felt scared again. She always knew she was being watched over. It had seemed like a dream but it was so very, very real.

Annie still did her bible reading every day, she received a huge amount of comfort from the scriptures. God was in control, he watched over them, God was a father to the fatherless, God had a special place in his heart for widows. God would provide, she need not worry. She was precious to Jesus, and He loved her and her babies. He would see her through.

Annie's milk dried up, overnight it just disappeared. She was devastated, as she had wanted to feed Janna for months, and had prayed hard that she would be able to. She had battled to feed Ben and had so wanted to make it work with Janna. Now her breasts were empty. It was such a weird feeling, her breasts so near to her heart and her heart feeling so empty and lifeless as if the evidence of it was manifesting through her milk production. She went to the doctor for pills, but the doctor refused.

"You have been through a terrible ordeal, you don't need the added stress of battling with breast feeding," he said.
"You have done well, very well, put Janna on a bottle."

125

Annie was bitterly disappointed but she knew that what the doctor said made sense. Janna went onto a bottle. Annie felt like a failure.

Annie had to start thinking about her future. Money was going to be a problem. Mitch had an insurance policy that would pay her out a lump sum. From that she would be able to handle the large moneys owed. She would be able to pay off the house, buy herself a decent car and pay all Mitch's funeral expenses. At the end of the day life went on. Bills had to be paid, they waited for no-one. She would get angry with the final demands she received in the mail. "Do they not know – do they not understand what was going on?" She wondered to herself.

She realised they had no idea and quite honestly they don't care – they just want their money – nothing else mattered. She tried so hard to be disciplined and pay things on time – it was difficult. She was not in the right frame of mind. Life had to go on but she felt as though she simply could not move. And she had to find a job. She had to be able to support the children and herself.

She was being cheated. Mitch's insurance policy was half of what it should have been. They had some cock and bull story and she had no choice. The company they had borrowed money from to buy the house was now wanting double of what they had lent Annie and Mitch. It was so unfair. Will interceded on her behalf, and sorted the house's price out for Annie. His calmness and excellent logic and brain worked it out for her, and he managed to save her a lot of money. Annie had never really been that good with money, she would always spend too much and now she had this large lump sum and had to be so careful with it. She had the children to think about, she had to raise them alone. She needed financial security, and the only way to ensure that was for her to go back to work.

She left Janna with the maid and found a temporary mornings only position. She could not work, she tried but it was difficult to apply herself properly. She would spend most of her working day in the toilet crying. She could not do this.

There was another problem, Annie's period had not come. She was convinced she was pregnant. She and Mitch had been making love and had used no protection because she was breast feeding. She could not tell anyone, she thought she would get told off for being so stupid, for having sex so soon after Janna's birth and more than that, for taking risks. They were not supposed to have had sex for six weeks after Janna's birth. Annie was secretly so pleased they had. "But, fuck, imagine if I am pregnant as well," she worried to herself. Every day she willed her period to start, it didn't and she became more and more worried. She considered abortion, but it was so against all the church teachings, yet she could not handle another child. She went to see a doctor and asked him to please do a pregnancy test. The doctor looked her in the eye and said "Annie, there is no way you are pregnant."

"But doctor," she said, "Mitch and I were not very careful, it is possible."

"No," he said, "impossible. Your system has gone through a huge shock Annie, it is normal for your periods to disappear, but lets do the test to put your mind at rest."

It was negative, and Annie was so relieved. She eventually came on about a week later, it was the best period of her life.

It felt so strange to Annie, that whilst she seemed to be coping so well and was feeling fine, that her body should just kind of freak out, as if it knew more than she did, as if it was saying all is not right. She had been totally unprepared for the sheer physical symptoms of Mitch's loss, and had always thought it would only be emotional, she felt as if her body was betraying her when she needed to depend on it. She had to stay well and healthy, she was the only surviving parent of two young children. As it was she was almost paranoid at home, she could not even put the kettle on without a cold shiver going through her. She was petrified of electricity, and would have terrible dreams, dreams in which she would be trying to do something and she too would be electrocuted. Ben would wake up in the morning and find her dead on the floor. It became all consuming, logic failed her, there were things Annie simply would not do. Like turn the pool on or off. Or change a fuse, or unplug anything. She would ask someone else to do it for her, she just couldn't.

There were other dreams, terrible dreams of Mitch. He was alive, and had left her, left her for another woman. He was in hiding from her and secretly laughing behind her back. He was happy and in love with someone else and she did not know, he never told her. There were still more dreams, ones in which Mitch was there, still alive, she would dream that they were making love. She would wake up, realise it was just a dream and hug herself and cry and cry and cry. She felt like she was limping through life, like she had lost a leg and could not walk properly, she could move but not fluidly. And she kept falling over, she could not stand for long. It would be fine for a while then everything would come crashing down and she would be in a crumpled heap on the floor. No-one saw this side of Annie, they only ever saw Annie made up and together, no-one knew the fear, pain and confusion she lived with, she simply could not explain it and knew that no-one would be able to relate to it.

Daina came through to help Annie pack up Mitch's belongings. It was a sad day, with so many memories. Annie and Daina would work on packing up his things, then cry, then find something funny, have a laugh, and continue. Annie loved Daina so much but Daina and the rest of her family were not Christians and Annie had to be careful that she was not influenced by her worldly family. She had been warned about this by the church. Her family would try and take her away from the church, she had to be strong and careful. As a result Annie withdrew from her family at a time when she needed them the most. Daina was the feisty one – she would not go quietly. She demanded Annie's attention and time and got it. They became very close again. But Annie remained wary. Daina took Mitch's clothes and got rid of them for Annie, Annie packed up most of his army memorabilia for Ben and she kept Mitch's gold cross for Janna. Their well used bar was taken apart and made into a coffee bar, his things were thrown away, given away or sold.

She had no use for his things now, they were just a constant reminder that he was not coming back. Annie felt as if she was trying to rid not only her being, but also her surroundings of Mitch, to make herself come to terms with the fact that he was gone. It made sense to her grieving heart. The doing away with Mitch's personal effects seemed to fit her state of mind, it was as though she was trying to rid her home of Mitch to enable herself to come to terms with his death. There was no escape from this, no right or wrong way to do things, Annie simply had to follow her heart and try and do what she thought was best - the only way through was to keep on going and feeling and weeping. The funeral parlour had returned Mitch's clothes. The ones he had been wearing the day he died. Annie had stored them at the back of his cupboard, the package was still there staring at her. Annie opened the well wrapped package. Mitch's smell hit her in the face. She sat on the floor holding his shirt and sobbed. She missed him so much. Daina joined her and they had a good cry together. Annie could not part with those clothes, not yet. She needed to keep them, for what she did not know, but it was the last smell of him and she could not let it go. She hid them at the bottom of her cupboard and was always aware of their presence.

In reality Annie had no-one to talk to. She was very lonely. She went for grief counselling three times but found it did no good. Nothing could ever make her feel better. She simply had to try and accept her fate and move on.

The guilt hit her. Oh the guilt – Annie felt so bad. How could she have been so terrible to Mitch during their marriage? Maybe if she had been a better wife this would not have happened. Maybe this was her punishment. Maybe God was punishing her for being so bad.

Then the anger – God the anger, Annie suppressed it well, she was so angry, so very angry at Mitch for leaving her with two children. She would mumble to him, "It is all right for you, you are sitting up there under fruit trees listening to the angels and I am down here with all the crap. It is not fair!" She also felt a huge suppressed anger at God for doing this to her, the God she was supposed to love so deeply. She was angry with many people and things, but mostly with herself, because it was all her own fault, it was her punishment for being such a terrible wife. She felt that she should have loved him more, should never have slept around, should have done more but had not known how to. It felt to Annie that as she recovered from one shit hand in life there was another just waiting to knock her down again. How she kept getting up, she never knew.

Suicide was an option, she spent long hours thinking about it, but it would be murder as well as suicide because she would never leave her babies. She used to wish she had gas in the house, a gas oven, then she would be able to close herself and her babies in the kitchen and they could all just go, go and be with Mitch in paradise. She would drive her car with the children in it and get the compulsion to drive into a wall or a bus or a tree, but the thought of her dying, and the children surviving was too high a risk and there was no way she could have physically killed her children, just no way. She would lie for hours at night scheming how she could do it, put them all in the car with a pipe from the exhaust was an option. But she had heard about people who had done that and at some point regretted their decision and tried to get out and were powerless to move, could she cope with being so mentally with it whilst watching her children die? What if she changed her mind and could not get them out? What would happen then? And what about God, God would never forgive her. She would not have time to repent before she met with her maker and then she would be banished to hell for ever and ever, burn in hell with Satan and all his demons while Mitch was in heaven with their children – they would still not be together, she simply could not take the chance.

Eating was not on Annie's list of priorities. Her small weight gain from her pregnancy was soon gone. If ever she did manage a meal, it would simply not stay down, she would feel sick and would go and vomit it up. She could handle small nibbles and no more. She always did her best to look good, always put on a brave face. She never left the house unless she was made up and well dressed. Almost as if she had to portray the image that she was coping, that she was together. To those around her she was being so strong. She knew that things were not the way they seemed, she was smoking again and it hounded her. She felt so guilty, knowing it was such a weakness. The church looked down on smoking.

The people from her church commented on how Annie was going to be such a testimony to so many. They were all so proud of her. God had chosen her for so much they told her. But she never felt chosen, she felt punished. The church explained that she would be able to help others because of her experiences, she would be a help to so many. "But I cannot even help myself," she thought, "how can I help others when I can't even help myself?"

Annie threw herself into her religion. She never missed church on Sunday. In addition she went to bible study every Wednesday at Rebecca's house. She was so brave, packing the children up and going home alone after the meetings. These were the only times Annie went out socially, she had retreated into her own little world. She hated the attention she received after Mitch's death, the way people whispered about her or when she was introduced to people they would say something like "Oh that Annie – oh yes we know all about you – shame how are you doing?" Annie would secretly want to punch them. She felt as if she had lost her individuality. She was no longer Annie, she had become Mitch's widow, a single mother. She was no longer a person. Her wants or needs were not important, there were too many others to consider. God came first, above all came God. Then the children. Her inner self came far down the list.

Serving God was all that mattered, she was loyal and faithful to him. She always strove to do her best and not to sin. She could not allow her old sinful nature to rear up again. She was a new creation, they had told her that, all her demons had been cast out of her. If there was any bad in her it was in her heart and she had to expel it from her being. She totally suppressed her sexuality. She refused to masturbate telling her grief counsellor "Masturbation involves fantasy, and I simply cannot fantasise about a dead man." God hated masturbation and God always knew what one did. God saw all. Even your heart and mind. You were never far from Him. He knew all. Every swear word that slipped out had to be repented for, if Annie had impure thoughts or anger she would spend hours praying for forgiveness. She hated any form of weakness in her self. She fought to be brave and strong and respected. She would talk for hours to people about the Lord and His goodness.

In the back of her mind was the nagging thought that this did not make sense, she did not understand why she had to follow these rules, why the God who she served and loved, and who supposedly loved her unconditionally and completely, took her husband and the father of her children. How could He do that to her if He was supposed to love her? Annie simply could not understand it. If she ever asked Rebecca about her doubts, Rebecca would always have a scripture to back up a theory and Annie simply could not argue against it. She had to accept that this was the way things were. She sang the loudest in church, she clapped more than anyone else, she praised more, she prayed more than anyone else, she did everything she could to keep herself together. So why did she still feel like such a failure? Why did she feel so broken, like her insides were a mass of broken pieces of internal organs, nothing in place, just all jumbled around in pieces, floating around aimlessly? Nothing solid or firm on the inside of her, just a mass of jelly and sharp objects that hurt so badly.

Annie's life took on a monotonous routine. Work, fetch Ben, go home, bath the children, cook, and if she felt like it watch the television for a while, and then bed. Wednesday bible study, Sunday church. When it all got too much she would go shopping but then Rebecca would crap on her, telling her she had to save her money. Annie had tithed ten percent of her pension from Mitch to the church, it had been a fairly large sum of money. She wondered why she could give it to the church but not spend it on herself or children? She found it hard to work out. Whenever she bought something for herself she never told Rebecca – who needed another sermon? She began to collect shoes. It was a mission in life for her to own every colour conceivable. She had over fifty pairs of shoes hidden in her cupboard. She had to keep walking. She had to keep going.

Annie received a British pension – she was overjoyed. She and Daina decided they needed to go shopping in South Africa. A shopping trip to South Africa for Zimbabweans was a rare treat. The shops were full of all the things one could not buy in Zimbabwe. It was totally indulgent and felt so wickedly normal to Annie to be able to have some form of pleasure. She would be able to buy birthday and Christmas presents for the children to put away, toys were virtually unobtainable in Zimbabwe. Daina was now pregnant and would need things for the baby. Annie welcomed the idea of being able to spoil this new life that was growing in Daina. She would be able to help Daina buy all the necessities for the baby. Vanessa, Annie's hairdresser was staying with Annie for a while and she looked after Ben, whilst Janna went to stay with Rebecca. Daina and Annie had a ball. Annie shopped like a demon and she and Daina would laugh for hours afterwards at Annie's antics. Daina would tell people later, "If you see Annie with a trolley move out of her way – quickly – or you may get killed – she is mean with a trolley, is Annie!"

Annie bought more shoes, clothes, make up, all the things she had not had the money for before. The future seemed so unimportant. Life was for living and money was to be spent. You never knew what tomorrow would bring. They spent their evenings talking and weeping and getting slightly tipsy. Annie had not drunk for well over a year now and it was a welcome release. She found she still had a sense of humour and could still enjoy herself. Daina was an excellent tonic for Annie. Her love for life and sense of humour was just the medicine Annie needed. The trip away did Annie a lot of good. Daina had managed to bring parts of Annie back from beyond, to the present to be enjoyed. Annie loved it – it was the most fun she had managed to have in ages.

Mitch had been dead for six months when Daina decided

133

Annie needed to get out and start living again. Annie was petrified, her confidence level was at zero. She had gone through the normal shuns from so called friends who thought they needed to lock their husbands away from Annie. In truth Annie was simply not interested. Gary had been to see her a few months before and made his intentions clear. He had arrived out of the blue one evening, Annie had put the children to bed and nearly jumped out of her skin when she heard a knock at the back door. She went through to the kitchen and asked who was there, "It's me, Gary" came the reply.

Annie let him in, he grabbed her and hugged her and told her how very sorry he was to hear about Mitch's death. He was now living in South Africa and had come up to Zimbabwe to visit his family and had learnt of Mitch's fatal end. He was so very sorry he told Annie. They went through to the lounge to catch up on all the years now passed. Annie felt so very uncomfortable with Gary there, she could not sit still and wished he would just go. Every time she looked at him it reminded her of the incident during the golf tournament and Annie had enough guilt to cope with at the moment thank you. She needed no more.

Annie made coffee and as she took Gary's coffee to him he grabbed her arm and pulled her to him. "Sit by me Annie," he cooed. Annie sat stiffly beside him, "Now come on Annie" Gary asked, "how are you coping in the physical sense?"
"I know what a hungry lady you are".

"Please, no, Gary" Annie gently pleaded, "I can't cope with this at the moment, I am coping fine, just fine thank you. I don't think about it".

"Well you know I would always oblige if you so wished" Gary pleaded.

Annie flatly refused. It would have felt like she was being unfaithful to Mitch all over again. She simply could not do it. She had totally suppressed and locked away her sexual nature. The truth of it was that Annie had locked it so deep within her, because it scared her to think of what would happen if she let it out.

Annie finally took off her wedding ring. The realisation dawned on her, she was no longer married. She was single and free. Everyone had told her she would marry again – God had a special man lined up for her. "True story," Annie thought.

Daina knew a single man from the town where she lived. She decided Annie needed to meet him. Annie was not convinced. He was not a Christian and the bible said you were not to be unequally yoked. Annie should only date Christians. Daina was persistent, and eventually a dinner with Chaz was arranged. Annie was very nervous about the arrangement. She made Daina and Jamie come in for the dinner and asked Sarah and Will to come along too. They met at a restaurant, Annie would not have anyone at the house. She was independent, she would drive there herself and be in control. No one could get passed her. She was too strong. God was so in control in her life. She made logical decisions and stuck to them. Emotions were not allowed entry.

Annie walked in alone. She saw him straight away. She had not seen a picture of him, but she walked in and she knew straight away it was him. He was standing alone at the bar getting drinks. Everyone else was seated at the table. Annie made her way to the table and greeted everyone. Chaz came back to the table, and they were introduced. He was divine, absolutely gorgeous. Very tall, blond, tanned, a big man, his stocky build was bordering on overweight but Annie did not care. He was divine. He had green, laughing eyes, a naughty smile and a wicked sense of humour. He had Annie laughing right from the start. They had a wonderful dinner, Annie only sipped at a glass of wine. After dinner it was decided they were going on to a night club. Annie went along but Will and Sarah went on home. Annie had forgotten how much she liked to dance, Chaz was a good dancer, full of energy. Annie loved the feeling of being smaller than a man, it was a new experience for her. She loved the way when they slow danced she could really nestle in. It was heavenly.

Mitch had been dead for almost seven months now. Annie had had absolutely no sexual release in that time, nothing. She had closed it down completely. It was the longest time that Annie had gone without some form of sex since the age of three. She had totally suppressed her natural desires.

It was midnight and Annie wanted to get home to the children, she said her goodbyes and made her way to her car. Chaz saw her out. She thanked him for a wonderful evening and said how pleased she was that Daina had insisted they meet. Chaz grabbed her, pulled her to him and kissed her.

It was over, the seal was broken and Annie was lost. Totally lost. She could have bundled him into her car right then and there and taken him home and fucked him all night. She did not know what stopped her. It must have been the children. It could only have been the children. Annie was flying, all her suppressed emotions rushed back through her in a few short moments. It felt like murder, absolute murder, for her. She wanted him, right there and then. She managed to pull herself away, explained that she had to go. Chaz asked her to come and watch him play cricket the next day, and she agreed without hesitation. They agreed upon a time and place to meet and Annie drove home. She was shaking, she had to stop the car, to puke her guts out, she was crying, and most of all she was horny, so fucking horny. "Oh shit, oh shit," she kept repeating, "what have I done?"

"The Lord will never forgive me, I have sinned so badly."
She got home and prayed for forgiveness and read her bible trying hard to concentrate on the words. Her thoughts kept wondering, wicked thoughts, totally wicked, and God could see them. She spent hours trying to purge Chaz from her mind but he would not go, she went to bed, wearing pants and trousers to stop herself from masturbating. It was so hard, so very hard. Sleep eluded her. She had it bad.

The next morning she was shaking and nervous whilst she

got the children ready. She made her way to Sarah's house where she was to meet up with Chaz. Jamie and Daina were staying at Sarah's and as Annie had arrived a little earlier than planned they all sat and had coffee together. They all made fun of her about the way she had taken to Chaz, and she could not fight them because everything they said was true. Annie was dreading seeing him. She hoped she had regained her composure, she needed to be in control.

He arrived looking so divine in his white cricket clothes. "Oh shit, I am lost," Annie thought, "this is too big, I can't fight it." The war within began, the war between the body, mind and spirit. Annie did not know which of the elements within her was going to win this one. But the body was definitely well out in front.

They went to the cricket game, Sarah looked after Janna and Ben went with them. Chaz was so sweet with Ben, taking him to the toilet and buying him drinks, it just choked Annie. Poor little Ben, his life was so unfair. He missed male company, she watched him almost cling to Chaz, and it was heartbreaking for her. Chaz and Annie sat together, Annie was all over him, she was embarrassed by her own actions, but could not control herself. She could not leave him alone, she wound her legs round his legs, she clung to his arm, she smelt his neck and his hair, she leant her head on his chest and listened to his heart. The smell, oh God the smell of a man, it was heady, it was divine, it was unfair, it was unreal. She wanted him badly.

Annie was far too intense for Chaz. He dropped her back at Sarah's and made his way back to the farm where he worked. He needed space. Annie, on the other hand, was a wreck. She prayed for help, but it did not come. She phoned one of the elders of the church to ask for help, and he told her to come round for prayer. He cast more demons out of Annie. "The demon named lust is a strong one Annie," she was told, "you have to fight it." She went home and phoned Chaz. She repented, she was a bundle of nervous energy. She still refused to masturbate. She loved this alive feeling, and never wanted it to end. But she wished it would. She wished she could get back in control but was too far gone. By now the whole church knew and Annie was being frowned upon. Her strength was turning to weakness. "The world has a grip on her," they said, "Satan has her in his grasp." She had to fight it, she could not give in.

Annie went to stay with Daina for the weekend. Only she did not stay at Daina. She went straight to Chaz. Herself and the children. How she managed to sort the children out and get them to sleep she never knew. She could not eat, she had a drink and another and another. She was so nervous, she was so horny. Chaz did not know what hit him. She grabbed the whiskey bottle and him and led him to his bedroom. She stripped him, examining every part of his body. God he was beautiful. She stripped, feeling no reserve. She lay him on the bed and began a journey with her mouth. She fell right back into the well known patterns, her instincts took over and she was lost. Her mouth found his erection, hard and throbbing. Her lips closed around it. It felt so natural, like coming home, a fleeting thought passed through her mind, that he was smaller than Mitch, it was there then it was gone. She was feasting, sucking, licking and sucking deeper. Chaz had lost all reserves and control, he came quickly – it had been a long time for him too – Annie drank him, sucked every last drop of his sperm, she swallowed it all.

"Divine," she thought, "just divine. Fuck I have missed the taste and smell of sperm." Chaz lay back mellowing, Annie grabbed the scotch and swigged from the bottle. "That's the only way to get the taste of sperm out of your throat," she laughed. Chaz lay her back and examined her body, she was so uninhibited. He touched and stroked and kissed and Annie floated somewhere far away, she was floating on a sea of passion. There was nothing else, just this moment, now. Ever so gently she climaxed, just a slight shiver running through her body. Chaz did not even notice and Annie never missed a beat, she just lay still and quiet enjoying every moment. She did not want him to stop, ever.

He was hard again, he entered her and Annie gasped and cried. She closed her eyes tight and the tears slipped down her cheeks. It was everything, the release, the coming home of sex, the familiarity of a man, the response of her body, the guilt and the feeling of being unfaithful to Mitch yet again. Chaz found a rhythm, he pushed Annie past the tears, she started to climb, Chaz kept going. Oh God he could make it last, he was so in control, she pushed him up and over and positioned herself on top of him. She opened her legs wide so as to feel him deep within her, she tightened her muscles and moved up and down, slowly, taking him into her ever so deeply with each thrust. She was building, she was building for a mother orgasm, when she came it was the most beautiful experience for both of them. Annie's juices flowed out of her, there was just so much, so much stored up, she came and came and came, her juices flowed over Chaz and down his balls, over his hips and on to the bed, he could hold back no longer he cried out in ecstasy as he filled her with his sperm. And she took it all sucking with her muscles she drained every last drop. She got off and collapsed on the bed, her breathing loud and laboured. She calmed herself and began to come down. "It should not have been that good," she thought, "it is not fair. It should have been awful then I would have been able to leave this alone." But it wasn't it was divine and she wanted more. Lots more.

They were so compatible sexually. They spent every free moment that weekend making love. They were both so open with each other it was unreal, they bathed together, laughed a lot, drank huge amounts and could not leave each other alone. Annie found it hard having the children there, they held her back and she so badly wanted to be alone with Chaz, she felt guilty for this, and felt bad for feeling selfish. But she was insatiable. It had been too long, far too long.

Daina had told Annie Chaz was twenty-five. "Three years younger than me is not so bad," Annie reasoned to herself. But Chaz was very immature. He was a good fuck, but when it came to relationships he had no clue about his own responsibilities. He gave Annie a hard time, he would not phone for days leaving her confused and angry. He would come in to town to see her and go out with his friends. She was not included, she accused him of being embarrassed about being seen with her. He explained that was not an issue, but he still did not take her out with him. Their relationship was purely physical, it was about sex and nothing else. Sexually they were magic together. Annie's weekends became a routine of going to Chaz's farm. Church took second place and God had to be put out of her mind while she was sinning so badly. She had been fitted with an IUD so there was no chance of a pregnancy scare, that was the last thing she needed. She was making up for lost time. She and Chaz were like animals when they saw each other.

Beth had met a man who lived in the same town as Daina and Jamie. Wedding plans were being made. Beth had finally seen the light after wasting eight years of her life on a married man. He would never leave his wife and Beth gave up. Her daughter Carrie was now five years old and Beth wanted a life. She had moved to the farm with Boet, her new man. He was younger than her and a bit of a party animal but Beth loved him. Annie got on very well with him, especially when they were drinking. Annie could drink most men under the table. They would have amazing parties at Beth and Boet's farm. The four of them getting pissed. They would drive from Beth and Boet's farm back to Chaz's farm late at night, leaving Ben and Janna with Beth, Annie would usually give Chaz a blow job on the way home. Often they would stop and fuck on the side of the road. They had even fucked in Beth's garden, they simply could not leave each other alone.

Annie realised at this point that she was allowed to live again, that one's feelings and emotions did not die with someone, they just got pushed back to allow the stronger feelings of grief to surface and then to leave, once they had been dealt with. Annie was able to part with the clothes Mitch had been wearing when he died. She took them with her to Chaz's farm one weekend and watched them burn to nothing in the old boiler outside Chaz's back door. She let it all go that day and took her life's decisions back to herself.

They planned a weekend away. Annie and Chaz decided they would go camping together with Daina and Jamie, it was a lustful drunken weekend. Sarah looked after the children for Annie. She needed the time alone with Chaz to be able to be herself. Annie found Chaz's passport that weekend, he had brought it along for identification purposes. He was twenty-one. And only just twenty-one. To Annie he seemed like a baby. "No wonder he was so immature in so many ways," she thought.

A relationship based on sex is never a strong enough foundation. Chaz could not handle Annie's total attachment to him, he still wanted his freedom. He could not handle the thought of a ready made family. He loved Annie's children but he did not want to be their father. That weekend away sorted out many of the issues that had been hanging over their relationship, they learnt things about each other and realised it was not meant to be. They had worn each other out after three months. Annie could not quite give up though, every now and again she would just arrive at Chaz's. He would be out and get home and find Annie in his bed. They would fuck for hours and then she would go and they would not see each other for weeks. But every now and again she would just pitch and so would he.

Annie went back to church but it was hard. She had failed in all their eyes. She had sinned. She was not as strong as they all thought. She could no longer be a testimony to the church. She was a lustful, fallen woman and to be avoided. Annie knew why – the men could simply never trust themselves. And the wives were insecure. Annie found it hard to believe that all these people who had loved her so much suddenly seemed to despise her. "How does this kind of love work?" She wondered, "this Christian love that you can turn on and off like a tap, it makes no sense. They teach me about unconditional love but they will only love me if I am doing what they say."

Annie felt like they were trying to put her in a box and she hated it. When she needed them all the most they were simply not there for her – they were too busy judging her behaviour, and they forgot to love her through it. They say that only the Christians shoot their wounded, Annie found this to be true.

"Well, when all else fails go back to what you know best," Annie thought, "I am free, single and why not?" She left the church men alone. There were a few easy targets there but Annie despised them all and their false love. They had let her down.

She started seeing another man, Daryl, he was shorter than Annie and it felt right. Annie gave him a hard time. He idolised her and she treated him like dirt. He was almost her lap dog. Whatever Annie said, he would do. She would tempt him and tease him but never let him fuck her. It drove him wild. Annie would get pissed and take a bath, she would ask Daryl to come and scrub her back. She would lay in the bath and masturbate while he was watching. It drove him wild and Annie laughed. "I don't need you," she would say, "I have ten fingers, I can do it myself. And you know what – it always satisfies."

CHAPTER 16

Annie had become best friends with Chaz's sister Amber. Amber spent a lot of time with Annie, they got up to a lot of mischief together. Annie loved her 'Fuck You' attitude towards people. One night Daryl was there with Amber and Dick, Amber's boyfriend. Dick had some good grass and they all indulged except Daryl. The children were sleeping and Annie was flying high. But then she had a bummer. She had smoked too much and was freaking out. The whole house was moving and Annie was scared. Daryl looked after her so well. He held her forehead as she puked for hours into the sink. She was crying and lost. "My babies," she kept saying, "my babies, promise you will look after them, look at me, look at me, I am a terrible mother," she was sobbing. "If my babies needed me now I would be unable to do anything for them."

"I want to get out of this," she kept saying, but she couldn't she had to wait it out. Daryl calmed her down, bathed her and put her to bed. He watched the children for her and sat with her all night, he did not leave her side. The next day she gave in and fucked him. He had proved himself to her, he had been there for her when she needed him and she was so very grateful. There was only one problem Daryl was very well hung. Annie was not very deep vaginally and Daryl hurt her terribly, she could not walk for two days afterwards, she was in too much pain. She never fucked him again. She also gave up the dope. She loved the feeling of getting high but hated the feeling of being trapped once you were there, you could not get out if it was a bummer. She had to be responsible for her children and she could not take the risk. Exit Daryl and dope.

Then there was Bryn, God he was divine. She had met him for lunch one day after chatting him up over the phone. They spent a very drunken afternoon together. After lunch Annie fetched Ben from school, took him home, hugged Janna and left the children with the maid. She was going out. She went back to Bryn's place, the party continued. Bryn's friend was there, just the three of them. They got so pissed that Annie fucked them both that night, and regretted it for months. She steered clear of both of them after that and never saw them again, it was just too embarrassing.

She felt as if she was in the whirlwind again. She was desperately looking for something to anchor herself onto but could find no solid ground. She simply did not know how to get out.

Vanessa, her hairdresser friend, had been away in the United States. She arrived back home, and went round to see Annie, and it was great. The time away had mellowed Vanessa and she and Annie sat drinking beer and listening to Bon Jovi - simply unacceptable in the church's eyes but they were having a ball. Who cared? Certainly not Annie.

"There is this boy," Annie said to Vanessa, "at church and I don't know what it is about him. He just seems to be there all the time. Every time I look around he is there. He is far from my type and I don't even fancy him but there is something going on." Vanessa demanded to know who – Annie said "Mike, his name is Mike."

Vanessa was stunned, she said "Mike is the nicest guy you could ever wish to meet, in fact, Mike was with me when I found out about Mitch, Mike comforted me and helped me so much. He is a very special person. I think I should introduce you."

"No!" Annie yelled. "Look at me I am a fucked out, failed Christian and he is so spiritual and superior. I mean he is an elder, and children's church teacher, and a bible study leader, I would freak the guy out."

Vanessa laughed. "No ways, he is a first class guy."

"You know Vanessa, all I really want is male company, a friend, someone to go to movies with or out for a meal or someone to come out with me and the kids, Ben misses male company and so do I – I just need a friend."

"He is perfect," Vanessa said, "absolutely perfect."

It was arranged Mike was coming for lunch on Sunday to officially meet Annie and the children.

On the Friday night Annie had met some guy through work, she now had a full time job working mornings only. He had come round for a drink and Annie had fucked his brains out. He reminded her of Mitch and he smelt of grease and she could not resist him. He had left and Annie had cried herself to sleep. She always seemed to fuck it up.

Sunday arrived and Annie went to church as usual, Janna decided it was time to have a puking fit and had totally embarrassed Annie in church by spewing up all over the place and all over Annie. Annie was in a state, Mike was coming for lunch. She rushed home and bathed herself and Janna, and gave Janna some medicine to stop the vomiting. Janna had a milk allergy – it always made her puke if she was given the wrong thing – it knocked Janna out and Annie was able to concentrate on getting lunch ready.

Annie was a good and capable cook, she loved cooking – it was the only subject she had done well in at school. She made a large tuna salad with everything in it and planned to serve it with large chunks of crunchy garlic bread. Dessert would be a fresh fruit salad and ice cream.

Mike arrived with Vanessa and Annie got drinks, a beer for Vanessa and a Coke for Mike. Mike was good with children, and knowing Ben from church they had an easy rapport with each other and got on famously. Janna was sleeping, thanks to the medicine. Mike and Ben spent the day swimming and playing. It was so sweet for Annie to see Ben responding so well to a man, he had dragged Mike to his bedroom and shown him all his toys, he would not leave him alone. Annie got very little chance to speak to Mike but he had already won her over – Ben thought he was great. Mike did commentary for the local radio and he had to go off to commentate on a soccer match, Annie invited him back for dinner afterwards, and he accepted. He left with Vanessa. Annie cleared up and got dinner going – beef stroganoff, her speciality. Mike was a chef so Annie was a bit panicked about cooking for him. She wanted it to be just right, there was something special about this man. There was something in him that Annie had not seen in any man ever before.

Mike got back later that evening, the children were down for the night giving Annie the freedom to be herself. They ate and chatted. They talked about everything, Mike was just so easy to talk to and he was so understanding. Not judgmental like most of the Christians Annie knew, he was different. Mike was over six feet tall, balding with blue eyes, he had an exceptional sense of humour and the most infectious laugh Annie had ever heard. Annie thought how wrongly she had judged this warm and loving man. He was special this one. They talked until two in the morning, Annie told him everything about her, he never batted an eyelid. She was surprised, she was convinced she would have scared him off with her unsavoury past but he was still there listening and understanding. He was amazing. It was time for him to leave, he had work in the morning and needed to sleep. Annie saw him off, he did not even try to kiss her good-night, he simply thanked her for a lovely day and left. Annie was stunned. "What's wrong with the guy?" she thought. "Weird, he never even tried anything."

On Monday she rang him before he had a chance to ring her. "I mean we are supposed to be friends so she could ring couldn't she?" She thought. He was full of bull shit and had Annie laughing early in the morning. She liked it. She invited him over that night. He said he had bible school – he was finishing his second year but would come after his classes at about eight thirty. "Fine, Annie said, "I will cook."

It felt good to Annie to have someone to cook for again, she was pleased to do the shopping and prepare a meal, it felt so normal. She organised the children and put them down. She was a strict disciplinarian, she felt that she had to be. Ben could not be allowed to think he could get away with things just because there was no father around. The routine had stayed the same. Annie had been very forceful about keeping things as normal as possible.

Mike arrived, they ate and talked and talked. He was there until three in the morning. Annie found out he was a virgin. She was shocked, he was twenty-seven years old and had never had sex, this amazed her. She would soon change that she chuckled to herself. He talked about his life and family and the church. He had been a Christian since he was fourteen and had served God fully ever since. He was still human though, he would have the odd cigarette and every now and again a swear word would drop into his conversation. Annie thought he was great, a human Christian, a very rare find. It was Mike's graduation on the Friday night and he asked Annie to come with him. She said that she would love to.

"That'll get the tongues going," she thought. She took Mike through to the bedroom to see if she would be taller than him with heels on – they were the exact same height. Mike kissed her. A gentle loving kiss. No passion just loving. Annie felt as if she was dreaming. This was not normal.

The same events played themselves out on Wednesday, Mike came for supper, Annie fed him in more ways than one. As they lay on the carpet kissing, she let her hand slip to his pants. He was hard, so very hard. She undid his pants and he did nothing to stop her. She freed his penis and ever so gently brought him to orgasm. She did not look down, she looked him in the eye the whole time. She covered his nakedness and went off to get a warm cloth to clean him up. She cleaned him and examined his most private of places. She found it so hard to believe that his penis had never been in a woman before. She was itching to fuck him but he was so innocent, so pure, she felt she did not want to taint him. Mike asked Annie to marry him that night. Annie replied "Um – I have to think about this ...... yes!"

Thursday morning Annie was an ocean of nerves. "Everyone is going to freak," she thought, "Mitch has not even been dead a year and I have agreed to remarry. I am in for a rough ride." But she knew it was just so right. Mike was her gift from God. He was the pleasure in all her pain. He was good and right and pure and true, just what Annie so desperately needed. He was stable and loving, kind and generous. Okay, he had no possessions but who cared? Annie had everything a house, its contents, a car, what more did they need? As long as they loved each other that was all that mattered. And Annie loved him already.

Annie had to tell Sarah, she knew Sarah was going to freak. She did not know how she was going to put it. They decided Mike would go and speak to her. It was arranged he would speak to Sarah on Friday, but first Annie had to introduce them – break the ice so to speak. On the Thursday afternoon they popped in to Sarah and Will's workshop. Annie had to collect something and she took Mike in to meet them. Just to casually introduce them and play it by ear. Annie flew in with Mike, they did not hold hands, they just stood apart. Annie was nervous, Sarah was always someone Annie feared. She knew Sarah's temper well. Annie made the introductions and they left. They were there for no more than five minutes. Mike dropped Annie home and went off to bible school.

When she got inside, the phone was ringing. It was Sarah. "So when are you two getting married?" she asked. Annie was gob smacked totally gob smacked. "How – how did you know?" she asked Sarah.

"It is just written all over you two, you just look so right together, perfect," Sarah said. Annie was delighted and relieved, the first and hardest hurdle had been passed with ease. Mike still went to see Sarah and asked if he could marry Annie. Sarah said it was fine with her.

Now they had to let the church know and make plans. They had to talk to the pastor and Annie had to tell Rebecca. Rebecca was going to freak. She had been through all the Chaz shit and she was most disappointed in Annie. Their friendship had eased a lot and there was a strain between them now. It saddened Annie, but there was nothing she could do. She simply could not be what Rebecca wanted.

The bible school graduation was as expected. All the tongues were wagging. They were the sole topic of conversation, but they did not care. They held their heads high and wore their feelings on their sleeves. It was the real thing, anyone could see that.

Annie had let Rebecca know, Rebecca was not impressed but what could she do? Nothing, big fat zero. They booked an appointment to see the pastor. They wanted to be married within six weeks. Mike had said he had vowed to stay a virgin until marriage and Annie knew six weeks was about all she could handle. They saw the pastor. He was very nice – they told him they believed God had placed them together and they wanted to get married, soon. The pastor said "If it is God now it will still be God in six months time. Go out for six months then I will marry you."

They had no choice really, Mike was well respected in the church and a leader, he had to conform. A date was set for six months later – to the day just about, they would wait not one day more.

Mike began bringing Annie back to reality. He was so good with her, he would pray with her and they would talk for hours. They were so uninhibited with each other. Mike would talk to Annie in the bath, while she was on the toilet, anywhere. They hid nothing from each other, they just could not have sex. Annie found it so frustrating. Had they not been Christians they would have been living together. They indulged in some pretty heavy petting. Annie loved teaching Mike. He knew nothing about woman and Annie delighted in showing him and teaching him where to touch her and what felt good and what did not. They did everything except 'the deed'. Mike was bringing Annie back to life. He was loving her and he was her very best friend. He was amazing with the children. So natural and they adored him in return. It was like a fairy tale – so perfect, in fact it was too perfect, Annie kept waiting for something to go wrong. But nothing did ever go awry. It only got better.

They went out for dinner one night. Annie indulged in a few vodkas as was her wont from time to time. It did not worry Mike; he loved all of her, every little bit. They got home and made their way to the bedroom. Mike always put Annie to bed before he left, he would lock the house and throw the keys through the window. At the weekends he would be there before she woke up and it would feel like they had been together all night. It was hard going for Annie, she wanted him to stay with her and he always had to leave, he was such a gentleman. She had only ever known bastards, no-one had ever treated her like a lady, the way Mike did. She loved the way he made her feel, like she was worthwhile and deserved to be loved and respected.

They were in the bedroom, Mike was putting her to bed. Annie was a tease, a terrible tease. "Come here," she beckoned. He came over to her. She undressed him. He did not complain. They touched each other and kissed and fondled. "Mike," Annie said, "how do we know it will fit, you know, maybe it won't," she teased. "Lets just try and see, just put it in me and let me feel then you can take it out again."

She was a bitch, she knew once she had him inside her there would be no stopping him. He resisted but not for long, she was a professional, she knew the moves. He was a bit awkward, not quite knowing what to do. Annie talked soothingly to him, gently and lovingly. She guided his penis into her, she was ready, well lubricated and inviting. He slipped in effortlessly. He held himself in check, Annie squeezed her muscles and he was lost. It took about three strokes for him to find the rhythm, not too sure at first, but then instinct simply took over and he was a goner.

It was beautiful, gentle and loving and one of the most amazing experiences Annie had ever had. He came, a long shuddering orgasm that kind of went on forever. And Annie just moved with him and took it all from him. He finished, opened his eyes and looked at Annie, so tenderly, so full of love. Annie felt like a total bitch. She had taken the most precious thing from him, something he had saved for twenty-seven years and she had taken it in three short weeks. She sobbed uncontrollably. Mike held her and let her cry it out. When she calmed down he soothed her and loved her and reminded her that even though he was a virgin he was no fool and he had wanted it as much as she did. They talked for hours after that, then they prayed, they asked God to forgive them and to help them to be strong in the future. It was going to be hard, the sexual attraction was strong and it was just such a completion of their love, so pure, so true, and so right. They were careful after that, very careful to stop before it got out of hand. Mike was stronger, much stronger than Annie and it used to really piss her off at times but she knew he was right. There was no way they could tell anyone – the church would freak and Mike would lose all respect and his position. They had to lie and keep it a secret.

The days were passing and Annie was powerless to stop them. It was coming up for the anniversary of Mitch's death, and she was dreading it. She would wake up with a sick feeling in her stomach. She was unreasonably paranoid and tense. Mike simply loved her through it. He would let her ramble for hours as she tried to put her feelings into words. She was so worried about hurting Mike, but he was so understanding.

"Mitch is no threat to me," he said, "how can I be threatened by a dead man Annie?" he reasoned.

"Mitch will always be a part of this family, he will always be Ben and Janna's father, nothing can ever alter that, we should be able to talk about him – he is just a part of us all."

Annie loved him for his logic and understanding. He was truly an amazing person. They decided to go to Daina and Jamie's for the weekend to get away, maybe the demons would not be so bad there. For Annie it felt like she was on some kind of journey, she was just being moved along and could not get off.

"I have to do this," she kept telling herself, "I have to pass this milestone". She had been warned that the 'firsts' were the worst. The first birthday without him, the first Christmas without him, Annie could not even remember Christmas, it had all been so surreal.

Once one had passed them all it got easier, she had been told. It was about to be put to the test.

She awoke in the morning of the eleventh of November and was surprised. She was fine, she had made it, she had survived the hardest year of her life. She had survived a year of grief. She had cried oceans of tears and she was now ready to fully live her life again. A peace came over her and she knew she had got over the worst of it.

"It can only get better from here," she thought, "I have Mike and we will be happy and fulfilled. He is my future and life now." She closed a chapter in her life and let go of all the anger and confusion that had accompanied Mitch's death.

Mike and Annie decided to travel to South Africa to buy an engagement ring for Annie. Janna would stay with Sarah, and Ben would come with them. Then they would then have to behave Annie reasoned. It was a special time for them all. Ben was pleased he was going to have a new Daddy. He adored Mike and the feeling was mutual. Ben was an intelligent and well behaved boy. He was loved by all of those who knew him. He had coped well through the trauma of losing his father and Annie had done a good job of bringing him up on her own, he was well adjusted and polite.

They spent five days away shopping and enjoying each other's company with no intrusions or judgements. It felt so normal, like they had been together forever. It was hard that they could not show their love for each other in physical ways, but they were determined to do it right. Annie wanted very much for this to be right, she had messed up so many times before and she was determined this was going to work. Ben took to following Mike around. When Annie was out of ear shot one day he said to Mike,

"Uncle Mike you are going to be my new Daddy hey?"
"Yes, Ben, I am," Mike answered, "and I am so pleased God has chosen me to be your new Daddy, I am a very lucky man. I can't be your father, Daddy Mitch will always be your father but I can and

want to be your Daddy."

"Can I call you Daddy?" Ben asked.

"Of course you can," Mike answered, "I would be honoured."
Ben asked Mike to keep it a secret from Annie. Mike respected his wishes. Whenever Annie was out of ear shot Ben would call Mike Dad and when Annie was around it was Uncle Mike. This lasted for a day and then Ben told Annie. Annie was overjoyed that Ben had made this decision on his own and that it was what he wanted. Annie reiterated Mike's words to Ben that his father would always be Daddy Mitch, nothing could ever take that away from him, but that Mike could and would be a Daddy to him. He seemed to understand. They chose a ring, a simple flat setting with three yellow diamonds. Annie thought it was the most beautiful ring she had ever seen.

Annie and Mike spent the next few months preparing for their wedding and marriage. Their nerves were constantly on edge and it was difficult for both Mike and Annie. Mike was nervous about the huge responsibility he was taking on and Annie was worried about marriage in general. She had become so independent and the church spoke strongly on the topic of the wife's submission to her husband and Annie hated the thought of losing her individuality. Mike was patient and loving with her. He worked hard to build Annie up spiritually and get her back on track with the church's goals. As he was a leader Annie would have certain responsibilities as a leader's wife. Annie hated the thought.

They worked hard at keeping their physical side suppressed. They would spend hours praying and talking, and became very close. A strong foundation was being built. They were the very best of friends. They could stand up against all the negative attitudes thrown their way. Mike's hard work paid off. Annie found a peace once again but still refused to give up the last little bits she considered her individuality. She still smoked, superstitiously almost, thinking "The last time I stopped something awful happened." It was now not breaking a habit but also a superstition. She still had an occasional

153

drink as well, but as Mike was a tee totaller she found very little satisfaction in drinking alone. God was back in place in her life and she was coping well.

The other task before they married was to find a home of their own. Annie did not want Mike to feel he was filling another man's shoes. They needed their own home. Annie sold the house she and Mitch had lived in for so long, the place both her babies had come home to, the place of memories, both good and bad. It was a bittersweet parting for Annie leaving that house. She would miss it so much. They found a larger house closer to town. Annie had made a good profit on her old house and they were able to put down a large deposit on their new home. Money was never an issue for Annie, if she had it or Mike had it, it made no difference, it was theirs to spend on their future. Mike was giving her things no money could buy, it felt right for Annie to pay the way. Annie moved into the new house a week before the wedding. Mike stayed on in the house he shared with a friend. It was murder for Annie being alone in their new home.

Their wedding would be a small affair. One hundred people would witness their marriage in a top hotel and dinner would follow. Mike and Annie reasoned they just wanted family and special friends there, no more. Annie had to invite Tom. Beth had married a month before Mike and Annie and Mike had met Tom at Beth's wedding. He had contained himself well. He hated Tom for what he had done to Annie but he suppressed his anger for Annie's sake, Annie hated a scene.

Tom's acceptance of the wedding invitation brought everyone's claws out and the family politics started. Annie hated it. She felt as if she was being pulled apart. What was she supposed to do? She simply could not please everyone and decided to please herself instead. At least then maybe she would be happy. She made her decisions based on what she felt was right. Tom would not give her away, Ben would.

The bridesmaids would be Vanessa and Amber, they would be dressed in cream and black pants suits. Annie was to wear cream, a low backed dress hand embroidered with pearls. It was beautiful. A short off the face veil, laced with fresh flowers in her hair and a bracelet of fresh flowers on her wrist. It was plain and tasteful.

Their wedding day arrived sooner than they thought possible, everything had been organised and it was now simply getting the procedures done. In Mike and Annie's minds they were already married. Amber and Vanessa led the way down the aisle, followed by Annie and Ben. Ben was dressed in a tuxedo, he looked so sweet and grown up and important. To Annie it felt right that Ben should be the one to give her away. Mike and Annie had chosen Phil Collins' 'A Groovy Kind of Love' to play as Annie walked down the aisle. Later they were slammed for breaking tradition and having non-Christian music at their wedding. It seemed to Annie that she could not get it right in the church's eyes. The tables were cream and black with touches of gold. They had black candles on the tables, something else they were slammed for.

"Black candles are used in satanic worship," they were told. People offered to pray for them for God's forgiveness and deliverance for being so totally wicked. Annie secretly laughed at them all thinking they were the ones who needed prayer. "Knives are also used in satanic rituals," she said to Mike "and I still have them in my house, do I need prayer for that as well?" Even the most special day of their lives came under stern criticism from the church. Annie felt herself being totally suppressed by them all. Daina was her saviour, they would sneak off to the ladies room for a cigarette and Daina kept Annie supplied with vodka. Annie thought their wedding was beautiful and special.

Mike had made the most moving speech that had caused everyone to cry. He pledged his love to Annie, Ben and Janna and promised always to be there for them. He thanked God for his beautiful family and told everyone how proud he was to be married to Annie and to be a father to Ben and Janna. Annie was deeply touched.

Annie got slightly tipsy, but Mike watched over her. They slipped off after all the normal formalities. They needed to be alone. They were staying in the hotel and Sarah was taking Ben and Janna home with herself and Will.

They had hardly made it through the door of their room when their suppressed desire came spilling through their carefully placed distance from each other. They closed the door and held one another, they stripped each other and ever so gently Mike made love to Annie. It was beautiful, like coming home she thought, just so right, as it should be. "He is a gift from God," Annie reasoned. His virginity had been the only pure thing she had ever had in her life. It was as if they had never slipped up, as if this was the first time. Annie had never known anything like it. It was pure and true and right and loving, everything it should be. Afterwards they bathed and went to bed. They did not get much sleep; they were making up for lost time.

They had two days away, it was enough. They both missed the children and were very eager to start married life together. Annie knew it could only get better. She loved Mike more each day, and his love for her was continuing to grow as well, and they marvelled at how blessed they were to have found each other. They also wanted to be a family in their new home. The six months of Mike commuting had taken its toll – they longed for normality.

Mike took to marriage and fatherhood like a duck to water. They were happy and secure. Mike and Annie had found an added bonus, not only were they the very best of friends, but they were very compatible sexually. It was the cherry on the top. They were open and uninhibited in their love making, giving and receiving pleasure. Annie found how well her body responded to Mike and his gentleness. He could make her orgasm over and over, like nothing Annie had ever experienced before. She would laugh and say to Mike, "I have been around babe, this you know, I have slept with many men and none of them has ever been able to make me climax the way you do."

He was so gently and lovingly and good. "Totally amazing," she would say, "are you sure you were a virgin? I think you must have had lessons," she would joke.

Annie took her role as a leader's wife seriously; she was careful to keep her nose clean and kept herself away from pointing fingers of so called do-gooders. They held a bible meeting at their house every Wednesday. Annie was an excellent hostess and enjoyed the evenings. Her love for her God escalated and she felt content and happy. She started dealing with her abuse for the first time ever. Being able to share it with Mike had helped Annie try and come to terms with it all. She did not have to pretend with Mike, she could let him know how painful it had all been. Annie had never, ever really been able to talk to anyone about it the way she had with Mike. Mike in turn had been compassionate and a pillar of strength, letting her ramble on and simply try and get it out. He never told her to forget it or to 'let it go' he would listen and then he would pray with her and ask the Lord to help Annie work through it all. Talking to Mike about it helped it become a little easier. She shared her testimony of how she came to know the Lord in bible study one night. Everyone was moved to tears by her words, they came directly from her heart. She spoke of her love for God and all the good He had done for her and how lucky she was to have met God when she did. "Who knows where I would have ended up if it was not for the Lord," she would say. She spoke briefly on her abuse explaining how very grateful she was to God for helping her with this.

"Abuse comes in cycles," she told them, "it seems to pass from generation to generation, I believe I have been chosen by God to break the cycle in my family. If God does nothing else for me but this, I will be eternally grateful to Him. It is enough that He has saved the next generation from abuse by stopping it at me."

"I have been through the deliverance's and the cutting of ties and they will not be passed to my children or my children's children. God has done a wondrous thing for me," she boasted. "Forever I will be grateful to Him for this and forever will I serve

Him."

Annie and Mike became advisors to many. Their good strong marriage and ability to work through things was hope for those around them. They were forever counselling or helping people. There were always people staying with them and they made everyone welcome. It was their duty to look after God's people.

*   *   *   *   *   *

The shit hit the fan, Jamie, Daina's husband of just over a year, ran off with Amber, Mike and Annie's bridesmaid. Daina was six months pregnant with their second child, their son Billy had been born nine months earlier. They had wanted their children close together. Daina was now alone with a baby son and was pregnant to boot. Jamie was not budging. They went through a living hell. The stress of it caused Daina to go into premature labour. She gave birth to a daughter Hannah at only twenty-nine weeks. She was tiny, a little miniature person but she was a fighter. She fought pneumonia and a host of other complications. Mike and Annie were constantly praying for her little life. God answered their prayers and Hannah survived.

Jamie and Daina sorted out their problems and got back together but it was never the same. The trust had gone. The worst was that Hannah had suffered nerve ending damage in her ears due to a side effect from the medication she was given to help her fight the pneumonia. Hannah was profoundly deaf and she would be a constant reminder to Jamie of his infidelity.

Changes always seem to come along suddenly. Something always comes along to burst a perfect bubble. Annie turned thirty and everything seemed to slowly fall apart.

CHAPTER 17

Janna turned three, a cute chubby little girl full of mischief and adored by all, especially Mike and Ben. Only Annie was allowed to bath her, and one day Annie simply freaked out. It hit her so hard. She was washing Janna and she had a flash back. She was Janna's age when Tom had started abusing her. Her vagina would have been as small as Janna's. The impact of what Tom had done to Annie finally surfaced, after years of trying to hide it away it was now staring at her right in the face through her own daughter. Annie could not take it. She silently fell apart. Her bulimia re-emerged again. She had controlled it well over the years only slipping back occasionally, but now it was raging. Mike did not know about it, he had no idea what was going on. It was as if from one day to the next it all just seemed to fall apart and he was powerless to stop it.

Annie became childish and irrational. She would lose her temper for nothing, screaming and swearing. Mike had to keep the children away from Annie when she was raging. She would lash out at them slapping and screaming, it was total freak out, total loss of control. Mike would pull Annie off the children and lock them away when she lost it. Eventually Annie used to know when it was coming and was able to get away. She would just run and run and run, leaving Mike to calm everything down at home.

The nights were the worst. If Annie was woken in the night, she would be locked into some old pattern, she would whimper and cry, she would be completely unreasonable. She was panicky, she would dive under the bed or into the cupboard. Mike would see to the children if they woke in the night because Annie was simply unable to. Suddenly there seemed to be too many demons hanging around in the dead of night for Annie. She became a bundle of nerves. She became extremely fearful of Tom. "He is coming," she would say, "he is coming to get me. He hates me and wants to punish me." Or, "he is coming to do things to me again and I can't stop him." She would not let Mike out of her sight, she would cling to him like a frightened child. She stayed at home and would not go out. Above all, she did not know what to do. Mike too, was unsure what their next step should be. He hated the pain Annie was living and he was totally powerless to help.

A friend suggested Annie speak to a psychologist. Annie laughed, "After my previous experiences, I don't think so," she would say. "No one can help me. God is the only one who can get me though this, only God." She went for prayer every week, she was constantly having demons cast out of her. She was headed one way, on a course of self destruction. She was in the whirlwind and did not know how to get out. She could not even work out how it had started. All had seemed fine and then everything just feel apart. It made no sense. "Why can't I just be happy," Annie would think, "what is wrong with me why am I so fucked up?"

One night she awoke from a nightmare, she did not know where she was. She did not know how old she was. She was sobbing. Mike woke up and went to comfort her. She freaked and he backed off. "He's there," she was sobbing, "there – outside the window. I can see him!" She made Mike go and check the house. There was no-one about. Mike never thought to refuse Annie's requests, so real was her fear that to do so would have made the whole situation far worse. He patiently checked every room in the house for Annie, then searched the whole of the outside property, when he came back in he found Annie huddled in her wardrobe and he gently talked her out and reassured her. He put her back into bed and held her for the whole night as she whimpered and cried in her sleep. From that night on Annie refused to be at home alone. "He will find out where I live and he will come for me when you are not here." She did not realise that she could say no to Tom. The thought did not enter her mind.

The bulimia in turn heightened the paranoia. She lived in a roller coaster of emotions, which Annie was riding, not knowing how to stop. She was vomiting constantly now. She had joined a slimming club and became a slave to the scale. She would weigh herself three times a day. She was addicted to laxatives and every time she ate she would vomit it up and swallow laxatives. This was the only secret she kept from Mike. She realised that she had to tell him, it was getting worse and worse. She was able to make herself sick without even putting her finger down her throat, she could simply bring it all up effortlessly. She was getting scared. She was out of control. It was all out of her control.

She sat Mike down and told him. She waited for him to do his nut, but he did not. He just held her. He prayed for her and he begun the journey of getting her back on track. He did not tell her to stop. He only asked that she tell him whenever she vomited. Annie reasoned that was fair enough. It was also enough to break the secrecy and expose it. It did not stop her bulimia completely, but it did help a lot.

Annie phoned the therapist recommended by her friend and booked an appointment. She was convinced there was nothing anyone could do to help her, totally convinced. Even God was struggling with her she would think. She arrived on time for her appointment. She marched in to the therapists office, sat down and said, "Hi my name is Annie, I was sexually abused and raped by my father when I was a child, I have attempted suicide twice, I have lost a husband, I have no faith in therapists due to a past experience, do I need you and do you think you can help me?" Patty, the therapist, was a star. She told Annie, "You will probably benefit from some sessions, lets see how it goes and if at anytime you don't want to continue that is fine, but lets just give it a go." Annie agreed.

After a few sessions Patty said to Annie that the most worrying part was how easily Annie could talk about her abuse. As if it had happened to someone else; a good friend or relative but not to her – Annie. They needed to bring Annie back from her locked childhood. They condensed a lifetime into eighteen months of weekly visits. The benefits were there for all to see. Annie controlled her bulimia, she learnt to talk, mostly to Mike, and she began to recover. It was a long slow process but it was working. Her punishment as she saw it was her body totally freaking out. She put on weight and battled to remain happy with herself. It was hard, so very hard, but Mike loved her through it. He would grab her tummy and kiss it, saying "I love it – I just love it – I love every part of you, every part, Annie. I love you for you and not how you look."

She hated it. She hated the excess, she hated feeling as if her body controlled her, she preferred to control it. But she had to ride this out – she had to believe her body would eventually come right and recover.

The elders in the church were voicing their concerns. They believed that Christians should have their problems solved in the church, psychologists were not advisable and most definitely not accepted by the church or the church's teachings. And when Annie found out Patty was a new age spiritualist there was no way she could go back and see her. They were on opposite sides of the fence and the war within Annie was too hard to fight. And anyway Annie felt she had done enough work. She was sane, she could cope now. Patty had taught her so much. It was time to test the waters and cope on her own.

Mike and Annie had decided they wanted a child together – just one. Annie battled to fall pregnant. It was a new experience. She had not had a problem before. They tried for over a year. Annie was convinced it was because she was carrying too much weight. It was her fault, all her fault. Her periods starting going haywire, weird things were happening to her body. She booked to see a gynaecologist. He suggested they do a D and C, give Annie's womb a good clear out and see if that would help. Firstly he would do some blood tests though. She would have the D and C in a few days time. Annie had the blood tests done on the Friday, she then went home to prepare for a surprise birthday dinner for Mike. She started bleeding, very heavily. She sat on the toilet, blood pouring out of her, confused and scared, she felt something pass through her vagina. She knew something was amiss. She had just had a miscarriage. She said nothing, told no-one.

On Monday she arrived for the D and C, the gynaecologist confirmed her pregnancy from the blood tests. Annie told him what had happened and he proceeded with the D and C. She awoke from it crying and wanting Mike. He needed to share this with her. He needed to be there. Mike arrived soon afterwards to take her home, he walked her to the car and she sobbed. Mike was confused, he had no idea about what had just transpired. Anne told him what had happened and the two of them sat in the car and held each other crying. It took a while for them to get over it but within six months Annie was pregnant and they were overjoyed. She had an easy pregnancy followed by an easy birth and their son Matt was born. It was a moving experience for Mike and Annie, a completion of their family unit.

Janna had always called Mike 'Daddy', she knew no different, Ben looked upon Mike as a father. They changed Ben and Janna's surnames so that they all had the same surname. It had been difficult for Ben at school having to explain why his name was different from his mother and father's and he simply did not always want to say that his 'real Daddy' had died. They were a complete family. There was no talk of 'step brother'. Matt was their brother, and that was that. Now they all had the same surname, it made sense. Annie felt strongly about it all, she refused to take Mitch's name away from his children, she simply added Mike's surname to the end of their names. Now they would have Mitch's name for life. It could not be taken from them, even when Janna married she would still have Mitch's name. It seemed a perfect solution. Matt was adored from the day he arrived. Janna was a perfect little mother at the age of five, and Ben an expert big brother at nine. Annie had a lot of help. She was running her own outside catering business from home and loved being able to be home with Matt. It seemed to make up for her having to leave Janna when she was a baby.

Janna seemed to change and after a short while felt pushed aside by this new intrusion. To say Janna was being difficult would be putting it mildly. She was used to being the baby. She seemed to revert to some kind of babyhood. She would lie on the floor saying "Baby can't walk, baby can't talk, carry baby." Annie found her behaviour very hard going and frustrating. Janna began to wet the bed. She was also wetting her pants during the day. Annie could not handle it or work it out. Annie decided to humour her, and then something clicked, Janna was crying out for a normal babyhood. Something she had never had. Annie babied her, put her in nappies, carried her and even allowed her to feed from her breasts. Janna had watched Matt feed and she also wanted to feed from Annie, Annie silently balked at the thought but was determined to get Janna through this. She allowed Janna to feed, Janna found she did not like breast milk and gave up. She wanted a bottle. Annie and Mike continued to humour her and her behaviour began to return to normal. She just seemed to slowly go through the years all by herself, she started crawling, then walking and then she came to her proper age. But still, something was not right and Annie could not work it out. Janna frustrated her terribly and their bond seemed strained. Annie was convinced it was because of her own background and Janna's likeness to herself. They were very much alike in so many ways and sparked conflict within each other. Mike was the referee. Janna adored him, but at the same time she hated Matt. They limped along trying to work through problems as and when they came up.

Annie was approached by one of Sarah's friends. They were starting a support group for adult survivors of childhood sexual abuse. Would Annie like to attend? Annie was so arrogant at this stage. She told them that she would come along, but she had done so much work it would be more to support their cause than anything else. It turned that this could not have been further from the truth; Annie did not know what hit her.

Things were going wrong in the church. Annie was secretly delighted to find out they were all so human after portraying their 'holier-than-thou' attitude. One of the elders was found to be associating with prostitutes. The drummer of the church band was sleeping with the lead singer. The guitarist was sleeping with a single mother in the church. One of the percussionists was sleeping with her boss. It became a huge scandal for the church. Annie found it highly amusing in light of how they had slammed her for her 'behaviour'.

Church then became like school. The pastor became the headmaster. The elders the teachers. Annie felt like she was five years old and back at school for real. Every Sunday they would all be rebuked and more demons cast out of people. It was a joke, a total joke. Mike and Annie left the church and joined another, quieter and less charismatic, church. All their so called friends now avoided them, they were bad, they had left, they were back-slidden. They had become the devil's toys. No hope for them, they were headed for the pit of hell. They simply did not care, they were happy with their move and choice of new church. Christianity had lost its appeal though, they had seen too much of the negative sides of it and they never really settled down at their new church, they went through the motions but something had definitely died. Christianity was not all it had been cracked up to be.

Annie threw herself into the survivors group. They would meet weekly and it was hard going. Very hard going. A psychologist and social worker headed up the group. In all there were eight abused women in the group, all coming from a similar background. For Annie it was comforting to be surrounded by people who felt the same way as she did. It was comforting to hear the others problem's, problems that were so similar to her own. She felt less like a freak and more human. The group was there to help them all break the secrecy of the abuse they had suffered. The aim was to put a group of women in a safe place, where they could talk without inhibition and without fear. No judgement, just a lot of positive affirmations and acceptance. Nothing was too terrible, nothing was a taboo subject. The women formed strong bonds in the group. They trusted and understood each other.

Annie worked hard, she wanted this to work, she wanted to have some chance at a normal life. She needed to exorcise her demons once and for all. Being able to talk freely and not be stared at as though she had two heads was a breakthrough for Annie. For the first time in her life she felt normal. Her feelings were normal. Her fears were normal. Normal in light of the life she had lived. It was a close and personally run group that achieved much. Personal therapy was also available if anyone felt they needed it but all were encouraged to talk about their experiences and fears within the group.

Annie found her bulimia heightened again whilst in the group. They discussed this at one session.

Annie shared how she had problems eating certain foods. Especially fruit. She hated the consistency in her mouth. Things always seemed to get stuck in her throat and the only way she could get it out was to vomit. They pushed her that day. "What Annie, what is stuck in your throat?"

"Oh God," she cried, "Oh God. No!"
"What Annie? What?"
"Sperm, it is sperm," she said "the taste of his sperm is still in my mouth and stuck in my throat and I can't get rid of it."

She was making the connection with the child within. The senses were coming back. The tastes, the smells and the feelings. Oceans and oceans and oceans of them. Annie was asked about her inner child. She did not know what they were talking about. Could she still feel herself as a child? Annie realised she had felt like an adult all her life. She had never felt like a child. She had totally separated her childhood from herself. But somewhere out there was the child Annie was and she had to bring her back.

The therapist worked hard with Annie, she showed Annie how to get in touch with her inner child. Write with your left hand, childish writing and see what happens. What happened was the start of Annie bringing herself back. Bringing all parts of her that she had hidden away, parts she had left in cupboards and under beds. Memories best left hidden and not looked at. Annie would go and look in the cupboard and freak out, close that door and run. They pushed Annie to work through this stage and Annie committed herself to work at it. She had to break past this once and for all, she needed the answers.

It happened one night. Mike and Annie were in bed. Mike wanted to make love to Annie and she could not, she simply could not. She was weeping and shaking. Mike was unreal, so in tune with Annie he knew exactly what was happening.

"Where is she?" he asked, "Where is that little Annie, the little one who is so sore and so hurt? Where is she?"
Annie choked and sobbed. She could not speak.
"Come on," he coaxed, "let her talk to me, let her out Annie, let her come to me."

"She is in the cupboard," Annie sobbed, "look, there she is hiding, hugging her knees there in the cupboard. She will not come out because she says you will hurt her. She knows what you want to do and you will hurt her."

"No I won't," promised Mike, "I won't hurt her, I will just love her, tell her to come."

Annie pulled that part of herself from the cupboard and drew herself to self. Mike held her, held them both waiting for them to become one. Mike then ever so gently made love to Annie, Annie kept her eyes open and watched. She made herself stay connected and to feel and see what was happening. The fear finally left her. A deep love replaced it. Annie gently wept and Mike held her. He held her all night, stroking her hair and stroking her all over her body, gently and lovingly. Totally non-sexual. As if he was feeling the real Annie for the first time ever.

Annie awoke early the next morning. She sat at the table with a cup of coffee and looked out the window watching the sunrise. It was beautiful, absolutely beautiful. It felt as if she had begun a new life. She felt complete and whole. Having this part of her back again was special and good. She was in control. She could take care of all parts of herself and best of all she could say no. No-one could ever hurt her again. She had been loved back to life. At the next session they celebrated, Annie had found herself. Now the real work could begin.

She drew, she wrote, she screamed at the injustice of it all, she sobbed, she raged, but it was controlled, it was right, it was a process she needed to go through. The memories all returned and with each one that came back she would share it with all in the group. She was breaking the secrecy, she was telling, she was telling it all. Everything Tom had done to her. She was exposing him and his perversion for all to see and it felt good and right and just. They would all talk about what they would do to their abusers if they had the chance. Annie's ultimate would have been to tie him to a tree, naked. To expose him openly for all to see who he was and all he had done. Most wanted to kill but Annie abhorred violence. She just wanted him to feel what it was like. She wanted him to know how she felt. How it felt to have no say in what happens to your body, how it felt to be humiliated and exposed. How it felt to have your choices taken from you. How it felt to be totally unable to control what was happening to you. The relief, the peace of the breakthrough she had achieved was a heady experience. Annie was alive, truly alive and living and coping and dealing.

She learnt to love herself, to feel compassion for what she had been through, she learnt not to judge herself so harshly. She learnt to live as a whole person. She found the joy of her childhood, and was able to remember the fun times. This helped to bring about the balance she so badly needed. It helped her cope with her own children and to be a happier mother. She learnt to love her children in a healthy way. Finding her own child within meant Annie was able to, for the first time ever, play with her children. Really get down on the floor and relate to them. Closing up her own childhood had meant she struggled to relate to them, there had always been a barrier. Annie found the joy of being childish, at times it was irrational and silly but it was all part of the process. Mike learnt to deal not only with Annie the adult woman but also with Annie the child. He understood her irrational, childish behaviour and was able to allow her to work through it. Annie learnt to laugh. Really laugh and it was good tonic.

Annie was unable to face Tom during this time. Her feelings was too raw and too exposed, the memories too fresh and painful. And as if by some unspoken understanding Tom was nowhere to be seen.

Her anger at Sarah was immense. "How could she not have known?" Annie would rage. "How could she have lived in the same house as him for that long and never know what he was doing?" The feeling of not being protected as a child was horrifying. She felt unloved by Sarah and totally rejected. It was completely irrational. Sarah had rejected her from conception. She had tried to abort her, Sarah had not wanted her. She had not protected her from her father. She had allowed all those terrible things to happen to her. Her feelings were so fierce because Annie knew how she felt about Ben, Janna and Matt. She would kill for them. Was there no-one in the world that felt that love for her? Was she only there for their pleasure and abuse? Why did Sarah not love her? Why had Sarah not protected her?

Annie and Sarah talked. They cleared up a lot of their past hurts. It brought the balance Annie needed. On the other hand, it opened many wounds for Sarah. They distanced from each other. It was hard for Sarah, she too lived with many demons of her own.

Daina and Jamie came to visit Mike and Annie. Their son Billy was now five and Hannah a cute four year old. Hannah was full of life and smiles, despite living in a silent world. On one of the days of their visit, the children were all off playing. Annie decided to check on them. Janna and Billy were found in an embarrassing state, Annie felt a chill run down her spine. "What are you doing?" she demanded. Janna looked at Annie and said, "We are playing the willy game mum." So blasé, so calm, like it was the most natural thing in the world.

Annie froze, her heart froze, her being froze. She removed herself from the room and called for Mike. Annie sat on her bed shaking. Something was wrong, she just knew something was very wrong. Mike came and talked to Annie. He explained that Janna had without fear said she and Billy were playing the willy game, like it was playing with dolls. Mike had asked her who had taught her this game. Judy's brother was Janna's reply. Judy was an ex-employee. Judy was her maid, the one who had been there through the trauma of

Mitch's death, who had been there when she brought Janna home, the one who had been her rock and sanity so many times. Judy's brother had lived on the property; Annie had housed him, allowed him to live there out of the goodness of her heart. Something curled up and died in Annie.

She phoned the group therapist. They had to wait to see the therapist, as she needed to get anatomically correct dolls. There were only two sets in the country. They waited two weeks. During those two weeks Annie just went through motions. She felt nothing, she saw nothing, she heard nothing. She took Janna to her therapist. Janna was taken to a private room to be talked to. Annie had not been able to speak to Janna. It was too painful, too close to home. With all Annie had gone through in the previous months this was just too much. She was locked into her own childhood and could not think straight. The therapist came out with Janna. She asked Janna if they could tell her mother what Janna had told her. Janna said that it was okay. Judy's brother, the therapist explained, had taken Janna to Judy's lodgings on the property, he had told Janna to remove her panties. He had rubbed his penis on her vagina. And he had masturbated while she lay on the floor. Janna had said some cotton wool had come out of his thing and he put it down the toilet. He had then told her she was not allowed to tell. She was not allowed to tell anyone. It was their secret.

Annie was totally emotionless. Her worst nightmare had become a reality. She could not speak about it. She could not comprehend it. She had tried so hard, she had not let Janna out of her sight, she had never let her stay away from home, Mike had never been allowed to bath her or linger in her bedroom at night. Janna had been protected. Annie had protected her so fiercely. How, how did it happen? The worst part for Annie was the fact that she was at home, cooking dinner in the kitchen when it had happened. She had been there and had not known anything was wrong. "And where was God?" she demanded. "Why had God not warned her or let her know Janna was in danger? Where was God and His protection that day? Where was this all seeing, all knowing, all loving God while her daughter was being violated? Where was He?"

"Liar, liar, fucking liar!" Annie's love for God turned to hate.

Once again Annie was limping through life. She felt she could not cope with the pain. Janna's abuse had been exposed. Janna was now going through classic symptoms. The bed wetting increased, Mike and Annie were called in to see Janna's teacher. She was in her first year of school. Janna was wetting herself in class. Janna was masturbating in class. Janna was not concentrating. Janna would not work. It was all so familiar to Annie. She became Janna. Annie seemed to float between childhood and adulthood. Some days she felt like a child. She could not work or cook or shop. She became almost a recluse. Mike took control and handled everything.

Slowly Annie began to talk. She continued with her group therapy, and they helped her through her new array of problems. They helped her separate herself from Janna. They showed her how to deal with her own abuse and with Janna's new found abuse.

Annie and Mike left the church. For Annie, God had failed her terribly. Her one unselfish request she had asked of Him gone unheard. He had betrayed her in the worst possible way. She could no longer sign her name to Christianity, to a God who professed to love so much and allowed a three year old girl to be violated. Janna's abuse had happened three years earlier and no one had known. Janna had carried the awful secret of it for three years. God had let Annie live in a false sense of security for three long years. He had allowed Annie to freely tell all how wonderful He was for breaking the cycles in her family. "How He must have laughed," Annie thought, "how He must have fucking laughed."

Annie slowly began to thaw, she started to come round. She was able to talk about Janna's abuse. The more she talked, the stronger she got. A huge righteous anger welled up inside Annie. She was going to do something. What, she did not know, but she was going to work through this.

Mike and Annie had decided not to press charges for various reasons. One being that the incident had happened three years earlier and Judy could be in Timbuktu for all they knew. How could Janna identify her abuser? How could they put Janna through that? How could they put her through a court case and investigation? It would be worse than the abuse. They did the hardest thing, they did nothing about what he had done.

As Annie came right she was able to work with Janna. They would talk for hours about Janna's abuse. Annie told Janna a little about her own abuse and a strong bond formed between them. A deep understanding kicked in and Janna found a trust in Annie. A bond formed between them that had never existed before. For Annie's part she learnt to really love her daughter, identify with her and have a compassion for her. Whilst this was good, it was incredibly painful. Annie would sob for hours at the injustices Janna had faced in her life. Never knowing her father or his love and then the abuse. It was so very unfair.

Annie would rage to herself and those around her. She would see black men, Janna's abuser was a black man, she would look at them all and wonder if it was one of them. She could not remember what Judy's brother looked like, he had only stayed on the property for a short time. She would see them walking while she drove and she would want to kill them all. It played havoc on her mind and she would stare for ages at them wondering if it was that one or another one she had seen, if it was the man at the supermarket check-out or the one walking down the street or the one filling her car with fuel. Reasoning seemed to desert her.

Annie's group decided they would no longer meet formally. They would still all see each other from time to time, but their main work was done. Annie had survived the worst of it. She was a true survivor. No longer would she be a victim. It was as if she had stepped from one level to another. She moved from 'victim' mentality to 'survival role' mentality. She learnt a very small word, one that had been erased from her vocabulary at an early age. One that she now put in place and used, it was simply 'No'. Annie learnt to say no. She had learnt she had a voice and was allowed to use it.

They started a group for young children who had been abused. Janna attended group therapy at the age of six. Annie and Janna would sit there alongside all those little girls and talk of their own abuse. It broke Annie's heart. She would sit and weep for them. Janna started keeping a journal and Annie helped her with it. Janna also attended private therapy. Annie was determined Janna's abuse would not be allowed to affect Janna the way it had affected her. Janna would not go through the promiscuous years, and Annie wanted Janna to deal with as much as she could at an early age thereby saving further trauma later. It seemed to be working. Janna was doing well, working hard at dealing with her problems. She became a loving little girl, she was coming right and Annie was relieved.

Janna attended a Christian school. Annie was fine with that. She did not want to move Janna because her own beliefs had changed. Annie was openly confronting abuse issues and people would often talk to her. Annie was approached by a friend who asked Annie if she knew that the school Janna attended had employed a known paedophile. Annie was horrified and extremely angry. She began a private investigation. The Christian school had re-employed a man previously fired for indecent behaviour with children. Their reasoning was that if the Christians could not accept him, no-one would and it was a Christian obligation to forgive and love him. Annie's reasoning was that one does not put an alcoholic to work in a bar. Give him a job in an office, not around children, were her own feelings on the issue.

Mike, Annie and a friend started up an investigation group. They had to be careful, as they were open to legal complications. They consulted lawyers and a private investigator. There was nothing they could do to remove this man from the school. They approached a member of the school board, but their hands were also tied. The headmaster would not budge, they were wasting their time even speaking to him, they would have to find another way. Annie prepared petitions and affidavits. By now the man was being exposed. Nothing was out-rightly said but there were rumblings. Annie was refusing to be silent.

Word soon got out about what Annie was up to and he was removed from the school. It was a huge victory for Annie, and for Janna, Annie reasoned. The children need to be protected. Annie spoke at tea mornings, she spoke at schools. She became very outspoken on the subject of childhood sexual abuse. She was not popular in some circles, but she did not care.

Mike and Annie fostered a teenage girl. She had been abused and was reacting negatively. Her parents could not cope with her and her father used to handcuff the poor girl to try and control her. He would handcuff her hands and legs then lock her hands to her legs like an animal so she could not move. This was done on the advice of a top psychologist. The poor girl was crying for help and no-one was listening. Mike and Annie took her in. They loved her and Annie spent long hours with her. She got her professional help. She managed to help get her off her medication that had been totally ineffective. She got her to talk about her abuse. This in itself was a milestone. They also managed to get Gail attending school on a regular basis.

They had an agreement. Gail could stay with them as long as she wanted. Mike and Annie would take no money for her upkeep. They simply wanted to help her as best they could. Gail could stay as long as it had no adverse effect on their own children, their own children had to come first. Gail also had to attend school and follow the house rules.

Refusing to go to school one day Gail slit her wrists in Ben's bedroom. Annie handled it very well, but after that Gail had to go home. There was no way Annie could subject her own children to this. There were other problems too and they had to admit defeat. Gail went home and sadly never improved. Annie would visit her and spend time with her but the poor girl was too badly abused. Annie felt guilty and such a failure. She had so badly wanted to help this

174

child, but she had to realise she was needed more in her own home and she had to learn to leave other people to work through their own problems in their own time. She could support and love but she could not make their problems disappear and she could not take their problems on as her own. Annie could not save the world. It was a hard realisation. Love alone is not enough. She learnt a good hard lesson here. In reality this was Annie's last step from victim to survivor. Once Annie realised that she could not make the world a better place but that she could save and protect herself, the mould was set. Annie as a victim was no longer, a new moulding deep within turned her to a true survivor.

CHAPTER 18

Mike and Annie found that their marriage had strengthened outside of the church. They had only ever known a church life and had been warned that the devil broke up non-Christian marriages. Mike and Annie realised how much they had been lied to. Their marriage, if anything, was stronger than ever. They were the best of friends and fell more and more in love with each other. Annie adored Mike, and he was besotted with her. They were like one person.

They found they were able to speak on taboo subjects. For the first time ever their marriage was totally open and honest. They talked about their fantasies and sexual likes. They began to experiment sexually. They watched pornographic movies. They did all the things that had been absolutely forbidden. They found their curiosity was healthy. They could watch and experiment, but if something did not feel right, they could also walk away from it. There was no perversion in it, there was no addiction, it was normal healthy curiosity, safe and within the confines of themselves and their marriage. Their sex life took on a whole new turn. An Annie free of fears and insecurities meant an Annie who was freer sexually. They found an incredible pleasure in each other. Annie was able to tell Mike about her sexual fantasies with women. Mike was totally unfazed.

Their social life took on a whole new lease of life. They enjoyed non-Christian company and became closer to Daina and Jamie. Beth and Annie also became so much closer. Annie had encouraged Beth to join a new group that was starting up and for the first time ever they were able to talk to each other about their abuse. It cleared up many past hurts, and built their relationship. They had much to talk about, and helped each other heal and became each others memories.

Annie and Mike had made friends with a couple who lived out of town. They farmed half an hour's drive away. It became a great friendship. The men got on very well and had much in common. The added bonus was that Annie got on well with Tamara,

Stuart's wife. Stuart and Tamara had no children, they had tried for many years but had been unsuccessful. Annie loved the freedom Tamara had without children and they spent a lot of time together. They would shop or meet for lunch. They spent weekends at Stuart and Tamara's farm. As they all got on so well the found they were able to talk about absolutely anything. The children enjoyed the visits to the farm and were totally at home there. Tamara would have made an excellent mother. She had such a natural way with children. She was incredibly beautiful, a short slim build, dark eyes, almost black, an olive complexion and long dark hair. She had Italian blood in her and it was very evident, a sensuous mouth, soft rosy lips and firm features. And a zest for life and living that was great fun. They found their sense of humours matched and would laugh for hours at silly things.

Mike and Annie still kept most of their old friends, the ones they had made at church. Most of them had also left the church, finally seeing it was not all it was cracked up to be. They shared common bonds. When Mike and Annie were not at the farm with Stuart and Tamara they were socialising and entertaining. They had bought a restaurant and were doing well financially. Annie loved the freedom the extra money gave her and she worked very hard. Annie still kept her own small business running from home. It was good for her, almost therapeutic, allowing Annie to see her worth and creativity. The children were growing, Janna was beginning to settle down at school. She battled academically but Mike and Annie knew this was due to the abuse. Janna had missed out on vital foundations when her school years started but they hoped she would come right. Janna received extra lessons and tried very hard. Matt was still at home and a constant attachment to Annie. He was so like Mike, sweet natured and loving. Ben was doing well at school, coming first in class and excelling at sports. Their life was on track, things were good. Annie had always said, "hard work reaps a sure reward." She felt as if she was finally seeing the rewards for all the hard work she had endured to get herself on track.

On Sunday nights the restaurant was closed and Mike and

Annie would devote this time to friends and family. There was often a Sunday roast at their home and a host of people would come round. Sometimes they would head out for the day with the children, or sometimes they would go to Stuart and Tamara's farm for the day.

It was late one Sunday evening. Annie and Mike had spent the day at Stuart and Tamara's farm and it was now time to leave. The children were asleep in the car exhausted. Stuart and Tamara walked them out to say good-night. Tamara came to Annie as they were walking out, she slipped her arm around Annie's waist, and they walked together comfortably. As they got to the car in the dark, Tamara lifted her lips to kiss Annie goodbye. It was the exact moment that Annie inhaled. Annie smelt the sweetness of her, Tamara's soft lips were slightly open, Annie tasted and liked. She liked it too much. She pulled gently away and got into the car. They drove home in silence. Annie was in turmoil inside herself. In just a few seconds her feelings toward Tamara had changed completely. She was thinking things she should not be thinking. She tingled all over and a heady feeling was there.

They got home and put the children to bed. They climbed into bed and Annie told Mike what had happened. They talked about this sudden change in events and Annie wondered if it was just her or if Tamara had felt it too. She and Tamara had talked about everything up until this point, but Annie had never told her about her secret desires. Annie and Mike talked for hours about it and Annie tried to decide what to do about it. Her mind told her to leave it, but her body screamed "No!"

The problem was she did not want to leave it. Mike understood and Annie assured him of her love for him. "This is not about you," she said "it is about me and my feelings." It felt like she had the opportunity to experiment with a life long desire. Suddenly so much came back to Annie and she spoke about these things with Mike. How she had played with her childhood friend. The pleasure the two girls had derived from each other's bodies. So much seemed to click for Annie. Memories of Amber, Chaz's sister, came back. She remembered how she would secretly watch her and banish the thoughts because of her religious beliefs. Her thoughts became almost scary, but very deliciously exciting.

The controlled person Annie had been for months now was slipping away and she was losing it, losing control. Her body was betraying her again. She had been faithful to Mike for six years, she had never been faithful to anyone before and she was so proud of that fact. But now, now she had longings and wantings. The difference was that she could discuss it with Mike. There was no longer the secrecy she had in her previous relationships, she could be open and be herself. There was no fear. Her environment was safe and loving. There was no threat to their relationship, first and foremost they were friends and they trusted each other completely. Annie saw such a difference here, in the past when someone had invaded her walls she would totally freak out, but this time Mike was so helpful and willing to listen she felt safe. She felt safe from herself. She had Mike to help bring the balance, she no longer felt alone. This feeling had been a long time coming and now that it was here it brought a peaceful feeling that helped Annie to work through the next stage of her desires.

Annie waited a day and phoned Tamara. "Lets meet for lunch," she said, "when are you coming to town again?" "Wednesday," Tamara answered, "where shall we meet?" They agreed to meet at a hotel in the city centre. They discussed the normal, children and husbands and said their goodbyes.

Annie was a bundle of nerves. How was she going to handle this? Could she risk losing a friend, and a good friend at that? Was it worth it? Almost overnight her feelings toward Tamara had changed and it was a scary time. She questioned her own make up and strength of character, she questioned her marriage and asked herself a zillion times why she could not just be happy with Mike and not feel the need for anything else. She worried about the children. But deep within she knew she had to see this through even if it meant losing Tamara as a friend. Annie was a wreck for the two days before the lunch date, smoking too much, not eating, shaking and dreaming delicious dreams. Mike was excluded from nothing. He knew exactly what was going on inside Annie's head, she told him everything. He held her and adored her, he never judged her, he knew it was not a deficiency in him. This was about something in Annie and he loved her so completely that he could accept all parts of her without reserve. He felt no threat, he felt no jealousy, just a deeper understanding and love for Annie.

Wednesday arrived, sometimes feeling like it took forever and at other times like it had come around far to quickly. Annie spent the morning bathing and getting ready. Every detail was thought out. Body shaved, creamed and perfumed. Underwear specially selected, she needed to feel sexy, clothes just a little revealing but not over the top. Subtle and sexy. High heels pushing her tall frame even higher, helping her chunky body to look slimmer, perfect make-up applied. It all felt so deliciously right.

Tamara was late, Annie was on her second vodka by the time she arrived. They kissed briefly on the cheek, Annie took the opportunity to smell deeply. Tamara always smelt divine. Heady perfume and sweet sexuality. She got Tamara a drink and they sat and chatted, arbitrary kind of stuff. They ordered lunch but Annie could not concentrate. Annie turned the conversation. She asked about Stuart and how things were going. Tamara confided that things were tense. Stuart was a most private person with a complex character and Tamara often found him hard going. He was putting a lot of pressure on her and she was feeling it. He was jealous of her and the farm's problems did not help. Tamara confided in Annie that if another man came along she would seriously consider having an affair. Annie saw her opportunity and took it. "What if it is not a man?" Annie asked. Inside her heart was hammering. Oh God this was it, she had done it, she had started the ball rolling now there was no way out. It seemed like forever before Tamara answered.

"What do you mean?" she queried.

"I mean what if it was a woman?" Annie spoke out bravely.

Tamara looked at Annie and it all became so very clear. A sexual intensity lit the air. They simply sat and looked at each other. Not saying a word for what seemed like the longest time. Tamara spoke first, "Well, I have never thought about it before, and I can't say the idea scares me. In fact it does the opposite. I am incredibly turned on." Annie was determined to do this as right as possible. "Let's not rush anything, Tamara," she said, "let's take our time here, once we start there is no going back. Let's make sure this is what we both want before we begin this journey. Let's take a week to think it over and meet here again next week and discuss it further."

They both agreed. A few more vodkas lightened the atmosphere further and they had a very special time together. They did not dare to touch each other, things were too close to the surface, they parted and said their goodbyes. No kisses this time, it would have been too much.

Annie floated home. She had been sure Tamara would be totally disgusted and furious with Annie. Annie had thought she would lose Tamara as a friend but her feelings were so strong she had to take the chance. Annie had a motto, 'expect the worst and anything good that comes is a bonus'. Annie had expected the very worst and she had been dealt a most wondrous bonus. She was ecstatic. She was tingling. She was in another world. She saw nothing or no-one – only Tamara.

Her safe place and reality was Mike, they talked for hours about it all. Annie felt she could be open with Mike about things and she needed this desperately. "Sex for me Mike, has always been so smutty and tinged with perversion but this feels so good and right and true, I feel like a virgin for the first time ever really, I feel as though I have a choice, I have my life back. It is as though I am divided into sections, a huge section for you and our marriage, sections for my children, sections for my family and there is this one little piece, just a sliver in the 'cake' of life, that is the piece for me. That is what is left after I have been divided up. That is the piece that is left is for me and Tamara fits it. I want her, and this, I want it to happen." Annie and Mike's sex life went wild, passionate hours of love making with Annie fuelling it with fantasy of what she would like to do with Tamara. Mike and Annie became even closer. They shared one of the most important parts of Annie, herself. The part of her that was for her. Her choice, almost her completion.

Annie and Tamara did not last the week. They met up just two days later at the same hotel for lunch. They could not eat or talk. They simply looked at each other, both bodies fully charged with sexual energy. They went to the ladies room, leaving their lunch on the table untouched, drinks half drunk. Alone in the bathroom, they locked themselves into each other, and allowed their first passionate kiss to erupt. It was a moving and amazing experience for Annie. She had never experienced anything like this before. So gentle, so loving and so sweet. Tamara's breath was like a warm summer breeze, tingled with sweet smelling flowers, grass and honey. Annie drank deeply from her lips almost as of she was feeding the deepest parts of her soul. It was like coming home, it was so right, so beautiful and fitting. Annie allowed her hand to gently, just gently, brush Tamara's breast. Oh God it felt so soft and warm and inviting, Annie longed to move her mouth downwards, to taste and feast.

They gently pulled away from each other, deep longing firmly fixed in each other's eyes. They looked deep into each other, as if they could each see to the very depths of each other's souls. It was a heady experience, Annie was floating, she wanted to spread her wings and fly, taking Tamara with her. She wanted to run away with her and never come back. Find a corner in the world just for them and lock everything else out. The sound of someone entering the ladies room brought them down suddenly, they stepped back from each other, no words spoken. They walked out together and made their way back to their table. They sat and looked at their uneaten food and got a fit of the giggles. They could not stop laughing. They pushed their food away and ordered another drink. Food was the furthest thing from their minds. They discussed booking into the hotel, but both agreed the timing was not right.

For them to have time together required careful planning

and working out. Stuart would have a fit if he found out about them. They had to be careful. "Thank God for Mike," Annie thought, "thank God he does not suppress me in any way, thank God he allows me to explore myself, to find myself and to be me. I am a truly lucky woman." The restaurant was now empty, tables were being cleared and Hoovers buzzing. It was time to leave, Tamara had to drive back to the farm. Annie wanted to take her home with her. They had to wait, it was as simple as that. They arranged to meet for lunch the following week. They agreed it was too dangerous to see each other over the weekend. Things were too near the surface and obvious. They could not allow Stuart to see what was happening.

Annie drove home feeling mixed emotions. Her head tried to be in control but her body was on fire. She needed Mike and his calm logic to help bring her down to earth. She got home and she and Mike spent time talking before they went off to their own restaurant for a busy Friday night's work. Annie regained her composure, took a deep breath and moved on. All she wanted to do was lay in bed and think and remember every delicious taste, touch and smell. But that would be bad news, nothing would get done and life had to keep moving.

Sunday they made excuses to Stuart and Tamara. "Family obligations," Mike told Stuart, "sorry mate we can't see you guys."

"No problem." Was Stuart's response.

It was all going so smoothly.

The weekend seemed to stretch on forever for Annie. She longed for Tamara and was desperate to just talk to her. But they had agreed to keep some distance over the weekend. On Monday morning Annie phoned her. They could not talk. The feelings were so strong for both of them. They arranged to meet for lunch on Wednesday – at Annie's home.

The days and nights were a blur, Annie was somewhere else,

things got done, Annie had a smile on her face from here to next week. The children loved the sudden festive atmosphere in the house. Annie played with them and laughed like she had never laughed before. Something had lifted in her. Some part of her had come home and she felt complete. She felt more effective as a mother and more loving and understanding as a wife. A part of her that had been suppressed for so long was finally being met. She came back to life and love, she pushed the fears and worries to the back of her mind and enjoyed the feeling of being totally in lust and in love and the feeling that life was most definitely worth living. She felt equal. She felt on a level, no longer pushed around or abused. She felt she had found a perfect balance. Mike, her friend, her true and only best friend and husband and lover, her children and family and now this last little piece. This piece of her coming home – it had always been there, Annie knew this, she had just never, ever allowed it access to her conscious mind.

It was as if the years of hard work of putting Annie back together were finally paying off. After years of confusion and not knowing who she was, Annie was allowing herself to see and feel and be. She tried not to judge herself too harshly. Preferring to allow herself to go with the feelings and see where they led. She wanted to explore this part of her being. She refused to push it away and suppress it any longer. Annie was coming together. Annie was taking control. She was listening to herself and allowing herself to learn exactly what was on the inside of her. For so long she had lived by other people's rules, parents, teachers, bosses and the church. She had no idea what her own values and feelings were. She loved the fact she could now find out for herself. She refused to allow guilt and fear to spoil this coming together of her as a person. For the first time ever her soul felt alive. She felt a depth to herself that had never been there before. A creativity sprung up and her confidence soared. She allowed herself to love all the individual parts of her being and allowed them to come to the fore. It was a totally new experience. In a sea of hormones and wants and lust and love and everything else Annie felt in control. At last, at long last she could take to the driving seat of her life by herself. She, and only she, would decide what was best for her as a person. Mike was there, always there to help and guide and be Annie's sounding block, but he did not try to control her or push her in any direction. He gave her the freedom she so badly needed to grow as a person. He did not clip her wings, instead he gave them flight.

Mike arranged to take the children out for the afternoon that Wednesday. He woke Annie as normal that morning, brought her tea, ran her bath but did not touch her. He allowed her to keep herself free of him. He did not want to confuse her in anyway. He held his own fears in check, knowing the time would come for them to talk about them. His love for Annie and hers for him was so deep and well in place there was no need to fear the worst. It would simply never happen. His total love for her was evidenced by allowing her the freedom she needed to explore herself. He could not suppress her, for to do so would mean he suppressed himself. He and Annie were one. Soul mates, joined at the very core.

Annie bathed at her leisure, did all the little things she never got around to doing. The atmosphere was kind and gentle and totally loving. Mike played relaxing music for Annie, knowing how nervous she must be feeling. She dressed ever so carefully. Tamara had said no perfume – she wanted to taste Annie, no perfume, just Annie. No make up, just Annie. They sent the staff off for the day. The children were to be fetched from school and Mike would keep them out of the house until five o'clock that evening. Mike helped Annie set up her seduction 'nest'. As it was a cold day, he lit a fire for them in the lounge. They lay the duvet on the floor, drew the curtains, placed pillows on the duvet, candles were lit around the lounge, champagne was chilling in the refrigerator, glasses were set out on the floor. Sandwiches made and a joint rolled. Annie and Mike had shared the odd joint together now and again and Annie had found she knew how much she could take in, what was okay and what was not, she had learnt to control it. It was not a huge part of her life, but every now and again she got the urge, in some situations it just seemed to calm her, today was one of those situations. Mike left before Tamara arrived, he did not want her to feel embarrassed in any way. Mike left and Annie smoked, she smoked a lot. She was nervous. Should she call this off? Was it too late? Could she go through with this? The thoughts all screamed around her head.

The gate buzzer went, Tamara had arrived. There was no going back. Annie had wondered if Tamara would be able to go through with it and now she was there. Annie opened the electric gate from inside, and went to the back door to greet her. Tamara came to her, came into Annie's arms with no reserve. She held champagne and flowers in her hands. Annie took the gifts, placed the flowers in water and took them through to the lounge where their stage was set. Champagne was opened and they both drank nervously and chatted aimlessly about complete trivia.

Annie said to Tamara "I have a joint, shall we smoke it and calm down here?" Tamara readily agreed. They lit and smoked the joint, comfortable sharing and blowing the smoke high into the air whilst sipping their champagne. There was no pressure, no wondering who was to do what. It all happened so naturally and beautifully. Annie asked Tamara to undo her top. Tamara unashamedly stripped to her underwear. Annie went weak. "Oh God," she thought, "this is better than any fantasy. This is the real thing." Annie stripped to her underwear, they reached for each other and kissed long and slow, deeply, passionately. Annie allowed her hands to wonder, so did Tamara. They were in complete synchronisation, no words just gentle loving movements and touches. No force, no push and shove, just delicious tender feelings. "Like a thousand butterflies on my skin," Annie thought. They lay back on the pillows, fire crackling, shadows licking the walls.

Annie licking Tamara. The surroundings became them. They were one, at peace and no shame or embarrassment was present. Annie gently undressed Tamara, taking time to look and study her most private of places, there was no shame, no reserve, it all felt so very natural.

Annie lay her down, she kissed her long and deeply on the mouth, sucking and drawing Tamara to her. She breathed her in, every smell of her, her hands gently touching her perfect pert breasts, pink nipples, small and erect, atop a perfect mound of delicious fleshy breast. Annie moved her head downwards and caught a nipple in her mouth. It was like nothing she had ever experienced before. Heady and delicious, Annie gently feasted, moving freely between one breast and the other, sucking the nipple, drawing it out, licking the underside of Tamara's breast, gently nipping the place where breast meets ribs, taking her tongue all the way around the outline of Tamara's breast, moving her tongue up under her armpit, drinking in the smell of her, sucking tasting and drowning in it.

Annie moved slightly, she allowed her tongue to trail down Tamara's perfectly flat stomach, she lingered at her belly button, pushing her tongue into it and licking and tasting. She moved down further, she flicked her tongue around the outline of Tamara's pubic hair, she moved her mouth to the top of her thighs and deeply sucked and nibbled the inside of her soft creamy thighs. She turned her over, she ran her tongue around the outline of her buttocks, she ran her tongue along the crack of her perfect butt, let her tongue ride the whole way up Tamara's spine. Annie nestled into Tamara's hair, long and dark, clean and fresh. She found her ears and sucked and kissed them, she moved back downwards, opened Tamara's legs and trailed a finger down her buttocks and let it find its way inside Tamara's warm, moist and inviting womanhood. It slipped in so very easily, Tamara moaned and started to move, totally relaxed and sensually turned on, her hips took on a natural rhythm. Annie removed her finger, turned Tamara over again and made Tamara watch her lick and suck her own finger which was dripping with Tamara's juices. Tamara's eyes darkened further and she flicked her tongue over her own lips, Annie pushed a finger back into Tamara, moved it in and out ever so gently. Tamara moaned and moved again but Annie withdrew, she took her finger up to Tamara's lips and said "Taste, taste how beautiful you taste, nectar, pure nectar."

Tamara opened her mouth and took Annie's sex soaked finger into her mouth, she feasted on the taste of her own womanliness. She drove Annie wild with longing through her sucking and feasting on Annie's finger. Annie withdrew her finger and gently traced it down the length of Tamara's body until it rested at her clitoris. She found the button, the one she knew would be ready and willing right now, instinctively she gently massaged Tamara's clitoris, feeling it grow and harden. She slipped her finger inside her again, withdrew it and continued to rub Tamara's clitoris bringing her ever so gently and lovingly to orgasm. The whole time their eyes were locked, watching the others reaction to what was happening. As Tamara climaxed Annie, shivered and found herself climaxing with her, no touch, just gentle waves passing through her body, their eyes watching each other come, their bodies so responsive and yielding. It was at that exact moment, then, that Tamara entered Annie's heart. Annie physically felt it happen. As though a gate opened and someone walked right in. And when they were in the gate was closed and bolted. There was no way out. Tamara was and would always be a love in her life. A rare and beautiful love, never to leave.

A tear escaped Annie's eyes, Tamara's eyes filled, they looked deeply into each other's souls and knew they had reached a part in each other that no-one had ever reached before. Annie felt as if she had just lost her virginity to a person she loved deeply. She had never had this feeling before, rape had meant the loss of this experience. Rape had taken something that should have been a beautiful moment in Annie's life and turned it into a nightmare. All this ran through Annie's mind and she unashamedly cried. Cried for the lost and the found. Tamara lay Annie down, stroked her brow and licked her tears. They kissed, more forceful now. Lips pressed hard together and they held each other so very tight. Annie did not know how she could ever let her go. How could she let her leave and go home? She wanted to lock all the doors and windows and tie Tamara up and keep her there forever.

Tamara began a journey, a journey of exploration. Annie felt a twinge of panic, she was overweight, how could Tamara, with her perfect body, possibly find Annie's abused and flabby body a turn on? As if reading her mind Tamara looked deep in to Annie's eyes and said "My God Annie, you are so beautiful, an artist's dream, all folds and soft and delicious, I want to feast on you forever."

Acceptance. Annie felt totally accepted for who and what she was. Her completeness came then. A deep understanding of who she was. Her depth arose and met in mid air with Tamara's. Their very souls seemed to collide and join. They stopped and drank more champagne, the sex seemed so very unimportant, here were two mature grown woman, igniting and joining on a level unexplainable. Totally at peace with each other and totally fulfilled, satisfaction would follow, this they knew. But for now the sexual buzz was electric and was to be savoured, to end it too quickly would be a compromise.

They lay down side by side, gently touching, stroking and loving each other's bodies. Tamara pushed Annie onto her back and lay on top of her, breast touched breast, stomach touched stomach and pubic hair met for the first time. Tamara rubbed her vaginal bone on Annie's clitoris, and it was wondrous. Annie marvelled at the new senses awakening in her. The new feelings and touches and smells never before experienced. Tamara gently brought Annie to orgasm, it did not take long, their passion was riding on the edge, a simple touch or look could take it over.

Tamara moved slightly higher and rubbed herself on Annie's bone, Annie watched her bring herself to a climax. It was beautiful, totally beautiful. As Tamara's orgasm shuddered through her body Annie kissed her deeply. Both holding their breath and then sucking in air from each other. Tamara rolled off Annie and clung to her. She wound her legs around Annie and her arms clutched her tightly. Annie did the same and they lay clinging to each other. They could not talk, the new feelings were too intense. This new experience was too wondrous to even try and put into words.

It was not over, gently Annie pushed Tamara away and moved her hand down Tamara's body, she pushed two fingers deep inside Tamara as if to try and feel the very core of her. She pulled them out, then pushed them in, slowly, the rhythm began, Annie began to move faster, her thumb massaged Tamara's clitoris whilst her fingers explored her depths. Tamara began moving faster,

Annie's hand a blur, Tamara grabbing Annie's hand and pushing it deeper into herself. Tamara's muscles locked and unlocked in wave after wave of orgasm. Tamara's juices flowed freely over Annie's hand and onto the duvet. Satisfaction. Tamara totally satisfied.

Annie was now incredibly turned on and needed the release herself, their love totally unselfish in its concept, Tamara lay Annie back and pushed her fingers into Annie. Annie was wild with want, she was brewing for a mother of an orgasm, she could feel it, it had been building for days, it was time to release it, and there was only one person who could do it – the person it had been stored for, the one who had the touch, the one who was here now. It was amazing how intuitively they knew what the other wanted or needed, this was not the time for gentle touches, Tamara, pushed hard into Annie, her nails raking Annie's insides. Annie did not care, she was too far gone. Tamara moved her fingers fast and strong, pushing deep and pulling, pulling out the release for Annie, when it finally erupted it took them both by complete surprise. Annie climaxed so long and wet. Tamara did not stop going, she did not miss a beat, she kept going, drawing and pulling out every last drop.

As Annie was coming down Tamara moved her mouth to Annie's pleasure and drank from her. She sucked the last drops out. She moved up to Annie's mouth and said "Taste, taste yourself from my lips." They kissed, deeply and passionately. Annie found that the taste of herself was not disgusting, it was beautiful and heady, the taste of her own sexuality brought Annie's psyche into synchronisation. Finally she could accept herself and her sexuality. Totally spent they lay side by side sharing a cigarette. They finished the champagne but did not touch the food. They had feasted on each other and were full and satisfied. Annie got up to go to the toilet and run a bath for them. She looked down at Tamara, totally relaxed and at ease, satisfied and fulfilled and she felt so tenderly for this new love in her life, as if she would do anything for her. She saw their juices mixed on the duvet and smiled gently, it was a beautiful sight. Annie wished the picture could stay like that forever.

They bathed together – giggling like school girls washing

each other and splashing in the water. They knew they had to get moving, Mike was due home with the children, but they wanted to make every second last. They felt as if they were in a bubble, just the two of them and they wanted no intrusions. But reality had to kick in. Things had to be done and the lounge cleared. They cleared up together, giggling at the state of the duvet, still wet from their love making. Tamara helped Annie to make the bed, suggesting they change the duvet cover.

"No ways," said Annie, "I want to smell us for ever, I don't think I can ever change that cover!"

Windows were opened to allow the smell of sex, champagne and dope to leave the room. The reality of watching their afternoon of delight disappear in just a few moments was sobering. They stood in the cleared lounge and held each other tightly. Mike arrived home, the house became a mass of noisy children and animals running through, their love bubble was now totally burst by reality.

Annie felt as if she were still floating on the ceiling, good sex and dope and the thrill of illicit love sending her higher. Mike could see she was flying and a stab of pain and fear hit him. There was a small part of him that had hoped it would be a disaster, that Annie would experiment and find she did not like it after all. The threat of a woman in Annie's life was not one Mike had ever considered. He always knew Annie would never leave him for a man – she basically mistrusted men, but a woman, he had never thought about. It hit him now, so tangible was the pleasure they had found in each other and so obvious their new found love and devotion to one another. He desperately wanted to know from Annie how things had gone on and what had happened. They both saw Tamara off, she had to drive back to the farm. She assured Annie that she was fine to drive, she needed the time alone to collect her thoughts before facing Stuart. She needed to repaint her face, she needed to come down and wipe the smile from her face. She hated to do it but it was the price they had to pay.

The children were in the bath and Annie and Mike went through to their bedroom for a 'de-briefing'. Annie had told Tamara Mike knew everything. She was stunned and fearful. She thought Mike would tell Stuart. Annie was able to explain Mike was not like that, their marriage very different to Stuart and Tamara's. "Mike is not a vindictive person," she said, "he also trusts me and loves me completely, as I do him." And because Tamara trusted Annie she in turn naturally seemed to trust Mike. Annie told Mike everything, she left nothing out, the magic of the afternoon entered their bedroom and Mike fucked her, hard. It was a bizarre ending to a perfect day.

Annie felt so complete. It was as though Tamara had awakened parts of her never reached before today. It was beautiful and right for both of them. Mike and Annie's sex life took on a whole new perspective, they could not get enough of each other. Annie's body felt so alive and pure. It was as though for the first time ever she had totally allowed herself to be drawn out – she allowed herself to enjoy and explore uninhibitedly. It was a heady experience. Far from pushing Mike and Annie apart – it made them closer. Mike understood and secretly enjoyed this new Annie. She was so beautiful, the lines on her face from the years of pain seemed to have been erased, her eyes sparkled like never before and she had a spring in her step. She walked lighter and for once Annie was totally happy. The past seemed so insignificant in light of the new experiences in her life. It was as though all the black parts had been painted over in dazzling colours. Annie had taken her life back. She was in control. She was well nestled in the driving seat and negotiating her own fate and future.

It was not all easy, Tamara had to live a double life, and it began to get her down. She longed to be free, she was jealous of the relationship Annie and Mike had. Through their relationship she saw the failings of her own marriage. She was also beginning to get jealous of Annie's children and the amount of time they demanded from Annie. Tamara was fairly selfish in this respect, never having had children, she had no idea of the commitment required. It was harder for Tamara than for Annie. Annie was complete – every side of her make up was being met. The feminine, the masculine, the

192

mother. It had come together and it fitted like a glove. Tamara still felt an imbalance, she had always longed for children.

Annie and Tamara spent long hours talking on the phone. It was their life line to each other. Annie was always woken by Tamara phoning and she loved it. It made Tamara feel so much closer. She was always the last thing on Annie's mind at night, it felt fitting she should be the first voice Annie heard in the morning. On one particular morning Tamara phoned later than usual, Mike and Annie were in bed together making love when the phone rang, Mike answered it and it was Tamara. He passed the phone to Annie. He was still inside her and continued to gently rock back and forth. Annie could not concentrate on Tamara, Tamara asked what was going on, Annie told her. Tamara said, "Carry on, I want to listen. I want to hear you come."

Annie told Mike to carry on, they were caught up in the moment, the thought of Tamara there with them. For Annie it felt so natural, she could hear Tamara softly moaning on the phone. Annie asked what she was doing, and she whispered hoarsely that she was finger fucking herself. It was enough, the image was enough and Annie rode away on a gentle wave of delectable orgasm. Tamara heard her coming and joined her. Mike saw and heard all and joined the two of them. It was the beginning of the coming together for all of them. Mike no longer felt excluded, he was a part of this, it felt so wickedly right.

Mike and Annie kept odd hours. As they worked late at night it meant they had the mornings deliciously to themselves. The children were at school and there was no pressure on them. Mike would always take the children to school while Annie slept in, he would then return home and climb back into bed with her. They usually made love every day. Mike would go into the restaurant at lunch time and Annie would stay at home. If she had functions she would be cooking in the kitchen. Annie had a wonderful maid, Annie had trained her and she was Annie's 'right hand man'. The one who helped with the children and who knew how Annie liked things done.

She could be trusted and worked well. It gave Annie freedom. Afternoons were spent with the children and in the evening Mike and Annie would go to the restaurant. Annie loved the work and the people and the festive buzz. She was liked by the staff and customers alike. Their businesses were going well and money was not a problem. They had everything they needed. They worked hard and played hard.

Mike returned home from dropping the children one morning to find Tamara there. She had come to town for the day, she and Annie were planning on going shopping. She had left the farm early and popped in for coffee and to wait for Annie to get ready. The three of them sat on the bed and chatted comfortably. Annie went to have a bath and left Mike and Tamara chatting. Mike was a great tonic for Tamara, she could talk to him like she could not talk to her own husband, Stuart. He understood about Tamara and Annie's affair and never judged them. Tamara was falling just a little in love with Mike. Annie did not see the signs.

She returned from bathing and proceeded to get ready, wrapped in a towel she asked Mike to rub cream on her feet. This was a morning ritual. She lay back and Mike gently rubbed cream into her feet. He then offered to do the same for Tamara. The two girls lay back and let Mike gently rub and caress their feet. The fire ignited. Annie and Tamara started to kiss deeply, Mike just watched, he did not stop touching them and caressing them both. Mike stood up, undressed and locked the bedroom door. He was totally at ease his erection hard, making a visual statement. Annie and Tamara looked at him they both smiled, Annie undressed Tamara, no words were needed. Annie lost herself in Tamara, touching, sucking and playing her sex. Tamara lay on her back, Annie opened her legs and exposed that secret part of her, she told Mike to look, Tamara felt no shame, no reserve, it felt so natural. Annie lowered her lips to Tamara's opening, leaving her arse in the air she gently licked and sucked on Tamara's juices. Mike climbed onto the bed behind Annie and gently entered her from behind. All three watched each other. The scene being played with no rehearsal. Just a coming together, perfect and fitting. Mike held his release in check, he did not want this to be over. He withdrew from Annie, Annie pulled him to the bed and took his hand and guided it over Tamara's body. Mike had only ever had sex with Annie, this was a new experience for him. Annie needed to show him what to do. It did not take long, he soon found the rhythm. Tamara had both Annie and Mike working her. She was history, she could not move, she was crying out for release. "Fuck her Mike," Annie whispered. Mike hesitated, Annie moved and allowed Mike access to Tamara's most private of places, she was open and willing and very ready. Annie moved behind Mike, grabbed his cock and ever so gently placed it into Tamara's begging pussy. Annie kneeled back on the floor and watched them find their rhythm, she watched how Tamara sucked Mike's cock deep into her and how he marvelled at this totally new experience.

"Don't come in her Mike," Annie whispered.

Mike withdrew and came over Tamara's pubic hair, Annie moved closer and rubbed Mikes come over Tamara and herself, Mike had been too quick, too turned on. His orgasm had come too quickly he had not been able to stop it, he had not wanted to. Tamara was climbing the walls, Mike took his expert fingers, long and thick and pushed them into Tamara, he worked her and milked her dry. While he was fingering her Annie was sucking on her breasts and kissing her mouth. She came, long and unashamedly totally lost in the love these two were showing her.

Mike and Tamara then pushed Annie onto her back and both began exploring Annie. Annie was wild. The contrast of Mike and Tamara's hands exploring her every crease and fold was mind blowing. The two people in the world Annie that cared about the most, loving her and exploring her was the best thing she had ever experienced. She was safe and in agreement, there was no fear or abuse, just love and lust and longings being met. Tamara worked Annie's breasts, they had always been such a turn on for Annie, very responsive and gave great pleasure. Mike was working her cunt, two fingers deep inside her, his thumb rubbing her clitoris and his ring finger and pinkie rubbing Annie's anus. The combination drove her wild. Annie's body seemed to explode in orgasm. She had been taken high to the peak and while she was there she rode it, she made it last and rode out the orgasm willing her body not to stop – ever. As she was coming down Mike moved position, he was hard again and ready to take her, he pushed himself deep into her and Annie gasped as he hit the spot in her he could reach so well. Tamara moved back and watched as Mike fucked Annie, she gently rubbed herself totally absorbed in their love.

Mike came in a long almost painful orgasm, screaming as he shot his hot seed deep into Annie. Tamara came soundlessly, to have made a sound would have broken the atmosphere. They were all so aware of each other but not needing words. They all lay back on the bed, Annie in the middle, Mike and Tamara either side, holding her and alternatively kissing her. She had allowed a wondrous thing to happen for all of them. They were grateful to her for her openness and sexuality. She had brought much pleasure into all their lives. And pleasure helps remove pain. They all came together this little threesome, their individual love for each other had been ignited and now burned strong. Three flames, joined and burning bright.

The three of them were now totally inseparable. Whenever they got the opportunity they were together. They avoided the farm, everything was too close to the surface. Stuart would have seen. Mike was able to tell Stuart they had severe work pressures and were unable to socialise. Stuart understood and there was no questions asked, just acceptance.

Annie and Tamara bought each other gifts, sent each other cards and spoke on the phone even more. They were building a little city within themselves and they had excluded everyone else. Annie cut herself off from her family again, not wanting anything to taint this perfect love she had found. She could not handle the judgement of others. There was also another problem, homosexuality was illegal in Zimbabwe. If they were caught it would mean prosecution. Annie could not be separated from her children. People die in Zimbabwean jails. Aids was rife amongst the inmates. It felt so very unfair to

Annie that she was breaking the law. When it felt so right and true how could it be so bad? They covered their consciences with their love for each other and totally excluded everyone else. Annie had time with her children when Tamara was not around. She found the balance and things were good, very good. She had never been happier. Her business flourished, the restaurant was doing well. All was well and good.

For a while anyway.

CHAPTER 19

Annie invited Tamara to their restaurant for lunch one day. The three of them feasted on oysters and champagne. They ate hungrily, selecting anything else they wanted from the menu. They drank copious amounts of alcohol. They had a ball. They sent all the staff home and locked the door. They drew the curtains and continued their party. Tamara was now calling the shots.

"Fuck her for me," she whispered to Mike. Mike fucked Annie. "Touch me now Mike," she demanded. Mike touched her, he licked her, he sucked her, he fucked her. He did not come in her.

Annie forbade this one thing, only this. Anything else was fine but Mike could never come in her. After all Tamara had been trying with Stuart for ten years to have children, the last thing they needed was Tamara falling pregnant at this time. It would be too confusing. Annie also liked to keep just a little of Mike for herself. She needed some control here. Her wishes were respected.

Annie found that Mike and Tamara were spending too much of their love making time on each other and Annie was beginning to feel left out. A bit like an intruder. She felt Mike was taking Tamara away from her and she felt Tamara was trying to take Mike from her. She was confused and angry. What had started so right and good felt like it was turning bad. Annie had to bring this in to line and quickly.

Tamara's petrol bill was sky high, Stuart was getting suspicious about the amount of time Tamara was spending with Annie. He could not understand why Tamara and Annie found time for each other but the four of them did not socialise anymore. Tamara told Mike and Annie and they all agreed it was time to go out together and test the waters. See how they would cope. It turned out to be fine, absolutely fine. They all played different roles and forgot about their illicit hours spent together. Annie and Mike started going to the farm again. They found it so easy to slip into other roles, too easy in fact to cut out the part the three had joined. When they were around Stuart it was just like old times, they all refused to allow their new feelings for each other to show. There was time enough for that when they were alone. It was fine, it was working out well.

Stuart had to make a business trip to South Africa. He was learning about artificial insemination for his cattle herd. He had a new breed of cattle and needed an update on methods. He would be away for a week.

Tamara spent two nights with Mike and Annie, they were all very careful with the children around. No touching of any kind was allowed while the children were around. But when the children went to bed, doors were locked, curtains closed and the games began. One night Annie went through to the bedroom, she pulled two of Mike's ties from the cupboard. She called the two of them through to the bedroom. Without a word she tied Mike to the wardrobe, naked. She stripped Tamara, lay her on the bed and made love to her. She made a statement. A silent statement. Telling Mike that while they all played together he belonged to her and her only. He was to remember his commitment to Annie. And he was to remember that this had been about Annie and her longings and completeness. It was not supposed to be about Mike and Tamara falling for each other. He was to remember he was tied to Annie for life.

With Stuart away they found they could spend their time together without reserve or fear. It was a special time. Annie wished Stuart would fuck off forever. She wanted Tamara to simply move in with them. To be a part of their lives forever. Mike had no objections to this, but Tamara did.

Things were growing and the fire was beginning to get out of control. Mike and Tamara were becoming too close and would sit together chatting and laughing while Annie was cooking or seeing to the children. Annie started to become very jealous. She felt like the outsider at times. Mike and Tamara were so comfortable with each other, they would openly kiss each other whenever they wanted to and Mike took to feeling Tamara at any time. It was not good, boundaries were being crossed. The fires were spreading too quickly. Annie had to douse it somehow. She could feel her marriage slipping. She could feel Mike's heart moving to another and she could not allow it. She would have to sacrifice her own desires for her marriage.

Annie arranged a lunch at a neutral place. Somewhere where they could not indulge in the pleasures of the flesh. She started the ball rolling. Annie had learnt in life that confrontation was good, especially if handled correctly. "Okay guys," she said, "lets talk, and lets talk openly and honestly. We need to know where we stand. We need to control this before it controls us." Annie detached herself emotionally from the scene and conducted Tamara and Mike like a director in a play. "Lets spit it out," she said, "lets hear where we stand and how we all feel."

Mike admitted he had fallen in love with Tamara. He loved Annie desperately but he also loved Tamara. He had no thoughts on leaving Annie but he wanted Tamara also. Tamara also admitted she had fallen in love with Mike, and Annie. Annie knew and told of her love for Tamara. They now had a difficult situation on their hands. The question was, how were they going to control it? They all decided they needed to take a break from each other for a while and let things cool down.

There was no way Tamara was leaving Stuart, she loved the lifestyle too much. Stuart was incredibly wealthy and Tamara's security was money. Mike and Annie could not compete with Stuart's financial status. Tamara wanted it all, and so did Annie. So did Mike. They talked about where things had gone wrong. Annie said it was because they had allowed Mike to become involved. What had started out as Annie's completion had spread to Mike and now it was no longer hers alone. She felt she had been moved aside and her completeness was gone. What was supposed to be for Annie was now for Mike and Tamara with her on the side. It had turned out wrong, totally wrong, and Annie would be the one paying the price. Annie called it all off. The stakes were too high. They made rules. They were not to be alone with each other – none of them. They would still socialise but always with Stuart present. No more time alone. They would meet again in the same restaurant in a month and see how things were going.

Annie was heartbroken. Her wheel of life feeling incomplete again, she limped along. The nightmares started. Fear entered her heart. She became convinced that Mike was going to leave her, that Mike and Tamara were seeing each other privately. Annie became a jealous, possessive woman. Totally illogical and childish. She could not help it. Mikes heart had failed her. The one man she totally trusted and loved had let her down. He had not been careful, he had allowed his loyalties to divide and Annie lost trust in him. It took them long hours of talking to work through this. Mike had to reassure Annie of his love for her on a frequent basis to win her back again. He could not bear the thought that he had failed her in any way. He felt so angry with himself for allowing things to get out of hand and he despised the fact that it was Annie who had had to bring it back into line. He was supposed to take care of her and look after her, he berated himself long and hard for his failings as he saw them. In so many ways he felt as if he hated Tamara for the feelings she had awakened in him and in a way he was angry with Annie for including him in her love nest. He had not wanted it to be that way, it had just happened. Mike learnt about the dangers of sex and how things can get out of control very quickly. These were lessons Annie had learnt long ago. Mike was on a learning curve. Annie could see this and while she was deeply hurt and angry with him she still found compassion for him. They decided to commit to working this out. There was no way they were going to allow their marriage to fall apart. They loved each other too much.

They agreed that the best way was to try and separate the 'marriage' bit from their relationship and just be friends for a while. After all, they were best friends and maybe as friends they could work through this. They continued to sleep in the same bed but they held their desires in check, allowing each other to sort out their individual fears. So much had stirred within Anne, and she was frantically trying to work it all out. Her years of therapy were being put to use, she had to see what the deeper meaning of all their experiences was. The only answer she found was that she saw her growth as a person. She saw how she had been able to handle a potentially explosive situation and bring it into line. It felt good. She saw that she was not falling apart like before, that she had no suicidal thoughts. In addition, she saw her strength of character and she saw the person she really was. She was able to commit to a relationship, she understood now that her marriage vows meant a lot to her and she took them seriously. She would work through this like she had worked through so much else. Her reward would be a stronger marriage.

It took Mike and Annie two short weeks to come right. They had to be totally open and honest with each other, it was the only way they could work through their problems. They had to work through the fears they had brought up in each other and each had to convince the other of their love and commitment to themselves. When the time came for them to 'pick up' their marriage it was special and loving and gentle. Afterwards they had held each other tight and cried and cried and cried. The healing had taken place, there would always be scars but the raw pain was healed. They were ready to move on now. They did not know how they would handle future situations but they knew they could overcome anything and everything as long as they stayed totally devoted to each other. They both promised to be honest at all times and committed to work hard to keep their marriage alive and well and healthy. They had learnt, they had grown, and they had grown closer.

The three of them met up again a month later as agreed. It was stiff and difficult. They had missed each other terribly but they all knew how dangerous things had become. They all decided to leave things alone. It was the hardest choice, it would be difficult and painful, but it was right, they knew it was right.

They saw Tamara less and less, it was too painful for all of them. They all knew they were handling it the right way but it did not make it easy. They just let their friendship slide. There was no other way.

Annie felt the loss of Tamara terribly. She missed the side of herself she had found and loved. Some days it felt so incredibly unfair. She was pleased to have had the opportunity to explore but the loss was great. She could not bear the thought of never again experiencing love with a woman. She studied her mind long and hard. She wondered if she was a lesbian. She reasoned that if it was not for Mike and the way he loved her, she would be. She had no trust or faith in men, Mike had restored that, but he was a one in a million. If it was not for Mike she knew she would have chosen the 'other side of the fence' so to speak. She told herself that it was not the end. That in time maybe there would be someone else. Maybe one day she would find someone to make her feel that way again. It was the only way she could move on.

For Mike things had changed within. He had tasted and enjoyed sex with another woman. He had always been so sure that Annie was enough for him. Now doubts were invading his being. Could he commit his future sexual experiences to Annie, and only Annie, or would he constantly wonder what things would be like with another woman? He had never had to 'compare' Annie before and he found himself doing so now. He felt so guilty and felt he could not tell Annie how he was feeling. He started looking at other women, looking at them like he had never looked before. His mind started playing tricks on him, he found himself turned on by other woman. This had never happened before. Mike had always been able to suppress his own sexuality and Annie had opened it so fully and quickly, he did not know how to bring it into check. He missed Tamara, he missed her wild sexuality and he missed the delicious hours of love making they had all shared. Could he now be happy for the rest of his life with just Annie? Could he settle down again and carry on as though nothing had happened? Something in him doubted this and he felt so very alone in his confusion. He had always been there for Annie, through so very much, could she now be there for him when he needed support? Could the roles be reversed? Did he want them to be?

The thought of Annie taking his role was frightening. Mike was secure in his role as Annie's support and husband. The tables turning would mean a loss of what Mike saw as his strength in Annie's life. Could Annie take this turn of events? Would she cope or would she crumble? And if she crumbled who would be there for her? Mike became nervous and jumpy. He snapped at Annie and the children, something he had not done before. It took Annie a while to realise what was going on. It all came together and bursting out one morning. Mike had returned from dropping the children at school, it had been a draining morning, the children had been difficult and the traffic on the way to school was heavy. Mike's patience was at end.

When he arrived home he was frustrated and irritable. He climbed back into bed with Annie and as normal Annie reached for him. She snuggled next to him and let her hand move over his body to feel for his usually erect and ready penis. Nothing. Annie was suddenly wide awake, her senses reeling, she instinctively knew something was wrong, very wrong. Mike had never rejected her advances before never. She felt a panic and her breath seemed to disappear from her body. Her heart was hammering something felt very, very wrong. She sat up and looked at Mike.

"Story Mike - What's going on?" she demanded.

"Nothing Annie, I am just tired – it has been a frustrating morning, the traffic was a nightmare and there are a few problems at the restaurant, nothing serious but I have a load on my mind," he replied. Annie was not convinced, she knew there was something else, something scary he was not telling her. Her mind flew to Tamara – it was just as she had imagined, Tamara and Mike had been meeting secretly and Mike could not cope – he was falling apart under the strain. He would not know how to tell Annie. Annie's fear quietened as she made herself face a worse case scenario. She calmed herself down in her mind and started the ball rolling.

"Okay Mike", she said, "out with it, I know you too well, we have been together too long for you to start trying to keep things from me, I know it is something else. You have to tell me Mike, I

204

can't cope with not knowing. When you keep things from me I always think the worst, you have to tell me Mike," Annie pleaded. Her own fears were now still, here was the man she loved who had been there for her so many times going through some private hell, Annie had the opportunity to give something back to him. She could cope, she could handle whatever it was, as long as he just told her the truth. Eventually Annie was able to coax it out of Mike, he was so broken, he felt such a failure and he was convinced he would lose Annie's love and trust. He poured out all his fears and feelings, feeling the release as each painful word left his body, feeling lighter as he voiced each thing, he left nothing out, he spoke it all.

When he had finished he looked long and deeply into Annie's eyes to see her reaction and his heart warmed. How could he have doubted her and her love for him? Worse still how could he have doubted her compassion and commitment to him and their marriage. They spoke, long and deeply, getting it all out. They learnt something that day – Mike was human and normal, and that was okay as long as he never shut Annie out. As long as they committed to always talking through these things and finding a compromise or balance they would be okay.

CHAPTER 20

There were problems in the country. Riots and strikes that were crippling businesses. Shortages also crippled their own business. Mike and Annie were being forced to make some serious decisions.

Ben was reaching teenage years. Janna was becoming fearful of black men. Matt was growing fast, he was no longer a baby. They needed to think about all of their futures. Mike wanted to get his family out of Africa. The problems and political rumblings were evident and he feared for them all. Aids was rife, official statistics revealed that there were seven hundred and twenty eight deaths a day due to aids related illness. No-one knew how many were dying in the remote areas, these deaths were never recorded. Annie lived in constant fear. Janna had been abused once, it could happen again.

There was a nasty rumour going around, that a witch doctor had told people who were dying of Aids that a certain cure was for the infected person to have sex with a white virgin. White woman were abducted and raped at knife point. One incident happened just a mile from where Annie and Mike lived. A friend of theirs was with her boyfriend late one night, on her way home. They were driving a pick-up truck and their windows were open. They had stopped at a traffic light and four black men had jumped onto the back of the truck. One of them held a screwdriver through the window at the man's throat. He was instructed to drive to a quiet bush area. When they had got there the four men had pulled them out of the vehicle and had taken turns raping his girlfriend while he was forced to watch, the screwdriver pushing on his jugular.

When they had all finished with this young girl, they then stole the vehicle and left the two abandoned in the bush. They made their way home and reports were made, but the men were never caught. The poor girl lived through three agonising months of hell waiting for an Aids test. It came back positive and her life was over.

Annie and Mike were not prepared to take the same chance with their daughter.

There was a growing fear in the country and Mike was very uneasy and fearful for his family. Ben would need to go to university after school, he was bright and talented, he needed a future. Janna would always battle with school but she also deserved all that life could offer her. She needed help in areas and there was little available for her in their home country. By the time Matt got to school there would be little left to offer him.

The cost of living was exorbitant. The unofficial inflation rate was forty-five percent. Annie would watch prices going up on a daily basis. Their money weakened against international currencies by the minute. Soon they would not be able to afford to educate their children. Corruption heightened. Mike and Annie felt a deep distrust in the government and felt they could no longer support it. They paid high taxes, sixty percent of their earnings went towards a government they did not support.

"So why are we supporting it financially?" they asked themselves. Annie had learnt to stand on her own two feet, she was independent of her family and although she would miss them terribly, she no longer needed them in any other way. She could live away from them. Mike had never been close to his mother, it would be easy for him to move on. He would miss his father and sister but they had each other and would cope. Life in Zimbabwe had taken on a surreal edge. What Annie called a reverse racism was well in place. The white people in the country had adjusted and changed with the country but now the blacks were discriminating against the whites. Blacks were preferred for jobs. Jealousy was rife. The government was going to take the white farmers' land away from them. Huge injustices were being inflicted on the white people, and Mike and Annie felt they could not be a part of this.

They decided that the time had come for them to leave. To move on for the sake of their children's future, and their own. Annie had a deep yearning to be near her grandmother. Agnes was now living alone, as Ted had passed away a few years earlier. Annie knew Agnes would not be around forever and had a burning desire to be near her when her life came to an end. She wanted to give back to the woman who had given to her at a time in her life when she had needed it the most. They sold their restaurant. Neither worked for six months. Instead they sold up their home and household effects. Living off their savings and profit they had made on the sale of the restaurant. Their beautiful home was to be sold. Annie had only four large boxes to pack her life into. Annie learnt to let go of all material things. She clung to Mike and her children fiercely believing they were doing the right thing. That their future was more important than a house and its contents. Strangely enough Annie handled the loss of a lifetime's collection of what made up her home well. The only part she battled with was leaving Tamara. But she had to be strong about that too. It could not be, there was no use wishing for things you could not have. Sacrifices had to made. Annie was prepared to make them, her thinking was that her immediate future was to be devoted to the upbringing of her children, her life could be picked up when they were older. Their children's needs had to be foremost.

England beckoned. They all had British passports. This family was heading for England. For a land of equality for all men. Where there would be no discrimination. Where they could love and be loved in their own right. Where they could start again free of the fears they had carried all their lives. Where they could freely love anyone they wanted irrespective of race, sex, colour or creed. They could be who they were without dictatorship or discrimination due to colour or sexual preferences. They needed to feel part of a majority. The white population in Zimbabwe was dwindling daily. It was official, the elephants now outnumbered the number of white people in the country. There were approximately thirty thousand white people in the country, and twelve million black people. Inflation and lack of money led people to desperate measures. The crime rate was sky high. The police unable to control it.

When Annie would travel in her car, she would have to lock all the doors and keep her windows closed. One had to be constantly alert to travel anywhere – even just to the shops. People had their cars stolen whilst they were sitting in them, they would stop for a red traffic light and tsotsis (bandits) would yank car doors open, pull the driver out and drive off with their cars. People were held up at gun point in their cars. People were advised not to wear their seat belts in case they needed to make a quick exit from their vehicles. People would arrive home, get out the car to open their gates and would be beaten with baseball bats and their cars stolen. The electronic gate companies made a fortune. High walls surrounded people's properties, with electric fencing on top of them. Security guards were everywhere. The fear was almost tangible. Annie wanted more for her children than this fearful existence. She wanted her children to be able to run and play and go places without fear. Children were kept in their own yards. They were not to venture out into the streets. They were not living, they were existing.

Annie and Mike wanted to do things right. There were a lot of loose ends to be tied up, emotionally as well as physically. Annie was taking strain from her family. They did not want her to go. While she full understood their reasonings her mind was made up.

"My husband and children are my immediate family," she told them, "the lives of my children are more important than mine." "They deserve a future with everything available to them," she said.

There was more too, Annie was desperate to further her own education, she wanted to work with abused children, there were many things she longed to do. There was no easy way to do this in Zimbabwe, as she had found out earlier with the episode at Janna's school. She needed to move on herself. She needed to let things go once and for all, to live and live whole without constantly compromising.

Annie spent days packing, clearing and running around. Mike dealt with all the legal things and property sale. Annie did the emotional things. She went back and visited the house where she had grown up. She wondered around the garden, peering into the windows and imagined herself as a child there. She was astounded at how small it all looked, it had seemed so big when she was a child. She found her big tree, the one she used to climb to get away from it all. She looked into her old room and saw the same cupboard where she would hide, she peered through the kitchen window and saw herself on the floor, Tom at the stove.

She wept for her loss of childhood. It seemed so fitting that the house was empty. It was as if she was being told all her demons had now left, she was free to move on. Annie always looked for the little signs in life. The ones that gave her confidence and strength to carry out her decisions. This was a sign. There was nothing left here now. The time had come to move on. She wondered around the house once more and her eye caught a cement block. She cleared the dirt and overgrown grass away and smiled. There were three little hand prints on that block. Three little hand prints with names under them. Beth, Annie and Daina. The block had been made when their swimming pool had been put in so many years ago, Annie must have been about seven or eight when it was done. She cleared all around it and lifted it from the earth, breaking fingernails and dirtying her clothes in the process, but she did not care. She struggled to lift it and carry it to her car. She placed it in the boot and wrote a letter to place under the door of the empty house. She explained who she was and why she had taken the block. She left her name and address and asked the owners of the house to contact her and she would gladly pay them for the block. She took the block home and scrubbed it clean. She tied a big ribbon around it and took it to Sarah's house and laid it outside Sarah's front door. It somehow felt fitting and right that Sarah should be the one to take care of it now. It was as if the girls had come home.

The owner of the house phoned Annie. He was very touched. He wanted no money for the slab. He was happy Annie had taken it seeing as it meant so much to her.

Annie and Sarah spent an afternoon together. They talked about all the things they had not talked about and should have. They cleared up many misunderstandings and found that under all the hurt and pain of years gone by was a deep love for each other. Annie could leave Sarah now and become a mother in her own right. She severed the apron strings once and for all. She found she was not seeking Sarah's approval anymore, she was an adult herself now. She made her own life's decisions and asked only for Sarah to always love her and respect her choices. They hugged that day, like they had never hugged before. The pasts now laid to rest they could move on. Annie had faced one of her biggest fears. Annie and her mother had survived, and it felt good. Another chunk of Annie's life fell into place. She healed a little more. Bitterness and anger and pain were leaving. Annie did not want to take this excess baggage, she had to let it all go once and for all. She was determined in her quest, wanting to leave nothing undone. She wanted to start her new life free of her past pain and nightmares.

She settled old arguments and trivia with friends. She spoke for hours to Tamara. Tamara did not want to let them go. She was clinging to them, heartbroken at the thought of the loss of these people in her life. Annie reassured her it was not about her but about their children and all of their futures. Tamara took the upcoming move very badly. She refused to accept they were leaving and eventually refused to discuss it. She was convinced they would change their minds. Annie knew there was no way that would happen. Things were moving ahead fluidly. Their house had been sold, and they made a good profit on it. The money would pay for them to move and take the small number of possessions they had decided to take. It would give them enough to live on for at least a year if they found no work in England. They were making huge sacrifices but deep inside themselves Annie and Mike knew they were doing the right thing. Their priorities had changed. Money was no longer the be all and end all of life. There was more to life than money, and they wanted more.

There was one other person Annie had to talk to, Tom. Changes had also come in Tom's life, his relationship with Melanie had ended when he met and fell for a woman half his age. He had met her while out at the pub one night. She was visiting friends who lived in the same town Tom lived in. She lived on the other side of the country to Tom and the thought of getting away from it all, getting away from everyone who knew him and knew what he had done appealed to Tom. He moved town to be with Belle, the new love of his life. He conveniently forgot to tell her about his pasts preferring to leave it all behind him and hoping it would stay that way.

Annie knew the talk with Tom was necessary but she was putting it off. She did not know how to do this one. She spoke to her therapist who helped her a lot. She was preparing herself for her final confrontation.

It all came together suddenly and well, Tom rang Annie. She could not believe she was hearing his voice after all her work in the previous months. It felt as if he knew what she was going to say to him, but he did not. He was phoning to tell Annie he was remarrying. He had been alone for twenty-three odd years now and was ready to marry again. The sad part was that Tom and Sarah had really loved each other. Tom never really got over Sarah. But he killed every drop of love Sarah had ever had for him.

Annie told Tom they were leaving the country and wanted to see him. They agreed that Mike and Annie and the children would travel the five hours to Tom's wedding. Tom invited Mike, Annie and the children to stay with him when they came up for the wedding, but Annie declined. There was no way she was having her children stay in Tom's house. They booked into a hotel. They rang Tom when they arrived and he invited them over. He wanted to see his grandchildren. He had never seen Matt who was now three and a half. The last time he had seen Janna was when she was a baby. They went round to Tom's house and met Belle, his wife-to-be. It was awkward and strained.

Annie was extra protective of her babies and Mike sitting silently giving support to Annie. Clutching her hand so very tightly. She was scared and nervous. She told Tom she needed to talk to him, he agreed to come to their hotel the following day. They stayed a while longer discussing the wedding and plans and filling Tom and Belle in on their future plans. It was amusing and comforting for Annie to see how Tom had aged. He no longer drank and was actually quite old and unthreatening. Annie was still bigger than Tom, she towered over him by a good six inches and was far larger in frame. She almost pitied the hollow man he had become. All fear of him left her and she felt in control for the first time ever concerning Tom. She saw he was no longer a threat to her in any way. She had grown up and was able to see her childhood fears for what they were. Just that, childhood fears that would never leave but could now be controlled. It was almost laughable to think that this little old man had caused Annie so much pain in her life.

She recognised her status as a survivor. Not only was she bigger in size but also in heart and mind. Tom was the one who had to live with what he had done, not her. She was the innocent. She felt strangely light and in control and a new emotion rose, forgiveness. Not forgiveness for what he had done to her, she could never allow that to be minimised, but more of a letting go and releasing him to his own life and choices and consequences. It was a cutting of ties and bonds that Annie no longer needed. That no longer served her or her life. She took back her life from Tom that night. She took her childhood to herself and locked it away in her heart. She took back the child he had violated and abused and brought her closer to her self and vowed to protect herself from now on. Never again would anyone have the right to violate her in any way shape or form. She was in control, she had survived and survived well.

Annie felt fine, absolutely fine. She was a little nervous about how her meeting with Tom would go but she knew she had to do this. Mike was wonderful, supportive and caring without pushing Annie in anyway. He was there for her, nothing else. He asked Annie if she wanted him to stay with her the next day for her meeting with Tom.

"No," Annie said, "I am fine Mike, I can do this alone. He frightens me no more. He is just a sad old man."

Tom arrived on time the next day. Annie brought him into the hotel room they were staying in and got him a cold drink. They sat on the bed. It was emotional for Annie, she loved this man. There was much she loved about him, there was much she remembered, not all of it was bad. He had loved her, in his warped way he had genuinely loved her. Annie saw this for the first time and it comforted her. She started the ball rolling.

"Tom," she said, she refused to call him 'Dad' feeling he had given up the right to being a father to her when he violated her, "I need to ask you some things. I need to know some things. I have been in therapy for five years and this is a part of my healing. I need to face you and confront you on what you did to me."

"The me who sits here now, not the child I had separated for so long, you see she is me, I have brought her back and both of us now sit here and face you. We want to know how and why it happened."

Tom handled himself well, as if he knew something like this would happen one day. "Annie," he said, taking her hand, "I will talk about this with you now, I will tell you anything you want to know but after today this subject is closed. I don't want to talk about it again. Is that fair?"

"Yes," Annie agreed, "that is fair."

Tom promised to answer any questions as honestly and as openly as he could.

"How did it start then? How did it all start, I want to know."

Tom answered slowly and painfully. "Annie it started out with a cuddle and a touch. I don't know how it got so out of control. I loved you children so very much, what started so innocently soon turned," he explained.

214

"That is why I had to leave, that is why I ran away with Debbie, I could not cope with what I was doing to you. And it controlled me I could not control it and I could not seek help. It all just got so out of hand."

There was pain in his eyes, Annie saw his pain and humiliation and the way he now had to live a reclusive life for what he had done, she saw that Tom paid a price for his actions on a daily basis, and this helped balance Annie. She saw she was not the only one who limped, Tom limped too. It felt right and just. He told Annie how he too had been abused as a child.

"Aha!" thought Annie. "I knew there had to be a tie somewhere."

Annie needed to know where it had come from in Tom. It did not take it all away but it made it easier to understand.

Tom told Annie about his time in jail and the humiliation he suffered on a daily basis. Child abusers were not treated very kindly in jail. He told how he would be pulled from his bed in the early hours of the morning. Annie secretly smiled at this, feeling such justice, now he knew how she felt, to be woken and humiliated. He would be taken to a room where prison officers would taunt him, jeering in his face.

"So Tom what are you?" They would demand, "You pervert, you fucking child rapist you, fucked your daughters did you? How did that feel Tom, how did it feel to fuck your daughters? How do you feel now?" they jeered.

"Still feel like such a big man?" Tom had needed to urinate, he was scared, they would not allow him to go to the toilet, they continued their verbal assault on him, Tom wet his pants, they all laughed at him. They broke him in that prison. They broke his very soul. Annie saw how justice had been done. Tom had paid, maybe not enough, but he had paid. Tom now lived with the demons, not Annie. Tom had led a lonely existence in prison, completely

215

ostracised by all around him he felt the pervert he was. It kind of cancelled a debt in Annie, she had not made him suffer as he had made her suffer, but at least he had suffered. It was enough, she could now let it go. Annie told Tom she could not allow him to be near her children. Tom took this like a slap in the face.

He thought about it a while and said, "Okay, I deserve that, I understand where you are coming from."

"I can't allow you to be a grandfather to my children," she told him.

That hurt, it hurt him deeply, but as far as Annie was concerned that was the consequence for his actions. It was his own fault. He could not get away with the things he had done unscathed. Annie now controlled him in so many ways. It was a sad reflection. Annie felt no superiority only a deep sorrow for a broken and perverted man whose life would never be whole again.

She said goodbye to Tom that day. She allowed him to die in her heart. She allowed the demons to die with him there. When she saw him off and she walked away from him it was as though an ulcer of pain melted from her being in the hot sunshine and she walked into a cool comfortable phase of her life.

Mike had paced the hotel smoking like a chimney, he had stayed close in case Annie had needed him. He was not out of ear shot. Knowing well how Annie could crumble and fall he needed to be close by to protect her. He would have killed Tom if he had hurt Annie in any way. But Mike trusted Annie's judgement and he knew Annie would never do anything to harm herself in any way.

After Tom left, Annie spent a little time alone. She wept for her losses. And she smiled on her victories. She watched herself metamorphosis from caterpillar to butterfly. And when she was ready she called Mike back in. Mike held her tightly and kissed her forehead. Annie told Mike everything and he listened and held her to him, stroking her and praising her for her strength and survival instinct.

Mike and Annie made love then, just the two of them, no one else to invade or spoil the love they shared. Annie's demons had left and she was together there and now. It was her and only her who made love to Mike that day.

They did not go to the wedding, there was no point. Annie had finished what she needed to do, they left town early the next morning. Annie had phoned Tom and made an excuse about a problem at home, she gave her apologies and wished him and Belle all of the very best. And she meant it. It was over, the final hurdle crossed. Annie felt so light and airy. They sang with the children the whole way home, Annie feeling happy, free and at peace.

The days were passing quickly, Mike and Annie found there was still a lot to do. They wondered if they would actually ever get on the plane. There were only two months to go and the reality of all the things left to do was beginning to settle in. Family and friends were distraught at their leaving but all secretly admired them for their ability to make the move. Many of them simply could not do it. They did not have the guts or the means available to uproot themselves. Mike and Annie spent their last months with their families and friends as if they were trying to absorb as much of them into their beings as possible. There were no arguments or fights, they treasured every moment they had with precious people.

Mike and Annie decided to spend their seventh wedding anniversary at a hotel. They needed a break and time alone. A friend came to the house to look after the children and Mike and Annie booked into a five star hotel. Five bottles of champagne adorned the refrigerator. It was going to be a wild night. They had booked in and were in their room, they had just had lunch and were getting themselves ready for an afternoon of total sex. Annie was desperate to just let go and scream and allow her body to climax over and over again. The previous months had taken their toll on Mike and Annie's sex life, there just never seemed to be enough time to make love. They still fucked now and again – a quick one fitted in amongst all the things needing to be done. They both longed for the release and indulgence of a full afternoon of uninterrupted sex.

Annie and Mike had a bath together a long luxurious bubble bath, they washed each other, lingering at private places, smiling into each other's eyes and seducing each other wildly. They moved from the bathroom to the extra large bed. Curtains were well closed, air conditioning buzzing, soft music played and they were on their second bottle of champagne, there was no rush. They were in a perfect sixty-nine position when the door bell went.

"Fucking hell, who could that be!" fumed Annie.

"Shit! Mike you had better answer it, maybe there is something wrong with the kids, the do not disturb sign is on the door, no-one would worry us unless it was an emergency."

Mike grabbed a towel, wrapped it tight around him to suppress his erection and went to the door. Annie listened her heart pounding. There was only silence. Eventually Mike came back in, closely followed by Tamara. He had opened the door and she stood there, finger to her lips instructing him to be quiet. She had walked in.

She stood at the foot of the bed. She was dressed sexily in black. Bright slut red lips and dangly ear rings. Mike climbed onto the bed. Tamara stripped for them. No words were exchanged. Mike and Annie lay totally mesmerised by her beauty. She came to them, she lay between them and kissed each of them passionately. Mike got up and opened another bottle of champagne leaving the girls to feast on each other's bodies. Annie was like a woman possessed, it had been too long, far too long. She sucked at Tamara and bit her desperately trying to absorb Tamara to herself. Fuck she loved this woman, how could she think she could ever live without her? How could she leave her? Their love was too strong, too perfect. Why couldn't Tamara leave Stuart and be with them forever? All this ran through Annie's mind as she gorged on every visible part of Tamara.

Mike came back with the champagne, fuck the glasses, they all drank from the bottle, huge gulps and then back to the task at hand. Annie worked Tamara, Tamara grabbed Mikes cock and pulled him closer, she pushed her bright red fingernails deep into the hole of his penis, Mike winced in pain and pleasure, all of them kept their eyes open, none wanted to miss a moment. They all found their parts so easily, it was like coming home, like Tamara had never been away, they all took turns, no jealousy, no hesitations, just lustful sex and abandonment and pleasure. Mike took turns between his girls, fucking one then the other, sharing himself equally between the two, moving away at the right time to allow them to explore and feel each other. Annie was on top of Tamara, rubbing her large full breasts over Tamara's, Mike took her from behind, penetrating deep into Annie, the force of his thrusts moving Annie's breasts over Tamara. Annie and Tamara's eyes locked together, total peace, total fulfilment, total pleasure. Kissing, licking, sucking, feeling, fucking. It felt like it would never end. No-one wanted it to.

Annie and Tamara changed positions. Mike fucked Tamara, good and deep, no holds barred. He withdrew in time, he contained his seed, he moved back and watched them at work, he quietly fondled himself while the two woman he loved the most in the whole world found pleasure in each other. It was intense, it was beautiful it was wondrous, it was so right and fitting. It was home for all of them.

Mike passed the champagne, time seemed to stop, there was no beginning or end, they were there, they floated somewhere else, they moved with no sounds, peaking and coming down only to peak again, orgasms flowed, juices mixed, love abounded. And when they were spent they all lay together and sobbed. Clinging to each other heart wrenching sobs emerging from them all. They all twisted legs and arms around each other, clung to the moment with all their might knowing it would be the last. Annie licked Tamara's tears, Mike licked Annie's, Annie licked Mike's, they drank from each other, physically and mentally, they tried to take parts of each other into themselves to hold this moment forever. None could let go.

Mike moved away slowly, he went to urinate and came back to find Annie and Tamara clinging to each other sobbing, totally sobbing.

"Hey, hey, come on girls," he reasoned, "lets not die here, life will go on, we will live again, this can't be the end."

But it was, it was the end. It could never be again. Not like they wanted. Not how they all needed. There were too many obstacles in their paths. Things could not be undone. Mike realised how futile he sounded, he climbed between them, held each to his chest and cried with them. And as they cried their love and lust rose, and Mike loved them both so very gently, freely moving between them he gently rode them and loved them completely. And when the time came for his seed to leave his body he simply came over them both, as they both lay there side by side he shared himself between them both. Shooting his sperm over their stomachs as if to mark them for life.

Tamara had to leave, they had been together for three hours and she had to drive home, it was all so flat and sad. They all wept freely without reserve. They all knew this was goodbye. Mike and Annie walked Tamara to her car and made sure she was safely in, how they let her drive out of the parking lot they never knew. How they let her go they never understood. The truth was they had no choice. Tamara had made the choice for them.

Mike and Annie had a very romantic dinner together, just the two of them lovingly gazing at each other, and reliving their afternoon delight. And when they went to bed that night Mike made love to Annie, just to Annie, all of him just for her. He made her watch his every move, he made her watch him climax, he made her feel his love shooting through her very being. He brought her back to him and held her tight. They both had to let her go and the only way they could was to lose themselves in each other. It was easy to push it all to the back of their minds, it had all seemed so unreal. The afternoon was never discussed, it was buried with all the other things that had to be left alone.

Annie busied herself with the children, preparing them for their move to a new country. They spent long hours together talking and planning their new future. Annie made her children feel their losses, she allowed them to cry and feel their pain. She sheltered them from much but not from their emotions. She knew how important it was to be allowed to feel as a child. She made them say goodbye to their friends, she held them as they cried. And when the time came for them to leave their house Mike, Annie, Ben, Janna and Matt walked through every room, reminiscing and feeling and crying. They said goodbye to their home and their life now past. It was time to move forward.

CHAPTER 21

They had done the farewell party bit, one hundred guests had invaded their home and partied like animals. A disco was hired and all neighbours invited. All friends and relatives and everyone they had been influenced by. Stuart and Tamara were there, but Annie and Mike had said their goodbyes to Tamara. Annie made a speech at their farewell, she thanked all her family and friends for what they had imparted to her life. She thanked them one and all for what they had given to her in life. She thanked them for the trying times which had made her learn and grow and she had thanked them for their love. It was emotional and from the heart. It moved everyone to tears. When Annie said goodbye, she did it properly.

They stayed with Daina and Jamie for two weeks before their flight left. They tied up any loose ends left, they saw special people and spent time with family. They went out a lot and laughed and reminisced. Their spirits had already gone from that country. When they got on that plane it was all over. The past was just that, the past, now they had a future to plan.

They had a holiday first. They had a night in Egypt taking in sights, Annie felt so very out of it. Her heart felt as though it was broken. She wondered if they had made the right decision. She wondered if she could see this out, the enormity of what they had done hit her hard. They were due to arrive in the United Kingdom with no-where to go. This little family of five had no home.

When they arrived in the United Kingdom they booked into a bed and breakfast, Annie cried all day, every day. Mike decided they all needed a holiday. Fuck the money. He booked a two week vacation in Florida. Disney World for his children and for the child within Annie. Annie had always dreamed of going to America, it was her life long ambition to go to America, ever since Uncle Errol had promised to take her to San Francisco Annie had wanted to see the country. Mike could and would allow her dream to come true. When the plane touched down in Florida Annie wept like a child. It was so overwhelming.

222

They spent a wondrous two weeks in Florida, it was a healing time for their family, they all needed it desperately.

Mike had arranged to stay with old family friends when they returned to England. The family friends lived in a small country town about an hour by train from London. It was a perfect resting place for them. Deciding they liked the area and schools they found a small house and began a family life again. Mike took his time finding work, wanting to find the right job and also make sure his family was settled. It was a time for them all to come together and feel the enormity of what they had done. Phone calls flowed between family and friends and Annie found it hard at that time. She always ended up crying. She found the English homes claustrophobic and the people most unfriendly. She missed her home and her family and most of all, Tamara.

Some days it felt like all the work she had done was non existent. She felt herself crumbling and fought to keep her sanity. She felt cut off, she had no-one to talk to. There was Mike but he was feeling the pain of all the leavings too and they began to drift apart. Neither seemed to be able to reach the pain in each other.

Annie wondered if they had really made the right decision. They had given up so very much and Annie felt cheated, terribly cheated. In this country she was a nothing and would have to work hard to gain her social standing again. Where she had once cooked for presidents and ambassadors and government ministers she was now at the bottom having to work her way up again. She did not have the energy to do it. She applied for a part time job in a local deli, they did not bother to reply to her application. "Fine," thought Annie, "Their loss."

Annie's saviour was her grandmother. After settling down Annie made a trip to Liverpool to spend time with her. It was a special time. Her grandmother was suffering from dementia but she knew Annie. They talked for hours and caught up and Annie listened to her for hours, fascinated by the tales of her youth. The two women shared a common bond, separated only by generations. Agnes had left England when she was young with two small children to live in Africa. It was like a reversal of history. Agnes could relate to what Annie was going through and helped her enormously. The confusion only helping as Agnes' early memories were vivid and clear. She became Annie's sanctuary and sanity. Annie always knew she had her grandmother there, somewhere she could run off to when it all became too much. Annie loved the time alone, the break from housework and children and meals. Guilt always accompanied these trips as Mike would be left to sort everything out. But he coped so well, as if he knew that for Annie to be more effective she needed her space.

Annie had tentatively planned to visit Zimbabwe six months after they had left. There was to be a huge family reunion of sorts. Family were flying in from all over the world. Annie felt scared about going but saw no way out of her obligations. She wondered if she would be able to leave again. She hated the thought of leaving everyone and getting used to life without them all over again. She was scared, but she was also very brave. She faced this like she had faced so much in her life. Her ticket was booked and paid for, plans were made. Mike was working part time and could cope with the children. Annie shopped and planned and had very mixed emotions. Excitement and fear.

A long flight flecked with minor upheavals left Annie arriving at Harare airport exhausted. She was met by Sarah and Jean, Sarah's sister who had arrived from Australia the day before. Jean and Annie had always got on well, they looked alike and were similar in many ways. Annie had not seen Jean for years and it was an emotional reunion. Sarah took Annie to her house and they all chatted and caught up on gossip. Annie was to stay with Daina and Jamie. A car was there for her to use and she had her freedom.

Annie spent days driving around, looking at familiar places and talking to people. She saw many of her friends. There was only one she wanted to be with. But she couldn't, she simply could not be alone with Tamara. Annie felt vulnerable as it was and she could not allow herself to be caught in a wave of emotion. She had to keep her feet on the ground, and Mike was not with her to catch her if she fell. She could not risk it. She distanced herself from Tamara those few weeks, confusing them both terribly.

Annie found her trip 'home' most therapeutic. It helped her to realise they had made the right choice in leaving. Things in the country were not getting better, they were getting worse. Morale was low and people were interested to find out from Annie how she was settling in England. Annie did not lie, she told them it was hard but good. There were so many more positive aspects than negative. The children had settled and were making friends. For Annie it was lonely though. She had made no real friends, she had been withdrawn and licking her wounds for months. She told them all how much of an adjustment it was, not something to be done lightly. She only saw Tamara in company so as to keep them both safe, they did not find time alone to talk, it was too raw.

Annie spent time at Beth and Boet's farm, enjoying the peace and serenity, yet feeling the fears and undercurrents of all farmers in the area. Times were hard, their land threatened, their futures unsure and unsafe. Money was tight. It was not easy for them and it would not get better. Annie found she had outgrown so much, she had learnt to stand on her own two feet. She had outgrown Zimbabwe and was yearning for what she now saw was her home, England. She missed Mike and the children terribly. She did not see Tom. preferring to leave that part of her life alone.

The Annie that arrived back at Gatwick was calm and together. She had laid much to rest, the trip to Zimbabwe confirmed so much for her and she was now ready to settle down and plan their future. As the plane had circled London and Annie had seen the green of England she had wept, it had felt like home. It really felt like home and she was overcome with emotion for the country in which she now lived.

They had all missed her so much, Mike, Ben, Janna and Matt. They all clung to her as she came through customs, they all huddled together and openly wept. It had been too long. They had been apart too long. They were happy to have her home and Annie was happy to be home.

Annie made some decisions. "I need to start living now," she told herself. Mike was working more and she had time alone. She bought a computer and it was a link to her family. Phone bills were too expensive, now she could have daily contact with family and friends in Zimbabwe. She found a balance.

Reading the paper one day Annie came across the personal advertisements. A double page of advertisements of people looking for friends and mates. Annie's eyes glanced to the women seeking women column. She read through it, her heart pounding. There was an advertisement and it seemed to be just for her. 'Married woman, early thirties, two children, bi-sexual, curious, seeking similar for friendship and possibly more.' Taking the bull by the horns Annie rang. She could not believe she was being so brave, or was that stupid? She had never done anything like this before. She left a message, replaced the receiver and then spent agonising hours wondering if she had done the right thing. But it was done, there was no going back.   That evening the phone rang, "Hi this is Jenny, you left a message for me." They chatted, an immediate rapport arising between the two women. They decided to meet. Annie invited Jenny and her husband round for dinner. It was a great evening, a lot of wine and good food, and there was more. Annie and Jenny just seemed to spark. The only problem was Jenny's husband. Feels like history repeating itself here," Annie laughed to herself, the difference was that Jenny's husband was keen to be involved in any sexual undertakings his wife ventured on. Annie was not available to have any outside influences. Not even Mike would be allowed in on this one, they had learnt that lesson the hard way. Annie and Jenny began phoning each other regularly, they made a coffee date. Jenny was coming to Annie's for coffee. Mike would be at work, the children at school. It was perfect.

Their morning together went well, they found pleasure in each other and found neither had any embarrassment or inhibitions. Jenny had not experienced a woman before, and Annie's knowledge was only slight. They taught each other, lived out fantasies and just enjoyed. There were no huge sparks, no emotion, just a physical release – well for Annie anyway. Annie's heart was closed, she did not want to allow another in, it always seemed to be too painful. Annie was relatively happy, she had found someone to share her preferences with without the emotional drain. The problem was Jenny, not Annie.

Jenny fell in love with Annie. Annie became Jenny's escape. Jenny's marriage was rocky and her children undisciplined and exhausting. Jenny loved the calmness of Annie's home, the way Annie's children did as they were told and the way Mike was so devoted to Annie. Jenny was jealous of everything Annie had. She wanted Annie for herself. She did not want to share, but Annie would not budge. "My terms or nothing," she would tell Jenny, "I care about you a lot but I don't love you enough to throw my family away. My commitments to them are strong and true. I will never leave them," she warned Jenny.

Their time spent together suddenly took on too high a price for Annie, Jenny felt that the more time they spent together the more Annie would give in. It did not happen. In fact it was the reverse, Annie got stronger. She could not allow anyone to upset her family life. Her desires were just that, hers. She could not incorporate her sexual desires with her family, they had to be kept separate. Jenny was now trying to make a move on Mike, suggesting to Annie that Mike join them one day. Annie flatly refused, and Mike spurned Jenny's advances. They had been down that road and no way were they doing that again, the risk was too high. Annie had to de-tangle herself from Jenny, it was the only way. It could have been so perfect but it was not. One could not control people's hearts.

Annie pulled back, Jenny was devastated. Annie called it off, and Jenny reacted by taking an overdose. Annie refused to carry the guilt. They talked but Annie flatly refused to be manipulated into continuing their relationship. Annie was gentle and loving with her, seeing her part in this but at the same time refusing to allow the situation to control her. Jenny left her husband and children. She begged Annie to run away with her, and again Annie refused. Jenny took another overdose. Annie nursed her through it. She sat at Jenny's bedside for days. But she refused to give in.

Eventually Annie managed to get through to Jenny. She helped Jenny to see that Annie was not her future. Jenny had to deal with her own demons, Annie could not take them all away for her. She had to work through her own shit. Just as Annie had had to do all her work alone so Jenny had to do it for herself. Annie encouraged her to go back to her husband and children and work things out. Jenny did this and Annie's role in Jenny's life took on a more positive note. Annie became a friend and adviser to Jenny. She helped her a lot and got her back on her feet. It was far from over for Jenny, she was only beginning to take healing steps. But she was heading in the right direction, and Annie would be there to help her every step of the way. They ceased to be lovers and became friends instead. It suited them better.   Annie found that the physical relationship with Jenny only heightened her love for Tamara, it felt like compromise. Like she was trying to replace one of the truest loves in her life. She realised she simply could not ever replace Tamara, it could never happen. Annie had to learn to live without her. She had to face facts and reality. It would never be. "Get over it," she told herself. But she found it hard. Too much had been opened.

Annie wrote and told Tamara that she had been involved with someone else. She was totally unprepared for Tamara's reaction. She did her nut. The letters that followed were hurtful and filled with deep pain. They spent a fortune on phone bills phoning each other and trying to talk it through. Tamara was heartbroken that Annie had been with someone else, she felt it had made what they had seem so unimportant. That was far from the truth. Annie was simply trying to find the balance again. Going about it the wrong way maybe, but she was trying, the only way she knew how, sexually.

Mike and Annie were offered a job running a pub about ten miles from where they lived. It was the break they had been waiting for. A new start, future and a stepping stone. Their ultimate dream was to buy their own pub but that was a long way off, they had to build up again emotionally, as well as house content wise and financially.

They moved and settled into their new position with relative ease. They refused to move the children to a new school, feeling they had moved them enough already. Mike did the school run in the mornings. It was like the only thing that had changed was the continent. Annie made trips to Liverpool to see her grandmother, Agnes was not well, Annie did all the necessary things with her, made out wills, discussed choices for funerals and basically the two of them came to terms with the fact that Agnes was ageing and ageing fast. Time seemed to be running away from her. They could not control it and neither tried to, they just talked through it all and tried to come to terms with the inevitable. Annie felt very torn at this time. She wanted to be with her grandmother, but also with her children and Mike, she wanted to move her grandmother to be with them but this would have been cruel. Agnes' confusion would have meant the poor old dear would not have known where she was. Annie did the hardest thing, she left Agnes where she was.

Now that Annie had moved further away, she and Jenny drifted apart. It was for the best. Jenny was getting professional help, there was little else Annie could do. Annie simply tried not to feel so guilty, it toughened her and made her resolve stronger for the future. She had to be careful, very careful.

Annie found that England agreed with her in many ways, she had lost weight, a lot of weight, it had just kind of slipped away as if Annie had managed to let go of so much. She was so pleased with how her body was coming together. She always knew it would take years for her body to recover from the bulimia. It felt as though at long last it was happening. Annie was more active, cleaning and running around, she never seemed to stop. She felt she had more energy, her health generally improved and she felt happy, not entirely complete, but happy. It had been a traumatic time for them all but finally things were working out and coming together.

She loved the work they now did, they adjusted very easily and made some very good friends. Life was becoming normal again. They entertained and started going out. They learnt to have fun and this healed so much for them all. The children were well settled and happy at school.

The biggest change was in Janna. It was as if she was a totally different child, all her fears seemed to leave and Annie found that Janna had learnt to laugh. A deep belly laugh replaced the nervous giggle Janna had once had. Janna was happy and settled. She did not mention Zimbabwe. Janna had no desires whatsoever to go back. She was doing well at school, things were coming together for her and the bonus was how close she and Annie had become. Things were as they should be. Annie was seeing the rewards of years of hard, painful work. Annie knew that the times would come when she and Janna would once again sit down and talk through Janna's abuse. It would never go away, Annie was so relieved it had only been one incident and that Janna had not been raped, she knew that abuse could never be minimised, abuse is abuse, but Janna would only have one nightmare to cope with, not a complete childhood.

Annie was prepared for the fact that as Janna grew up and things changed in her body and mind Annie would have to handle things differently with her. It would be a process and at each stage of Janna's development Annie would work with her and help her through it. She wanted to be there for her, it had to be different from her own abuse, there had been no-one for Annie and Annie felt as if she had an opportunity to positively help Janna. Never would it be put away to be forgotten about, things never worked like that, but they could leave it for a while and pick it up as and when circumstances dictated. Annie knew that as Janna got older she would have a deeper understanding of exactly what had happened and this would be painful for her. Annie wanted to be able to be effective in Janna's later years, someone once told Annie she was the perfect mother for Janna, they could relate to each other and Janna would be able to really talk to Annie and Annie would be able to deeply understand. Annie liked this philosophy. She was a firm believer that positive builds, if she could find a positive note in any situation this is what she would cling to, knowing she could build something healthy from it. "Negative only destroys," Annie reasoned.

Ben was growing fast, starting his teenage years. Annie was dreading them but Ben seemed to be handling them well. They had had a few disagreements but they always seemed to be able to reach a compromise. Annie made herself approachable for her children, and treated them with respect and a firm hand. She allowed their personalities to develop and she tried hard to be a good mother. She did not want to suppress her children or break their little spirits, she wanted them to grow up healthy and balanced and she knew this could not be achieved by ignoring issues or letting discipline slip.

At times it felt like she and Mike were like children playing house. Trying so hard to do and be the right people without totally fucking up their children's lives. They both had no real example to learn from and had to go on instinct alone. Only time would tell if they got the balance right. But for now things seemed well. Matt probably took the longest to adjust, he missed the maid and the garden and the pool. He missed the outdoors. Annie and Mike did what they could to help bring a balance to his little life. They would take the children to beaches and parks and spend family time together when they were not working. Mike started playing cricket and Annie and the children would go and watch. Annie loved getting out and being outdoors. Summer was heady in England. Lazy warm days and always so much to do and see. They had survived the major life changes and they were doing well. They were on the right road and it felt comforting.

Annie found that the nightmares never really disappeared, the time between them simply got longer and longer, she was going for months now with no freak outs. The removal of herself from her country of birth seemed to bring a deep healing. There were no

231

familiar sights and smells to trigger fears. She felt safe in England, protected and safe. The only thing she would have changed was to have Tamara closer. She was still Annie's weakness. And she did not know how she would ever get over her. She tried, she tried so very hard. Some days were fine and others were murder. Annie would sit and read all the cards Tamara had sent to her and weep for her loss. She missed her terribly. Not only the physical contact, but the deep friendship also. She missed the constant phone calls and contact. She missed not knowing what was happening in Tamara's life. She wished it would all fall apart and Tamara would come to her but these were pie in the sky wishes. It would simply never happen. Annie had to learn to live without her. Annie threw herself into her marriage, her children and work. It stood to reason something would fall apart eventually. Annie was imbalanced, parts of her were not being met or reached, she had suppressed them rather than deal with them for she did not know how to deal with them. There just seemed like no way out of this one.

Annie felt as if she was caught in a whirlwind again and did not know how to get out. She was going through the motions but living a half life. In trying to purge Tamara from her self she had totally suppressed her sensuality and she had totally suppressed her physical longings because of the pain it seemed to cause in her life. Annie could not work out how to balance this one. She had tried with Jenny and that had been a disaster. Annie missed Tamara more and more. She seemed to look for her everywhere. On days when there was no mail Annie was depressed and withdrawn. She wrote to Tamara constantly, convinced Tamara would make some changes in her life. She had been so upset about the Jenny incident, maybe just maybe it would have given her the will to leave Stuart and come to Annie. Annie knew she was being unreasonable and wishing for things that would never happen but that was all about fantasy. When the real world seems so fucked up fantasy is a good place to be.

Even though Annie battled to find the balance in herself she found that they were settled and happy in England. People had starting to pop over to visit, Jamie's sister had spent time with them at Christmas and they had had a ball, enjoyed each other's company and laughed a lot. Annie found that this was the hard part. No life long friends, all relationships were at the beginning. There was no-one she could phone for a chat or when things got her down. She felt so very alone at times.

CHAPTER 22

Annie's computer, her lifeline to her family had freaked out. Ben had done something to the computer and she was seething. She placed a call to her computer boffin as she called him. Heath was a good ten years younger than her, brilliant, quiet and brooding with the most amazing dreamy sea green eyes that Annie had ever seen. There was just one more thing – Heath was a good six inches shorter than her. Shit, why had she not noticed that before? She usually felt just a little ill at ease with him not really knowing how to take his aloneness.

It had been a day from hell. The vodkas had started at about fiveish and it was now seven o'clock, Annie was beginning to fly, food had not been on her agenda for the past couple of days and she thrived on the heady light feeling of hunger. Almost as if she was punishing her body and depriving it of any form of pleasure. The walls were closing in again and she was desperate for a door to escape through. In walked Heath. Those eyes, those fucking eyes. When Heath looked at her it was as though he looked right into her very soul. They penetrate deeper than most people's and at times Annie had felt almost naked when he looked at her.

She got him a drink and another for herself. He sat and worked on the floor and she slid down the wall to be at his level. Mike was busy working downstairs, the children watching television upstairs and she and Heath were relatively alone. She began her seduction. It had started with her seeing things about him she had never noticed before, the way his slim fingers worked over her computer, the way his neck just peaked out from the collar of his shirt, his flesh looked so alive and so soft and dreamy, just like him.

The conversation changed and they were talking subjects never before broached. Whenever a chance arose Annie gazed upon all visible flesh and her juices flowed. Fuck, she wanted him. She remembered the week before she had been on a train going to visit her grandmother and on passing through Manchester a flash of Heath has passed before her eyes. She had wondered about his nipples, of all things, his fucking nipples. Where did that come from? As she explored the feeling she realised she had an urge to see him naked, this was the starting place of her passion. Did he have a hairy chest? Or no hair? And his nipples, are they large, or small with hair or without hair? And what about that part where the stomach vees towards his pubic area she wondered what that looked like, smooth or flecked with hair or lots of hair? The rhythm of the train had fuelled her thoughts and she had almost drifted off to sleep thinking thoughts best left alone. She had almost forgotten this experience until now.

Now she understood why she was so pissed off about Ben fucking up her computer because it meant she would have to face Heath after all her mind's wanderings. No wonder it was a day from hell, no wonder the vodka had called so early in the evening. The memories drifted through her mind as she sat with Heath on the floor. Jesus her fingers itched just to touch him, just to feel what he felt like. The back of his neck almost beckoned her and she sat on her hands almost as if to stop the thoughts. She longed to just sink her teeth into his neck and lick his skin just to taste him, he looked so divine, and she felt like an animal starving for a feast. Her whole body tingled and Heath's eyes lit the fire. Conversations started and stopped almost in mid sentence – she kept losing track of what she was supposed to be saying and it was not the vodka.

Her courage built the more she drank and she almost pushed herself to voice her most private thoughts. The thought of the aloneness of him, the fact he lived alone, he was single with no children, no demons in his eyes just a deep knowing and understanding of so much fuelled her further. The moment broken when she heard her voice propositioning him.

"Oh fuck what have I done?" she yelled internally. It was too late she had taken the step, she had passed the point of no return. Biting her lip she listened for his reply. He was so controlled, so at ease, almost as if he was used to this happening to him, almost as if he was propositioned by frustrated wives on a regular basis. He smiled, oh fuck his smile so tender so delicious, she pinned herself back to the wall to stop herself from sinking her lips to his. She felt so alive every sense in her body screaming. He ever so gently brought her back to earth. He was so skilled. She landed gently back in reality and heard him out. He needed to think this one over, he needed some time. Patience was not one of Annie's stronger features, but he made her feel so alive, she was prepared to wait. Shit it had been ten years since someone had made her feel like this, ten years of being convinced no man could ever penetrate her well placed walls, so she could wait.

He asked for the weekend to think things over and that he would let her know the following week. "Fuck it feels as though I am selling him a car," she thought, "but maybe this is the way to handle it."

"This is not about love but about passion and sex so maybe the clinical approach is what is needed."

She agreed and Heath packed up to go home. As he was leaving she asked him if she could please satisfy her wonderings about his chest. With a shy grin he pulled his shirt from his pants, Annie's stomach lurched and she fought to control her desires. "No," she said "don't show me, I want to feel." He stepped closer and she moved her hand up to his chest and ever so gently felt over the starting place of her fantasy. Like a slap in the face she felt not hair or skin or flesh or nipples. She felt his heart and the outer core of his very soul. She was totally taken aback by the whole new surge of feelings this brought out in her. Sobered by this whole new turn of events Annie said her goodbyes and Heath left.

Sleep eluded her that night. She lay for hours and hours trying hard to piece the puzzle together. How did it happen, what was it about him that got her going again, where was that sane controlled person that was her and had been her for so long?

"Shit not again please not again, I can work through this," she thought, "I can."

She lifted the buzz of Heath from her being and peered deeper into her feelings. As she lay and examined the feel of Heath's chest she was bewildered at first by what she saw. Heath had been so closed, his heart and soul totally closed to her and her advances. She knew then without a shadow of a doubt they would never enter into a physical relationship. With this came an overwhelming sense of relief but also a burning shame at being so forward. She was totally unused to being turned down, being so physical and sexual she had always got her man, she knew which buttons to press. She knew men's weakness so well, it was one of her greatest strengths.

"Shit," she thought, "why couldn't he have just said okay and then I would not have to try and fucking work all this out. God, all I wanted was some form of escape some release from the norm and the shit, something just for me almost to play with, something totally mine that I don't have to share with Mike or the children or family or anyone, just Heath and I locked away somewhere private. I just want to run away some days she thought, some days I don't want to be a mum or a wife or an employee or that together person – I just want to be and do what I know best, I want to indulge in the pleasures of the flesh and lose myself in sexual release and freedom."

"Fuck, why the complications now, why couldn't it have just been so easy, just for once, why is it always tied to something deeper, why do I have to keep digging and finding the parts of me that are lost and have to bring them back?"

Annie needed Mike to help her through this one. She knew that he suspected something was going on. He had not been faced with Annie's wanting another man before and Annie was unsure as to how he would take it, she did not know how to tell him this time, she could not find the words and she was afraid of hurting him. But Mike knowing her so well had played her perfectly and exposed her hand. He had pushed her hard, knowing expertly which buttons to press to get Annie talking from deep within. She had been so quiet and withdrawn after Heath had left, Mike had left her alone that night. The next day however he started, dropping little things here and there to test Annie's reaction. He was trying to find something to spark her, something that would get her going. It was important he did this, and soon, as the longer he left it, the harder it would be for them to talk about it. "So, how did it go with Heath last night?" he asked. "Did he manage to sort everything out for you and is everything okay now?"

Annie was not in the mood for conversation, she was too busy trying to piece it all together inside her head. "Yeah, yeah, it's fine – working fine now thanks," she answered.

"So what was the problem?" Mike asked, "I mean he was here for ages, it was late when he left – after one in the morning."

"What the fuck is this?" she spat at Mike, "A fucking inquisition? Don't you trust me – do you think we were up to no good up here last night. Is that it Mike? You think I fancy him don't you?" she taunted.

Annie, I know you fancy him – it is so obvious, don't forget I know you and I know you well – you can hide from many but not from me," Mike reasoned.

"Fine," Annie yelled, "if you want to know I'll tell you okay – I asked him to fuck me – okay – are you happy now – and guess what he turned me down, the little short fuck wit turned me down okay – can we leave this now!" she yelled.

"No," Mike said, "we can't leave this Annie – we have to talk about it – what is it about him, what has he got that gets you going? There must be something."

"Mike, this is not normal," Annie pleaded, "how do I tell you of all people that I fancy another man, for God's sake, I can't tell you anyway until I find some answers for myself. I don't know what it is about short men, every time a fucking coconut, heartbreak." She ranted.

Mike continued to push her, he was not letting up now, he had to push her, force her almost to spit it out. Mike won, he got it out of her, she ranted and raved, she cried and sobbed, but she got it all out.

The freak-out had been his way of forcing her to face her feelings and to look deeper into what was going on. Once again Mike knew it was not about him or his inadequacies, this was about Annie and her life. It stood to reason that every now and again something would flare up and set her off again, no-one could live through what Annie had lived through with no repercussions. The difference was that Annie worked through her shit. Mike knew how to get her to the place of searching, healing and fitting things together. Heath was not the problem here, there was something deeper in Annie and she had to find it. To leave it now would simply mean it would crop up again, there was no use wishing these things would just go away. They had to be confronted and dealt with. If it was not Heath it would be someone else, it was that simple. They had to work past this one.

After Annie had finished bathing and dressing the day after she crumbled, Mike took the children to school and returned home. He sat with Annie and they talked.

"Tell me all Annie," Mike encouraged.

"Ah Mike, I just don't know," Annie said, "it feels so very weird, I was so sure of me and who I was and what made me tick. I was so sure I had found it all, the balance and that my life would take on a level now."

"Fuck you know how hard we worked at this. I can't understand where these things come from. I understand that there will always be attractions in life, that is just the way it is, I will always find men and woman attractive – there is something about certain people that just does things to me."

"But with Heath I am so confused; I don't know what I am looking for there. All the pain of Tamara and the shit with Jenny. I think I was trying to find out what my stance on this subject is. Is it really woman I am attracted to or am I simply just a fucking sex maniac who can never get enough? It feels like Heath has opened something in me and I can't work out what it is."

"Okay," said Mike, "let's look at this logically, let's remove the emotion and look at it for what it is. What attracted you first, Annie?"

Well," said Annie, "if I have to be totally and brutally honest I think it must have been his size. I seem to have always had a weakness for short men."

"Okay," said Mike, "why do you think you have this?"

Annie sat and thought and a light just seemed to click on inside her. The tears came and she slowly nodded her head.

"Okay. Okay, I see it now. It's Tom. It feels as though I have spent my life trying to replace him in my life. Does that sound perverted Mike?"

"No," Mike answered, "it kind of sounds natural. Tom has been a major influence in your life. Good and bad. You loved him Annie. For all his perversions you really loved him. I suppose it makes perfect sense that you would spend your life looking for him again. What you need to do now is let this go. You have done the work, you simply need to realise Tom can never be a part of your life. You have to let all parts of him go now. The good and the bad. You have spent so much time dealing with the shit and the pain and clearing that. You now need to let go of the good stuff as well. You need to simply accept all parts of this and now let it go once and for all."

"The hard part was letting go of the sore stuff Annie, I suppose we just never realised you would have to let go of the good as well. By letting that go it means you have left it all, does that make sense?"

Annie thought about it. "Yes," she replied, "I think you have hit it on the head there. It was like I was trying to work the shit but keep the good stuff. That can't be, I have to let it all go. I have to accept I don't have a father in any sense of the word. I can't have the good or the bad. Heath was just a trigger really, it was like I wanted to hold on to some part of Tom and not let it go. I suppose I reverted to what I have only ever known, sex. And by trying to find some part of Tom to fill the void in my life I looked for it in the ways he taught me. I know it is not just that with Heath. He really moved me, Mike. So deeply, and I could feel his passions, I see the connection but it is deeper than that. I mean if I was searching for some kind of father figure I would have gone for an older man."

"Yes Annie, I know, Heath was just a trigger that's all." Mike explained. "There have been other men you have felt attracted to during our marriage," he reminded Annie, "the difference being you never felt the urge to do anything about it. We have been through a hard time, we have left everything we have ever known. You are searching for something familiar. You started at the place you know best. You took one thing about a person and built it up in your mind. It felt familiar and good."

Annie had to agree, how well he knew her. "Shit this is a man in a million," Annie thought. "He knows that it is not about him and I can talk to him and tell him all my deepest darkest secrets and he never judges me, he just loves me."

"Sometimes I wonder what I have done to deserve you," Annie said to Mike. "You have been so much to me during our marriage. You have helped me more than you will ever know. Thank-you for not suppressing me Mike, thank-you for allowing me to work this out. You know this is not the end yet, the pieces are just starting to fall into place, I need to work this one out once and for all."

Things this deep don't just disappear overnight but Annie was determined to see it through. She was so grateful to Heath, he could have just jumped in and that would have been disastrous. Annie realised this much. Yes, she missed the sensual passionate sex she had found with Tamara, Heath's depth had moved Annie's passions. It was not about sex really, it was about sensuality. Heath was one big bundle of so much. Annie learnt from this. She learnt Tom could never be replaced in her life, she had tried that so often and it had ended up in disaster. In fact when she looked back it had nearly cost her her life on two separate occasions, Gary and Curt. It was weird that she never noticed it before. This time it was good. It was positive stuff and good healing work. Annie had crumbled and freaked but she had not been shattered into a million pieces. She had seen the answers with Mike's help and had made the decision to work through this. This time she had not fallen head first into a bottle, she had not tried to take her life again. She saw her own growth.

This was just the final little coming together. There would always be something or someone who triggered things in her, that was normal. The best part was that Annie had the love and support to work through these issues, it was comforting. Annie also had to let go of Tamara. She had to accept that things could never be the way she wanted them to be. Annie accepted the fact that she would always love Tamara but that she could let her go and this she did. She released her. The memories she had would always be there to treasure but it was over, finished. No going back - ever. Annie learnt that her completion was deep within herself. She did not need to look to someone else to complete her. The completeness was simply an understanding of her own complex character and acceptance of all sides of her. The searching was over. Completeness was just like a giant jigsaw puzzle, you tried different pieces to see if they fitted, sometimes you left them there for a while thinking they were in the right place but as you got further into the puzzle you could see where you had placed pieces wrong. You could then move them around until they found their rightful place in life. Tamara, Jenny, Heath – so many names and faces and people, they had all just been pieces of the puzzle called her life, she had moved them around to find the best place for them. They were a part of her and always would be, they just had to be put in the right place, the place where they fitted and helped complete the picture. When the pieces had been wrongly placed she felt the imbalance and would have to search over the picture of her life to see where she had gone wrong, she did not need to break it all up and throw it away in frustration. She had to learn to take the time and be patient with herself, to find the wrongly placed pieces and move them to more comfortable zones.

She lifted the piece of the puzzle called Heath. She examined it and she found its place in her life. Now she had to tell him. As best as she could Annie tried to tell Heath. She felt embarrassed, but there was something stronger. She needed to do this right. She felt a stronger emotion here, gratitude. Heath was one special person. He could so easily have simply used Annie, broken her, but he had depth and he had soul. It was not his way. He had refused Annie's advances, but in return he received her friendship. They cleared the air, and found that they had much in common. They became good, firm friends. Heath's piece of puzzle had been moved to where it should be. It was good and right and comfortable. Every now and again Annie would look at him and her heart would lurch, he was so incredibly divine. Every so often she would think about what it would have been like. But in reality sex is just sex.

It can be exciting with someone new but that soon wears off. It soon becomes the same. You have to learn to be happy with what you have and not spend your life looking for more. Friendship lasts forever. Annie and Heath would be friends forever. Had things been different she would never have had this special person in her life. She would have fucked it up badly. So, more than anything, Annie felt gratitude. The fact that Heath chose not to take advantage of her only heightened her feelings for him, and for herself. She had broken the self abuse cycle, with his help. She wondered if he would ever really know how much he had done for her. He had made her face herself and work it out. Annie knew that there would be other times in her life when people would invade her but she knew how to handle it now. No longer would it destroy. She

243

had learnt to build from all of life's experiences.

And as for Tamara, Annie filed her away in the depths of her heart. One day maybe there will be someone again, Annie would 'never say never'. But if and when it happened it would be so very different.

"I will not seek again, I will just live my life as best as I can. I won't try and be something I am not. I will simply accept and move on and as and when things come up for me I will deal with them," Annie reasoned.

"I can't determine my life's path and I won't try but I will commit to working through issues. I won't give up I will continue to place one foot in front of the other in my life and I will live my life as best as I can, remembering to be kind to myself. I will strive to be the best that I can in light of my life's experiences. I will choose to build from the positives. I won't allow the negatives to destroy me. I will search for the positive in everything and learn and grow."

*   *   *   *   *   *

Annie received a call from Liverpool. Her grandmother was very ill. Annie did not hesitate, she packed a bag and got the first train out. She arrived in Liverpool late at night and made her way directly to the hospital. She spent time at her grandmother's bedside, Agnes recognised her and was so pleased she was there. She told Annie, "I knew you would come."

Annie went back to her grandmother's flat to sleep and eat. She then spent the next few days sitting at the hospital until all hours of the night. She could not leave her grandmother alone. Annie wanted to be with her when she died. She wanted to be there for her and love her, just as she had loved Annie.

Annie rang Sarah and Jean. "I think you should come," she told them, "don't waste time, just get here." Sarah and Jean both arrived on the same day. The three of them spent all their waking hours at the hospital.

Death came for Agnes on a Saturday morning. It seemed fitting that it was raining, as if the angles were crying. Annie, Sarah and Jean were with her as she passed from this life to the next. Annie held her as she died and spoke of her love for her and thanked her for all she had done in Annie's life. She kissed her a hundred times from all the family. Annie's face was the last one Agnes saw before she left. Her eyes were soft and full of love and peace. And when she had gone, Annie covered her with a blanket and kept her warm. Sarah and Jean came and kissed her goodbye. They sat with her body for a while and all said their personal goodbyes. Then they left, Sarah had a plane to catch. Jean and Annie would be organising the funeral and the packing up of the flat.

Annie was determined that this death experience for her would be done right. She wanted to feel and see and experience it all. It was a way of exorcising the demons that had invaded her being after Mitch had died. She picked clothes for her grandmother, she viewed the body at the mortuary. Feeling thankful she had. The body that lay in that box was not her grandmother. Her grandmother was somewhere better. Annie found she could let her go, she could let the shell that lay in that box be burned in cremation. Annie felt so strongly about it all that she decided to conduct the funeral service herself. She did not want a stranger talking about her grandmother's life. She could do it better.

She met with no resistance, Annie had written beautiful poetry and obituaries for Agnes. The service was small and personal and very moving. Annie said goodbye properly this time.

She buried her grandmother's ashes next to her grandfather's. She laid flowers upon her space in the ground under the trees, she whispered her last goodbye to the woman she loved so deeply. She understood that this was one thing she would simply have to learn to live with. She would miss her every day. Annie and Jean left Liverpool and Annie returned home to her family and normality. She needed to feel life, after experiencing death. Things had been done, paperwork organised, furniture moved and Annie now needed time alone to grieve.

Annie moved another piece of the puzzle in her life. She removed the piece that said death was only ever traumatic and devastating. She had seen the positive process of it all. She had faced it. It was so unlike her experience with Mitch's death. She had been so very afraid then. This time she had faced it smack on and not run away. She had made herself see and hear and feel every aspect. No nightmares followed Agnes' death, Annie's dreams were full of happy times and life. She found she was more able to came to terms with Mitch's death and allow the demons to rest. She covered it with love and thanks. She could leave it now.

As Annie sat and looked over the picture of her life she saw there would always be pieces that would need moving. "But you know what, there is no rush," she told herself.

"We have the tools now, we can work through this." So much had been brought into its correct place. And when the time comes for me to move any pieces I can and will do it. Confidently and with compassion."

Her life was only just beginning.

LAST NIGHT I DID DREAM
THAT YOU GAVE YOUR LAST BREATH
I FELT NO SADNESS AT YOUR PASSING
BUT RATHER A SENSE OF EASE
THAT MAYBE TODAY MY PEACE WOULD REIGN
BUT AS YOU PASSED ME THE DEMONS STAYED
AND I REALISED THAT WHEN YOU GO THEY STAY
IN THIS LIFE TIME OF OURS
IT IS FOR US TO EXORCISE OUR OWN DEMONS
YOU TRIED TO PASS YOURS ON WITHOUT
ACCOUNTABILITY
AND YOU WANTED ME TO DO IT FOR YOU
NOT ONLY DID YOU TAKE THE MOST PRECIOUS PARTS OF
ME
BUT ALSO YOU DID LEAVE YOUR DIRT FOR ME TO CLEAN
AS I WONDER OF THE FAIRNESS OF IT ALL
I REALISE THAT I AM THE LUCKY ONE HERE
YOU LIVED YOUR LIFE WITH THE DEMONS INVADING
YOUR BRAIN AND BEING
WHILE I SPEND MY LIFE EXPELLING SAME
SO WHO IS THE VICTOR AND WHO IS THE LOSER?
WHEN I DIE MY FATHER
I DIE MY OWN PERSON WITHOUT ATTACHMENT
FOR I SPEND MY TIME CLEARING AND SEEING AND
WORKING TO BE THE ME I AM
YOU SPENT YOURS IN ESCAPE – I TRIED THAT PATH
IT ONLY BRINGS PAIN AND LONELINESS
SO MY DREAM OF DEATH – WAS REALLY ONE OF LIFE
FOR I TAKE MY LIFE FROM YOU
THE ONE YOU FEEL YOU GAVE TO ME
I PLACE BACK WITH YOU WHAT IS YOURS
AND KEEP FOR ME WHAT IS MINE
WORK YOUR SHIT AND I'LL WORK MINE
AND WHEN I GO I KNOW I LEAVE MY DIAMONDS FROM
COAL
AND YOU, WELL
THAT'S YOUR CHOICE.